BEEN WRONG SO LONG
IT FEELS LIKE RIGHT

BEEN WRONG SO LONG IT FEELS LIKE RIGHT

A KING OLIVER NOVEL

WALTER MOSLEY

MULHOLLAND BOOKS

LITTLE, BROWN AND COMPANY

NEW YORK BOSTON LONDON

Mulholland Books / Little, Brown and Company
Hachette Book Group
1290 Avenue of the Americas, New York, NY 10104
mulhollandbooks.com

First Edition: January 2025

Mulholland Books is an imprint of Little, Brown and Company, a division of Hachette Book Group, Inc. The Mulholland Books name and logo are trademarks of Hachette Book Group, Inc.

The publisher is not responsible for websites (or their content) that are not owned by the publisher.

The Hachette Speakers Bureau provides a wide range of authors for speaking events. To find out more, go to hachettespeakersbureau.com or email hachettespeakers@hbgusa.com.

Little, Brown and Company books may be purchased in bulk for business, educational, or promotional use. For information, please contact your local bookseller or the Hachette Book Group Special Markets Department at special.markets@hbgusa.com.

ISBN 9780316573269 (hardcover) / 9780316584470 (large print)
A Library of Congress control number is available for this title.

1 2024

MRQ-T

Printed in Canada

For my friend Jerome Hairston

BEEN WRONG SO LONG IT FEELS LIKE RIGHT

The greatest mysteries are the ones we never suspect.

1.

MARLEIGH MIRABEL MANN, that was the name she gave. She was somewhere around thirty-four years of age and well schooled in the arts and graces of civilized decorum.

"What do you do for fun, George?" she asked me.

We were sitting across from each other at the Versailles, a French restaurant housed within the Cordon Bleu Hotel on the northern border of midtown Manhattan. I was wearing a tapered blue suit with an off-white dress shirt and a maroon tie.

"Didn't they tell you about my job?" I asked, even though I understood her question quite well.

"Yes," she said, "of course. But..."

The woman calling herself Marleigh Mann wore a one-piece frock that was a slightly darker blue than my ensemble. The dress was made from the kind of silk that relaxes on the body, making her seem upscale and yet informal. Her skin was the tone of rich blond ivory, her eyes gray like mildly tarnished silver. Those eyes opened wide, almost glittered.

"...I don't know," she mused. "I just wondered about whatever you do that makes you feel happy."

"I have a daughter."

Those gray orbs darkened ever so slightly.

"What's her name?" the lady asked.

Improvising, I said, "Magdala."

"That's a very interesting name. Where's it from?"

"It was an ancient Middle Eastern city. My ex-wife, her mother, named her."

Marleigh knew when to stay quiet. After all she was a very special class of escort, one of social, not carnal, service.

"When Lena, my wife, left me," I said, "I kind of fell apart. She wanted Magdala to go with her to California, but Maggie decided to stay with me. She was still in high school then. Since we both needed, I guess, um, continuity, in a way we were able to save each other. You know what I mean?"

"Yes," Marleigh Mann said.

I could tell by the tone of her voice that she'd found a way to feel good about our...transaction.

We were having lunch that day for both of us to see if we were going to be a good fit.

The name I'd given her agency was George Westerly, a vice president at a large New York investment bank. That bank was starting a specialized sub-branch that would cater to what they were calling the African American middle class. Marleigh had been told that I was a wealthy businessman who needed a lovely, age-appropriate woman on my arm at various social gatherings around an upcoming banking conference.

"Magdala is the center of my life. My North Star, I guess you'd say. But, um, I'm a..."

What I wanted to say was that I was a high-level loan coordinator and then roll out the rest of the lie concocted to get this woman, my prey, where I wanted her. But the words wouldn't come.

My client was a man named Anthony Orr. I'd never met or even talked to the man, who lived in Santa Barbara, where his wife, Marigold Hart, had walked out on him, taking with her their seven-year-old daughter, Antoinette. Marigold had been spotted by a family friend, the art dealer Jason Manheim, somewhere in New York, but she was gone before he could get to her. Acting as a representative of Tony Orr, Jason got in touch with a contact he had in the mayor's office; this contact (I never knew their name or gender) put Jason together with Gladstone Palmer, an NYPD dispatch sergeant and jack-of-all-trades, asking him if he could help find Marigold without setting off an official police investigation.

Sergeant Palmer called me.

"Listen, Joe," Glad said over the phone. "They're willing to pay twenty-five thousand to get her in their sights."

"Not gunsights, I hope."

"No, not at all. The man just wants his daughter back."

"And what do you want, Glad?"

"Ten percent and a good bottle of hooch."

The dispatch sergeant and I had a rocky history. Once, back when I was still a police detective, he betrayed me in order, he said, to save my life. It was the flip of a coin how I felt about him at any given moment, but that ambivalence went into abeyance when there was twenty-two thousand five hundred dollars on the table.

"Have your guy Manheim get a one-page description of

everything pertinent about the wife: what she likes to eat, what kind of schools her daughter is used to, the clothes she wears, her education and expectations of life. Get me all that and a five-thousand-dollar retainer and I'll give it the old high school try."

"Okay, boyo," my best frenemy said. "Expectations of life might be over the top, but I'll tell Jason to get all he can from Orr."

"Have him get me pictures too."

So I got my sometime foot soldier, Oliya Ruez, to take the picture of seven-year-old Antoinette and her mother and hang out around the various upscale private schools in Manhattan and Brooklyn.

It worked.

"I saw the child at Bennett Academy on the Upper East," Oliya told me at my office on Montague Street, Brooklyn. "Her mother came to drop her off. I followed Mom home and managed to get her name off the doorman."

"How'd you do that?"

"His name tag said William, but his accent was Portuguese. When I called him Guilherme he started liking me. After that all I had to do was pretend to remember a woman from the building who had a kid at Bennett, where I had been a janitor."

"Are you from Portugal?" I asked her. Oliya was a fairly new acquaintance and about as tight-lipped as the sphinx.

"I spent some time in Equatorial Guinea."

She's on the short side, maybe 145 pounds without an ounce of fat. I'd once seen her knife and kill two merc-level men in less than half a dozen seconds. Olo, as I call her, is not a pretty girl, but she's a striking woman.

"What do you want with her?" Olo asked.

"Why?"

"She just seems kinda nice," the killer said. "I mean…are you sure the husband isn't some crazy?"

It was a good question, but after a few highly moral, yet fiscally irresponsible, decisions, I found myself needing the cash this job promised.

Looking for Marleigh Mann through the various search engines available to me, I'd found her face on the Maximillian Escort site. They took pains to explain that their escorts were not for any lascivious purposes and that they were very expensive. Their sole purpose was to make the client look good.

The client, George Westerly, explained that all he needed was arm candy. From there we set up a lunch meeting, which I'd have to pay for, plus five hundred dollars for Marleigh's time.

All that and I came up short when it was time to seal the deal.

Oliya's question came back to me while we talked at that French restaurant. I had no firsthand knowledge of Anthony Orr, and Gladstone wouldn't have concerned himself with the subtler nuances of sanity.

I could have given Glad Marleigh Mann's address and collected my fee without ever thinking about the lady again. I might have done so if, at one time, I hadn't been dropped into Rikers Island on charges of crimes I hadn't committed.

The well-mannered escort could see my hesitation. Her smile was the soul of empathy.

"They told me that you needed someone to come with you to a few social gatherings having to do with your job," she said.

"Uh-huh, yeah," I answered, trying to get back into the groove. "Cocktail parties and a couple of dinners."

"I was wondering why you didn't ask for a Black woman to come with. Considering the job and, and you . . ."

It was this kindness, this innate level of understanding, even through my lies, that derailed the setting up of Marigold Hart, aka Marleigh Mirabel Mann.

I gazed into her eyes wondering if anyone could ever truly understand another human being. But Oliya was right. Why hadn't Orr wanted to go through official channels? What was this woman's reason for running away with her daughter, working as a chaste escort under a false name?

My thinking took more time than I wanted.

"What is it?" she asked.

The new challenge was to change the course of our interaction without causing her to run screaming from the restaurant.

"I know why you're doing this kind of work," I said.

Her eyes tightened but didn't exhibit any real fear. She was probably thinking that I simply wasn't the right fit for her kind of service.

"Oh?" she said easily.

"Bennett Academy costs just south of a hundred thousand a year."

This unexpected intelligence brought out a bit more concern in those gray eyes.

"How do you . . ." she said and stopped. "How do you know about Bennett, George?"

"My real name is Joe Oliver," I revealed as a kind of offering. "I was hired by Anthony Orr to locate you."

She reached for her purse.

"I can understand you wanting to get outta here," I said. "But don't you think you should hear me out before you go?"

"I will never go back to that man." Her voice was steely.

"I know. That's why you and Antoinette left Santa Barbara."

This last piece of intelligence set up a slight tremor in the stalk of her neck.

"How much does Tony know?" she asked.

"Nothing from me. He gave me a retainer and your picture. So far, I haven't given him a thing."

"And what is it you want from me?" She was no longer friendly or engaging.

"I want to understand why."

"Why what?" Her sneer pleased me, made her seem more like a fellow mortal.

"Why you left. Why Anthony is after you. Why he didn't want the police to know, officially, about this investigation."

Through an act of sheer will Marigold Hart calmed her racing mind and concentrated on me and my invasion of her life.

"Why would any of that matter to you?" she asked, almost civilly.

"Because someone I trust has told me that you seem to be a good person."

"Who's that?"

"You've never met her."

"How many people know about me?"

"Right now, just me and my friend."

"How much is Tony paying you?"

"Five thousand down and twenty more when I give him your location."

"And how much do you want from me?"

I considered this question. Mr. Smith from the Maximillian Escort Service told me that it would cost eight thousand dollars, plus expenses, to obtain Marleigh's services over an extended weekend. She'd been gone from California for more than a year. If she had two jobs a week, she might have cleared more than half a million dollars...

But no. By milking her I would have committed a betrayal of myself worse than Gladstone Palmer ever had.

"I don't need your money, Mrs. Orr."

"That is not my name," she said stiffly. "If you want to call me anything, it can be Hart."

"I don't need your money, Miss Hart."

"That doesn't make any sense. If you don't want the money, then why are we here?"

"I'm here because this is my job. I find missing people or, at least, those that others have trouble locating. I'm a detective. I like the job. But every now and then I get the feeling that I might be being used. I don't like being used."

Marigold calmed down a bit more, realizing, I think, that I wasn't an immediate threat.

"No one knows about my daughter's school?"

"Not at the moment."

The woman whose life I had come so close to destroying took a few moments to compose herself. During this time the waiter, a squat Caucasian in woolen trousers and a dressy purple vest, brought her a fancy Niçoise salad and me an oval platter of frog legs Provençal alongside green beans almondine.

"Bon appétit," the waitperson wished us.

"I can't prove it," the upscale escort said after the waiter departed. "But I'm pretty sure that Tony killed his first wife."

"How'd you get there?"

"He's a brute, Tony is. Not physically, at least not with me or Annie. Not until the end, anyway. But psychologically, you know?"

I nodded, taking my first bite of amphibian.

"One day I realized that I just couldn't take it anymore. I got a lawyer and told Tony that I was leaving."

"What'd he say?"

"Nothing that day. He just grunted and walked out of the tearoom."

"Tearoom? You had a tearoom in your house?"

"Tony's rich. He's into construction all over Southern California. When he built the house, he wanted a tearoom with a big window that looked out on an English garden."

"I already hate the guy."

Smiling, she went on. "The night after I told him I was leaving he broke into my bedroom. I'd locked the door, but he kicked it in. He dragged me out of bed by my hair and told me that no woman was ever going to take either his money or his children. That's all he said. Then he threw me to the floor and walked out.

"That night I looked up his previous wife on the Internet—Natalia Henly. I knew that she had been murdered during what Tony called a botched burglary, but after he broke into my room I began to wonder, and to worry. An article in the *LA Times* reported that she'd been strangled in her bed while her husband was away on a business trip to Mobile, Alabama.

"That didn't prove anything, but the next day Annie and I were on a train headed east."

"Huh," I said. "Wow."

"Yes," she agreed.

We ate for a few minutes in silence, each of us looking up now and then.

"I'll tell you what," I said. "I got to say somethin' to your husband. But I can wait a couple'a days. I'll tell him about Bennett Academy but not your apartment. You can pull Annie outta there and then come up with another name, another place."

Her gray eyes had widened.

"This is a lot to take in," she said after a minute or so.

"I can see that," I agreed, "but not nearly as much as if Tony had found a less considerate PI."

She smiled again and gave me a side nod.

"Do you have any advice?" she asked.

"How much money you got?"

"Enough for a year or so."

I gazed at my prey-cum-client, feeling good about who I was.

"You have two days to think about what you want and what you might need," I said. "Maybe you'll get on another train and pick a city that your husband won't guess. And if it seems too hard, I'll give you my number and we can talk again."

2.

I'D MADE IT back to Brooklyn, to my Montague Street office, by midafternoon.

Aja was there at the reception desk visiting with an unexpected guest, a diminutive, black-skinned, and very old woman.

"Grandma B," I said as the woman rose from the visitor's chair set before my daughter's worktable.

"Well, well, well," aged Brenda Naples tsked. "There you is comin' into work when most decent people gettin' ready t'go home."

I bent over to kiss her lips, as was our custom.

"I—I didn't know you were comin', Grandma. I'd'a been here otherwise."

"That's okay, Joe. Aja got me a Dr Pepper out the icebox and been tellin' me what you and her been doin'."

I pulled up another chair to join my familial generations.

Grandma B took half a step back, reaching behind to right herself against the arms of her chair before slowly lowering into the seat. This caution was not unusual for a ninety-four-year-old woman. But Brenda Naples and her boyfriend, billionaire silver magnate Roger Ferris, had been in the habit of nearly daily ballroom dancing for the past few years. That kind of regular exercise, along with their morning constitutional around the grounds of Roger's Manhattan mansion, had given Brenda renewed strength. So it was noteworthy that she needed extra time to sit.

"What brings you out here to Brooklyn, B?" I asked.

"I was sittin' in the windah room lookin' out at the Hudson and it come to me that I haven't been to see you in years. Years! So I said to myself that I better gather these old bones up and make it out here before another day has passed."

"Grandma B's been telling me about your uncles and cousins all over Mississippi, Alabama, and Tennessee," Aja said with great pleasure.

"Ain't she talk nice, King?" Brenda said, the smile on her face reminiscent of some celestial being, deeply satisfied with its hand in creation.

"She's the best of both sides of the family," I agreed.

"Oh my God," Aja complained. "I want you guys to remember that when you meet my new boyfriend."

"You got a beau?" Brenda asked.

"Yes, ma'am."

"You think he might give me some great-great-grandbabies?"

"Grandma!" Aja's eyes went wide, her mouth forming a perfect O.

"It's only nature, child," Brenda explained. "Where you think you be if your daddy didn't get your mama with you?"

Putting up her hands and shaking her head in denial, Aja said, "I have work to do."

This tickled my grandmother to no end. She laughed, slapped her chest, and shook her head in approval.

"Girl, you are, blood and bone, a Naples child," Brenda blessed. Then she turned to me and said, "Why don't we go to your office, King, and let somebody out here do somethin' productive?"

My office is a quarter the size of Aja's. She needs more room because it's her job to maintain the printer, computers, office supplies, and file cabinets, and also to manage my clients and guests when I'm busy in the inner sanctum.

I have two visitors' chairs. Brenda took one and I the other.

Once seated, she craned her neck to look out the picture window onto Montague Street. That artery, once the main-stay of working-class Brooklyn, was now the center for gentrification. Workingmen and -women had been pushed to the outer limits of the city, struggling to pay rent and buy boxes of cornflakes without going into debt.

"It's such a nice place you got here, King," Brenda blessed.

My middle name is King. My father named me that as an honor to both me and my namesake, King Oliver, Louis Armstrong's mentor. Dad loved jazz, thought that it was what distinguished Black identity in America and the world.

"Jazz is the distillation of all the music of the world," Chief Oliver would tell me when he still lived with us, before they trundled him off to prison.

"It's so nice that you got your own office," Brenda confided. "It belongs to you. No white man can come in here and fire you and send you away with your tail between your legs. That's the only way to live like a human bein'."

Even as she said these words, I could tell that she had

something else on her mind. It was how she wasn't looking directly at me that was the giveaway.

I stayed silent, waiting.

When Brenda realized what I was doing she regarded me.

"I got a tumor," she said behind that steady gaze.

I've been shot twice in my life, and neither time was near the trauma I experienced hearing those four words. I couldn't speak. I tried to keep the pain off my face but probably failed at that too.

Brenda smiled ever so gently, seeing the love in me, I believe.

"It's a cancer," she said. "Prob'ly anyway. The doctors say it's between the heart and lungs and because'a that it's gonna be a bitch to operate on."

"Roger will get you the best surgeons in the world."

"I ain't told Roger."

"Why not?"

"Baby, this is my load to bear. I got a very good doctor and she's handlin' it."

I felt lightheaded and helpless. Brenda Naples was the backbone of our entire line. She and my grandfather had always been there for everybody. Everybody, no matter how far they strayed or what they did wrong. When I was sent to Rikers Island, she and Granddad were there every visitors' day.

"What did the doctor say?" I asked.

"It don't look too good. The operation would be tough for anybody, and my body is a helluva lot older than that."

"So—so what are you gonna do?"

"They runnin' tests now. Doctor got a whole hospital full'a specialists been pokin' me all ovah an' wirin' me up to machines bigger'n your car. I told 'em that I won't do chemo. No, no. Too many people I seen done been cut low by them poisons." Brenda leaned back in the chair, set her jaw to granite, and gave me a curt nod as if daring me to try to gainsay her decision.

"Is there anything I can do to help, or . . . something?"

I expected dismissal. Whenever I wanted to do something, anything, for my grandmother she'd tell me, often brutally, that she could take care of her own damn self.

But instead, she whispered, "Yes, child, there is."

"Wh-what?" I stammered.

"I want you to find my son, your father, and bring either me to him or him to me."

Where hearing that my most important elder was maybe dying had caused me pain, just the mention of my father brought about numbness in my heart and mind.

"Chief's in prison," I said. "All you got to do is go see him on visitors' day."

"No, baby. He got out nine years ago. They—what you call it—they appealed his conviction and sprung him outta Attica."

"Out? Why didn't anybody tell me?"

"I didn't know it myself until I heard it from Andrew Williams. He told us that Chief was out but that he was keepin' a low profile."

"Even from you?"

"Andy said that Chief said he was ashamed. I guess that makes sense. Anyway, I didn't tell you because you was in all that trouble. And you were so mad at your dad that I thought it was bettah just to let it lie."

Chief Odin Oliver had been sentenced to prison for

robbing a convenience store in Brooklyn when I was thirteen years old. The prosecution claimed that in the commission of that crime he shot two men with deadly intent. One was named Ira Gross and the other Felix Corn.

When I came along with my mother to visit Chief at a meeting with his lawyer, he assured me that he hadn't done anything wrong, nothing at all. But at the trial, he refused to speak a word in his defense.

He refused to help his lawyer, Bernice Appleton. I knew this because one night she came to the apartment and begged my mother to get him to talk to her.

"If he doesn't help in his own defense," Appleton said, "there's nothing I can do."

"He's just so proud," my mother replied. "He doesn't want to give them the satisfaction."

I didn't understand any of it. We'd been evicted from the house I was born in, and my mother cried all the time. They said that my father robbed the little store but his friend Andrew Williams told me that "those white men owed your father that money. He made them a loan deal and they thought they could just turn a niggah away without any bad-lash or backfire."

"Then why didn't he tell the judge that?" I had Mr. Williams's phone number because we both read comic books and he was my father's best friend.

"He just feel like he don't got to answer to stupid," Andrew said.

Mr. Williams was an exceptionally thin, very black-skinned man who smelled of chemicals that I could not name.

I called Bernice Appleton's office from a pay phone across the street from my middle school. She wasn't there but I left her the information I got from Mr. Williams. It didn't make any difference. My father was convicted and then, not long after that, my mother, Cicily Oliver, had a nervous breakdown and was sent to an asylum. Three months later my grandmother said that she had died.

My grandparents took me in. They loved me and doted on me, but for all that care and good upbringing, I could not forgive my father. In my mind, up until the day my grandmother asked me to find him, I hated Chief Oliver for the pain he brought down on his family.

He had named me King, but his parents named him after the king of the gods and still he couldn't do right by his wife and child. I hated him. I didn't want to. I tried to get myself to visit him in prison. I tried to read his letters and to write to him, but I couldn't do either. All I could do was to grow up and become an NYPD cop in order to somehow blot out Chief Odin Oliver's many crimes.

"Joe."

I hadn't thought about my father, other than in passing, for years. He abandoned me and deserted my mother over stupid pride. He shot two men over money. He refused to bow his head for the sake of his own blood.

"Joe."

"Yeah, Grandma?"

"I know how you feelin'," she said. "But this is somethin' I need. I wouldn't ask if you wasn't the only one could help me."

"Nine years."

"It's a long time. But Aja tells me that if you put your mind to it, you could find just about anybody or anything."

I could see the strain in her face. She had looked out for

generations of Olivers, Napleses, and other clans descended from her bloodline. She had given victuals and love, hard words and even blood to protect and uplift us.

I still hated my father, but the look on my grandmother's face dismissed the heart behind that loathing. The hot blood no longer flowed to that passion. It was a kind of forgiveness; forgiveness without love.

"Has he ever reached out to you since he was convicted?" I asked.

"No."

"Not a letter or phone call?"

"The only letters he ever wrote was to you, Joe."

"And I threw them away."

"Yeah, you did. But what you didn't know was that your grandfather plucked them all out the trash."

"You still have 'em?"

"'Course I do. Chief is my son, my blood. And you are the best'a him."

That was an afternoon of revelations. From the moment I saw her sitting with Aja, laughing and maybe dying, I knew that my life would change.

My grandmother wanted me to find her son. She had letters he'd written me but that I'd not read. Just by asking me to find my dad she cured me of the virus of living hatred, turning the disease cold and dead in my depths.

"What did the letters say?" I asked.

"I don't know."

"You didn't read 'em?"

"They wasn't my letters to read. Me and your grandfather decided to put 'em away just in case you wanted 'em someday."

Grandma B and I lived in different worlds. In her realm

there was only right and wrong. Two separate paths that brought you to either Heaven or Hell.

In my world there was no such a thing as absolute good or undeniable evil. Sometimes you had to embrace iniquity to achieve grace and at other times you had to turn your back on innocence.

I believed my view of the world was more practical, but I had to admit that my grandmother seemed to exist on a higher plane.

"Where are these letters?" I asked her.

"They at Silbrig Haus." This was the mansion where Roger Ferris, Brenda Naples, and his staff lived and managed his worldwide mining and investment empire.

"I guess maybe we should go there," I said.

"Thank you, baby." Her smile was my fee.

"But there's one more thing," I admonished.

"What's that?"

"You need to tell Roger about the tumor. He's your man and, no matter what you say, he deserves to know."

"Where you guys goin'?" Aja asked when we came back into the front office, headed for the door.

"I'm gonna take your great-grandmother back to Roger's," I said.

"For dinner?"

"We might eat sumpin'," Brenda admitted. "But it's mostly family business we got to take care of."

"So, I can't come?" my daughter grumbled.

"Not this time, honey," were my words, but Aja more likely responded to the set of my eyes.

"Okay, Dad."

3.

SILBRIG HAUS IS a private bastion on the Upper West Side, beyond Riverside Drive and on the shore of the Hudson River. Comprising more than a few blocks of prime Manhattan real estate, it is fortified by high walls of stone and stainless steel, surrounded by an immense, parklike lawn, and guarded by at least a dozen well-trained men and women, all of whom have been instructed to shoot first in the case of incursion.

The front gate is composed of thick, crisscrossed steel slats and always defended by at least two armed guards.

I pulled up to the blockade, rolled down the driver's side window, and waited.

"What's your business?" I heard the woman's voice before seeing her.

She came from her post to the left of the gate, behind the Great Wall. She was tall and bulky. The latter because of the weaponry she carried and bulletproofing she wore.

"Joe Oliver," I said, "delivering Brenda Naples."

The woman leaned forward, peering through the dim

twilight into the windshield of my ultracompact Bianchina automobile. Her face was handsome in the extreme, with no trace of prettiness. She had brown eyes and a confident mien.

"At ease, Doral," a masculine voice commanded.

Immediately Doral backed away, making room for the giant Forthright Jorgensen.

Forth was six foot five and looked to be hewn from stone. He was an anarchist who had decided to work for Roger Ferris because King Silver promised to, one day soon, turn over all his ownings to his employees.

"Hey, dude," I said.

"Joe, Miss Naples," Forthright replied.

As the words passed his lips, the great metal gate rose into its slot in the upper wall. Doral and her male counterpart took up their posts at either side of the entrance — semiautomatic rifles at the ready. Forth moved out of the path and, twenty feet up the road leading to the mansion, seven granite buttresses rose to block the way just in case my car was loaded with explosives.

I drove on, and before I got to them the blockades lowered into the concrete lane.

"Grandma B, King," greeted Richard Naples, also known as Rags. He was standing at the threshold of the huge, elegantly mismatched front doors of the manor.

Rags was a tough ex-soldier, ex-mercenary, ex-bodyguard who had most recently worked as a *specialist in delicate extractions* before taking the job as personal bodyguard of our grandmother. I say *our* because Rags is my first cousin. Brown-skinned and wizened, Cousin Rags wasn't big or impressive to look at, but he was deadly and completely without hesitation in dangerous situations. Between gigs, he took the job guarding Brenda because they were blood and she liked having him around.

"Hey, cuz," I said.

"Baby," Brenda added, kissing him on the cheek. "Roger here?"

"In the library, I think."

"Good. Why don't you show Joe to my room and let him in?"

"You got it," he said to her, and then: "Follow me, Joe."

The three of us moved into the huge foyer of Silbrig Haus. The walls of the grand lobby were painted sunflower yellow under a multicolor crystal chandelier, all supported by a bright white tiled floor. There were five doorways off that hall, leading to the rest of the house. Between each entryway and the next stood a wooden podium supporting a white porcelain vase, each of which contained six or seven deep red peony blossoms. I remember thinking that this would have been a good entrance for either a wedding or a funeral.

Brenda headed out through the doorway that stood second from the right, while Rags led me to the entrance at the far left.

I'd never been that way before, but, then again, I hadn't seen most of Roger's palatial home.

By almost every standard, Roger Ferris was considered the richest man in the world.

He lived up to that designation.

Along the wide corridor there hung paintings done by many of the old masters. Goya, Rembrandt, van Gogh, and one painting of a powerful woman done in the baroque style. The woman warrior was naked, armed with a short broadsword and battered wooden shield. Surrounded by darkness, she was in the process of leaping into battle.

I stopped in front of this last masterpiece.

"Pretty cool, huh?" my younger cousin said.

"Who did this?"

"Artemisia Gentileschi."

"Who's that?"

"She was a sixteenth–seventeenth-century Italian painter. This one is called *Judith on the Cusp of War.* But you won't find that title anywhere."

"Why not?"

"Because it was never on public view. Rich men passed it down through the centuries until finally Mr. Ferris got it."

"You know how much he paid?"

"Nuthin'."

"How does that work?"

"The story Grandma B got was that this was a gift for him from a Peruvian artichoke plantation owner. Not just one plantation neither."

"He just gave it to him?"

"I guess it's worth a lot to be friends with Mr. Ferris."

We walked on through the gallery until coming to a battered and weathered pine door. The portal had originally been painted white, but years of sun had peeled most of the coating away.

"What's this?" I asked.

"She told me that this was the door to her shotgun shack outside of Jackson, Mississippi. Her and Granddad brought it with 'em in the truck they came out here in. She said that she took it with so that she'd never forget the door they came out from."

"And she had it put on as the entrance to her room," I concluded. My grandmother certainly did come from another world.

Rags took a key chain from his baggy military pants, searched around, and finally found the key to the lost door.

"There's a phone in there with tabs for different ones of us. You could call me or Forthright if you need anything."

Brenda Naples's room was as much a relic as its door. Smallish in dimension, maybe thirteen feet by twenty, it was the kind of space that many people, even today, call home. There was a metal cot on which lay the thinnest cotton mattress and a desk, constructed from white pine, that had once been painted red. She had both a chamber pot and washbasin in there. On a three-legged stool, set next to the head of the bed, stood a brass and glass kerosene lantern that might have come out of Mississippi too. There was no window, hardly anything to dispel the idea that she was back in the woods outside Jackson.

The only modern item was a flat phone unit set upon the pine desk. It was fashioned from orange-colored plastic with a bulbous receiver, a digital number pad, and a double row of sixteen buttons with name tags handwritten by Grandma B.

At the foot of the bed stood a dark and deeply nicked walnut chair, its seat smooth from years and years of use. The legs were slender but strong. I could imagine my grandmother sitting on that chair, knitting a baby blanket for some cousin or neighbor while the moon rose and armies of insects ventured out, looking for blood, the skies above filled with bats ready to feast on them.

I pulled the sturdy chair up to the desk, sat, and leaned over to open the bottom drawer on the left side. This was where Grandma B told me to look. The only content of that drawer was a stack of seven letters held together by a withered rubber band. When I tried to pull the still-sealed envelopes out from the elastic it crumbled.

Sitting at the small desk, it felt as if I was a child again, having taken a shortcut across the cemetery and regretting it.

Those letters from my father were like huge graveyard headstones—evil, unapproachable. I knew I was there to read them. I knew they could not hurt me. But it took many long minutes before I could screw up the courage to tear the first one open.

They were stacked in order, by date, and I read them in that sequence.

Only the first and last letters had anything to do with my grandmother's request. The front of each envelope had as a return address Chief's convict number and the printed words **ATTICA STATE PRISON, NEW YORK STATE**. The letters were all addressed to Mr. King Oliver. The hand my name was rendered in spoke volumes to me. My father had taught me my letters. I recognized his printed characters as if having seen them only that morning. I could hear him telling me that *plain printing is the only way you can know for sure that people will understand what you're writing down.*

The first letter had arrived maybe six months after he went to prison. It read:

King,

I know I let you down at the trial. You're young and still excited about books like the Three Musketeers and movies about Superman. In stories like that the good guy is always the strongest and sometimes the smartest. But in real life heroes are the people that stand up to what they call insurmountable odds. You might have to look up that long word but I think you know what it's like to be small and bullies trying to make you feel even smaller.

I love you, boy. You need to know that.

You also need to know that I am not guilty of the crimes they blame me for. My lawyer Miss Appleton told me about your phone call telling her about the money those men stole from me. You were right. I don't know how you found that out but that was good detective work. You were right but that wasn't all of it. Misters Gross and Corn pulled out guns on me when I faced them. They meant to kill me so I did to them as they meant to do to me. Well, I didn't kill them but I shot them pretty good. All I got was a graze on my arm. I went to Ruby Lee's house and she patched me up. After that the cops chased me down and put me in chains. Miss Appleton told me that there were no guns found on the men I shot and that they said I cut my arm running away from the police. She said that there was no way I could claim self-defense. She wanted me to make a deal with the prosecutor. All I had to do was tell them about the illegal criminal businesses Corn and Gross were into. But I told her no. I could have gotten a reduced sentence by snitching but that would have been wrong and I'd have still missed you growing up.

And that's another thing. I told your Grandma B that I don't want her coming here and that I don't want you here neither. I couldn't bear it. I couldn't stand to have you see me here like this. I don't want you to never be in a place like Attica Prison. We will see one another one day when we are both free men breathing free air.

I love you son
Chief OO

I didn't cry over that letter right then, but I felt like it. I understood my father understanding me and I could see, clearly, how alike we were. It was as if his incarceration was an evil spell cast upon me—all I could see and feel. And this letter, the one I had thrown into the kitchen wastebasket, was the counterspell.

The next five prison posts were more technical. He wrote about the prison schedules, classes, and the library, about solitary confinement and how much he was hurt by isolation. He studied plumbing, electrical engineering, and carpentry because he knew that any kind of fancy education like law or premedicine wouldn't get a man like him, an ex-con in the free world, anywhere.

It was the last letter that gave me any hope of finding him. It came twelve years after his sentencing.

King,

I don't blame you for not writing me son. I don't want you seeing me in here and you probably can't even think what to say with the wound your young heart must feel. So this is going to be my last letter for a while. I just want you to know that I've made peace with my time here in prison. I read a book I got from a teacher name of Bernadette Broadman that's been talking to us about reading and writing. The book was a novel called The Stranger and written by a man named Albert Camus. It was a story about a man like me. A man that shot somebody. The man went to prison under a death sentence. He wasn't so much bothered by the gallows but more about a life without freedom and cigarettes. But as time went by he got used to his situation and learned how to be free in his mind. When I read that I thought that it was true for me and I hope beyond hope that it is true for you to.

I love you
Chief OO

p.s. The one thing you need to be free is to let go of hate. Hate is like a acid that eats away at your heart. If you hate you can never love.

Along that line—One of the men I shot, Felix Corn, was arrested a few years later and sent to prison for three years. He became a Christian and wrote me when he got out. He said that he was going to go to my lawyer and admit that him and his friend Ira had pulled out guns on me.

It was a deep pain that felt good, reading my father's letters. He was a good man and somehow it felt like I had always known that, even if I didn't know that I knew.

4.

SITTING AT MY grandmother's desk with Chief Oliver's letters strewn around, I realized that the diffuse light allowing me to read those dispatches from hell was somehow coming from the corners of the ceiling. This was a surprise because I expected that the kerosene lantern would be the sole source of illumination. Brenda, I was sure, would have preferred the smell of burning oil in her little den, but, when I thought about it, I realized that she probably didn't want to incinerate Silbrig Haus with a toppled lantern.

She had given up part of the desire to re-create her origins because the new world she lived in needed her to modify herself. In the same way, I needed to adjust my heart.

For nearly thirty years I'd been like a two-thousand-pound bluefin tuna hooked by some unknowable angler. Thirty years of pulling away, of feeling a pain inside, of diving down into darkness, thirty years of leaping and then plummeting, of crying out for help that would never come. It was so much like the impending doom facing my grandmother that I truly felt that I was about to die.

"Joseph?"

Hearing someone call my proper name when facing the specter of death felt otherworldly, as if God or the Morning Star were calling to me. But then I realized that it must have been the speaker on the garish orange phone unit.

"Roger?"

"Brenda told me that you were in her cabin."

"Yeah, okay. What do you need?"

"Thank you for getting her to talk to me. I knew something was wrong, but she never wanted to talk about it."

"No problem, Rog. I did it so you could back her up."

"That's all I want."

"Good. As long as you remember that she's going to make up her own mind, you two should get along just fine."

"I know," he murmured, then he added, "She says that she has you doing something for her."

After a few seconds I said, "Yeah."

"What is that?"

"Private."

"Like her tumor?"

"Look, man, this is Brenda Naples we talkin' about. If she wants you to know what she's up to, she will tell you, okay?"

Roger Ferris was not someone used to being told no. He was the guy you gifted an unknown priceless masterpiece, just because. The silence he rolled out after my refusal underscored that expectation.

"Anything else?" I asked.

"Brenda told me to tell you that she was going to bed."

"Tell her I'll call tomorrow."

My apartment is one flight up from the second-floor office. One big room and a toilet, it also has big windows along with a small stove/oven and a big iron-footed bathtub. I could access that flat from the stairs leading to the third floor or by climbing a rope ladder through a hatch that I'd cut in the ceiling of my office.

I had just run the hot bathwater and was about to step in when my cell phone chimed.

"Hello?"

"Mr. Oliver?"

"Miss Hart."

"I've been thinking about it," she said. "I need your help."

"I thought you might. I mean, I know how hard it can be when you're on the run alone."

"What can I do?"

"Pack what you need and then keep Annie home from school tomorrow. I'll send somebody around about two. Her name is Oliya Ruez, and she will take you someplace safe. After that we'll figure out exactly what to do."

"I can pay you for whatever is needed," she asserted.

"If it comes to that, I will take your money."

The bath felt great, almost like a baptism after a lifetime of self-centered sin. It was a moment of grace. So much so that I took up my cell phone and engaged one of the oldest numbers I had.

It rang eight times before a voice answered, "Glad."

"Sergeant," I said.

"Ah, if it isn't my black Irish brother. How goes it in the civilian world?"

There was music and loud talk brewing around my friend.

"Where are ya, Glad?"

"At a celebration in New Jersey. They wanted me here

because I'm one of the few left who knows how to dance. Do you have news for my friend?"

Because I didn't trust my Irish brother I said, "Not quite yet. But I need a favor for another job I'm working."

"Let me get out pencil and paper, my boy." I could hear his grin.

"Come dance with me, Mr. Palmer," a woman's voice said from somewhere in New Jersey.

"In a minute, darlin'," he replied. "I'm just gettin' a shoppin' list from me dear mother."

A moment later he said, "Go on, King Joe."

I gave him a list of names and their approximate ages along with other identifiers.

"What kind of job is this?" Gladstone asked.

"Family business."

"The nastiest kind."

The quality of my sleep that night was different. It had been so long that I bore the weight of hate for my father that it had become an unconscious burden, a fifty-pound growth on my back, a pocket of intensified gravity that followed all the days of my life. But now I was floating like a shark in warm waters with a current of fresh brine wafting through my gills. Life was peaceful and easy, a state of bliss.

Even the singing phone didn't disturb me.

I reached for it among the blankets and pillows, engaged the call without looking to see who it was on the other end of the line.

"Hello," I said wistfully.

"Joe?"

"B."

"You asleep?"

"What time is it?"

"Two thirty in the mornin'."

"Well then, yes, I am most probably asleep."

"Are you okay?"

"I am."

"Should I call you later?"

"What did you want, Grandma?"

"I woke up in the middle'a the night, worryin' over what I asked you to do."

"You mean findin' my father?"

"You don't have to, Joe. It was just a crazy old lady's dream. Let sleepin' dogs lie, that's what my mama used to tell me."

"This dog has woke up from deep hibernation, B. He's up and he's hungry. You couldn't throw him off the scent with a bullwhip or shotgun."

"Are you all right?" she asked again.

"There's a smile on my face in my sleep."

"That could mean you crazy."

"If I am, I'm satisfied with it, and I promise you—I will find my father and bring him to your door."

"Call me in the mornin', King, when you're awake. We can talk then."

"I love you, Grandma B, and I will tell you that again in the morning."

Two hours after my grandmother's call a single note chimed loudly. My eyes opened wide and all the exhaustion of the years of inner anguish was gone, at least temporarily. I got up out of bed, naked from the bath the night before, and went to the twelve-foot-high window that looked down on Montague Street.

It was still dark at 4:32 a.m. A couple of solitary souls were walking in opposite directions across the street from each other.

It wasn't winter yet. It wasn't cold, and I felt like primitive man, Cro-Magnon, at the end of the ice age, gazing at a future filled with possibility. My father was back in my heart if not my life. My grandmother was alive. She could call me in the middle of the night, and I would answer.

The chime was notification of a text message.

Gladstone Palmer had looked up the names I'd given him the night before. Following them down was the plan for the next day, maybe two. And then there was Marigold and Antoinette. They needed a protector and, possibly, that job would fall to me . . .

"Hello?" he said on the first ring.

"Mel."

"Joe. What can I do for ya?"

"How do you feel about putting up a nonsexual female escort and her eight-year-old daughter for a few days?"

The ensuing thirty seconds of silence was expected. Melquarth Frost was as removed from this world as my grandmother. He'd been wrong since the day the rapist impregnated his teenage mother, since that mother raised him in the church without even a shred of love, since he found his father, killed him, and then reduced his emaciated body to sewage waste. For Mel to take in two innocents was akin to a lifelong pacifist finding himself in the role of commander on the front lines of a forever war. The silence was indicative of him trying to find a way that he could be human and civil with noncombatants.

Mel was not a sane man. He was not a citizen in any true meaning of that word. Untethered from rote fealty or meaning that wasn't scented in blood, Melquarth found one day that he needed a friend. He offered me the position because there was some sort of resonance between our ethics.

"She some kinda S and M worker?" he asked hopefully.

"Just an impressive date for men who don't have the capacity for long-term relationships."

Another pause.

"Black?" he asked.

"Old-school white, like you."

"And they're in trouble?"

"Can you do it, Mel?"

"I only ever talk to citizens when I'm pretendin'," he said.

"I know you think that, but the truth is you know how to talk, be friendly, how to share. They just need a place to sleep and eat and be safe."

"But what if...I mean..."

"Look, you don't have to do this alone. If you agree to take 'em, Oliya will bring them and stay with 'em too."

"Oh."

"You're still seein' Olo, right?"

"Yeah. She'll stay?"

"I'll ask her to."

"Well then, okay."

After talking to Mel, I had to sit down for a while. He had been a killer, a kidnapper, and a knife hand. He'd broken every law, every one, because that's what he was created to do. But he was trying to change, and I believed in him—mostly.

*   *   *

I fell asleep sitting naked in a hammock-chair hung next to the bed. It was 8:07 a.m. when I awoke again. My breathing still came easy, and I had shed the spectral Dickensian shackles forged so long ago.

Donning pants and T-shirt, I made yet another call.

"Hi, Joe," she said lightly.

"Hey."

"Mel says that you're sending me to that church of his with the ladies I tracked down."

"I decided you were right," I agreed. "I mean, if the husband hired me to tell the cops that his wife was here with their kidnapped daughter, I would have probably seen it through. But the way it is I have to look deeper."

"You think he might try to hurt them?"

"Ask me that in a few days."

5.

I WAS DRIVING my tiny Italian car up the FDR Drive, just past Fourteenth Street, when the cell phone sounded. Connecting the call, I turned on the speaker.

"Hello?"

"King?" my grandmother called out.

"Yeah, B, yeah."

"You in your car?"

"Headed to the first interview on the trail to Chief."

"I asked you to drop that."

"You did, but you must have forgot that I'm almost as stubborn as you."

"Who you goin' to talk to?"

"You don't know her. Just some woman might have a crumb or two."

"I want you to be careful, King. You know your father was always on the rough side."

"If my math is right, he's gonna be sixty-six in two months. I think I might be able t'take 'im."

"This ain't no joke, boy."

"What's wrong, Brenda? Yesterday you was all up on me finding him. Now you act like it's some kinda sin."

"Roger was very kind to me yesterday," she said in answer. "You were right about that."

"And what does that have to do with the king of the gods?"

"Do not blaspheme to me, Joe."

"What does Roger have to do with Chief?"

"Um, I was just thinkin' that maybe I spend a li'l too much time with my head in the past. You know what I mean?"

"Maybe so."

"Roger in my life, right now, today. He sat down with me, held my hand, and kissed each and every finger. He was that grateful for my trust and that sad ovah sumpin' got nuttin' to do with him."

"He loves you," I agreed.

"I haven't talked to Chief since his trial. He been out all this time and haven't called me, not once. I got you and Aja, Rags and my sister down Mississippi; people that love me even though I can be a bitch on wheels."

I was coming up on the Forty-Second Street exit and smiling.

"I should'a read my father's letters," I confessed.

"I should have made you read 'em," she answered.

"You don't have to be mad at yourself because Roger feels for you, B. It's like Granddad used to say, life is the journey."

"I don't want you puttin' yo'self in peril lookin' for my son, Joe."

I laughed out loud.

"What you laughin' at, fool?"

"You been usin' that word *peril* since Mama had me in short pants."

"What's wrong wit' that?" There was a smile in her voice. "It's a very good word for knuckleheads like you and your father."

The traffic was light, and I was making good time on East River Drive.

"You remember what that minister in your church used to say all the time?" I asked.

"Hand of God," she testified.

"That's right," I averred. "Minister Charles always said that we are just game board pieces being moved by him. That's you, Grandma."

"What you mean me?"

"He the one put Chief in your mind so that you would give me those letters. He put those letters in my hand so that I would finally do what was right and go out to find my father and ask his forgiveness."

I both believed and did not believe in the words I spoke. Maybe there wasn't a God, but there I was on my way to a fate that felt preordained.

"Baby."

"Yeah, B?"

"Be safe," she whispered.

"Always," I lied.

I got off at the Ninety-Sixth Street exit and took the first left down eleven blocks, where I turned right and even found a parking space on the street.

Her apartment building was made from red brick that had turned almost black over many years of Big Apple pollution. The front door was no larger or more imposing than the hatch Brenda Naples brought up from Mississippi. To the right was a double column of fourteen names each; 4F was S. Pearlman.

She answered my ring over the intercom. "Yes? Who is it?"

"Is this Bernadette Broadman?"

"Pearlman," she corrected.

"But you used to be Broadman when you taught literature at Attica prison." This was not a question.

There was an understandable pause after my claim.

"Who is this?"

"Joe," I said. "Joe Oliver. The son of Chief Odin Oliver."

"What's your middle name?" she asked at the end of a long corridor of silence.

"King."

Her hesitation made sense; after all it had been a quarter century since those days. She'd been married since then and separated, maybe even divorced, since that.

"How did you find me?" she asked.

"The Internet is an amazing tool," I stated. It wasn't a lie even if it wasn't how I found her.

"What do you want?"

"I haven't seen nor heard from my father since I was thirteen. The other day I came upon a letter he'd sent back then. He said that you were his teacher and that you taught him about Albert Camus."

"Mm," she uttered in what sounded like appreciation.

"Reading that letter made me want to reach out to him. But when I got in touch with the prison, they said he'd been released almost a decade ago."

"Are you a policeman?"

"Certainly not." But I wondered why she would ask.

"Do you have identification?"

45

"Yes, I do."

Another pause, then: "Fourth floor," and the door buzzer sounded.

Once, before Aja was born, my soon-to-be wife, Monica Lars, and I had gone to Paris for ten days. One of those days we took a tourist bus to the Palace of Versailles. It was summer and too hot, but we trudged down every hallway that palace had to offer. What struck me most was the little rooms set aside from the sleeping quarters of both the king and queen. These were the areas where servants awaited the pleasure of the royals.

Bernadette Pearlman's compact living room reminded me of a miniature waiting room for some servant. It was well appointed but somewhat cramped, friendly if somewhat utilitarian. There was too much furniture but that wasn't my call.

I sat in a barely cushioned armchair and she upon a backless cherrywood bench set before a maple desk.

When I handed her my driver's license, she studied it closely.

"You're from Brooklyn?" she said.

"I live there."

"Where is Montague Street?"

"Brooklyn Heights."

"And what do you need to know about Oh-Oh?"

I smiled at the initial-driven nickname.

"He was my father and then he was gone," I said simply.

"You could have visited him."

Rather than try to defend myself I asked, "Why did you ask me if I were police?"

"They come around every year about this time asking if I'd seen him."

"The police, not his parole officer?"

"They want to put him back in a cage."

"Why?"

"You don't know anything about him, do you?" she accused.

Bernadette Broadman-Pearlman was around five-two with just enough padding to make her huggable. She had to be in her fifties, but her eyes and skin were youthful.

I explained that he'd written to my grandmother and said that we were to never visit him in prison.

"He didn't want us to see him like that."

That earned me a little sympathy in those fetching eyes.

"He got me fired from my job," she said.

"How he do that?"

The way her eyelids lowered I knew it was not what he had done but what she had.

"I was engaged to Pearlman way back then," she said. "He didn't want me teaching at Attica. We were living together, what they used to call living in sin. But...I guess there wasn't enough sin for me. Your father showed me things that my Sam would never learn."

"And that's why they fired you?"

"I married Sam after that because...I don't know. We were already engaged. But then one day your father came to the door and asked if I'd go have a drink with him."

"Did you tell your husband?"

"He was there in the house when Oh-Oh came by. Sam told me not to go with him, but he might as well have asked the sun not to shine. I lived with your father for three years and never regretted it, not one minute."

"You left your husband?"

"Never even looked back. We might still be married for all I know."

"Why did you and my father break up?"

"We didn't."

"You got him in a closet or sumpin'?"

She smiled, showing me what my father saw.

"The police were after him."

"What for?"

"They said he murdered a man named Ira Gross."

"But . . . he shot Ira back when I was a kid."

"Somebody finished the job a few years ago."

"And the police set their sights on Chief?"

Ms. Broadman studied me. While she calculated and weighed, my mind was filling up with meaningless questions. What was her life like before my father? Did he snore in the bed next to her? Was he kind?

"I need to find him," was all I could say.

"I don't know where he is."

"You don't have any idea of how to reach him?"

"He called me one night," she said longingly. "Some friend of his out in New Jersey had been approached by New York detectives. They wanted him for questioning. He'd already heard that that man Gross had been murdered. He told me that he had to run. I—I—I offered to go with him, but he wouldn't hear about it. He said that he wanted to think of me making tea in my little kitchen."

"He didn't give you any way to get in touch with him?"

"I don't understand."

"I want to speak to my father," I explained.

"I hear that, but what I don't get is, why after all these years?"

48

"His mother, my grandmother, Brenda Naples, is very sick."

"No. What's wrong?"

"Cancer."

"He talked about her all the time. He said that she was the toughest person he'd ever known."

"She wants to see him before the operation."

"How old is she?"

"Ninety-four."

"That's too old to be cut up like that."

"Probably."

My father's lover leaned back against the desk, a look of sadness and mild distaste on her lips.

"I haven't spoken to him since we talked that night on the phone," she said. "And that was years ago, like I said."

When I was a detective with the NYPD there were differing levels of resistance to interrogation. Most criminals didn't have a moral compass or, at least, not one that worked. They'd sell out their cronies if the offer was good enough. Sometimes they'd sell each other out for no good reason whatsoever. In other cases, there was the challenge of fealty to a gang or maybe a culture. This was the blockade of omertà, refusal to betray the trust of the gang, almost a sense of nationalism among thieves. But even here there were chinks and flaws. The refusal to inform on a coconspirator could be undermined by proving to the man being questioned that the people he was shielding were willing to inform on him. Sometimes you just had to keep the person being grilled apart from his people. Often, if you spent enough time with a crook, if you brought them a certain delicacy they coveted or discussed favored sports, he would, or she would, switch allegiance and share their innermost secrets.

The toughest nut to crack in the interrogation game was always love. Love cannot survive without the object of its passion. Love is not a citizen among equals. Love cannot escape, cannot switch loyalty, cannot exist without its yang. And, in my experience, a woman truly in love with her mate cannot be disabused of her commitments. Like a river, love must run its course, and if it is true love in the heart of the woman being questioned, then that truth will keep its own counsel.

Bernadette loved my father. I was sure of that. Maybe it was the way he kissed or how he shared laughter with her. Maybe he was her first real lover, like she claimed. It didn't matter. The why of love was not a science, no more than most humans' certainty that they had a soul. Love, like good music, was a feeling that could not be deconstructed.

I was pretty sure that some of what Bernadette was telling me was lies, but I had no refutation that had a chance against her passionate heart.

"I understand what you're saying, Bernadette," I said. "He wanted to protect you and so had to keep you in the dark."

She looked as if she wanted to cry.

"If I find him," I continued, "I'll tell him how you've kept the home fires burning."

That softened her a bit.

"I'm gonna kick up a lot of dust looking for him. And he might reach out to you when I do. So I'll leave you my number. If he gets in touch, tell him what I told you. Then, if he wants to talk, he'll know how to call."

I took a little pad from my sports jacket breast pocket and jotted down my cell number. When she took it from my hands there was a static shock between us.

We both smiled at that.

6.

I HAD PLANNED to go see Gladstone Palmer after bracing Bernadette Broadman. She might have known something worth chasing down about my dad, and the perfect New York cop could access files that had been closed to me since I'd been dismissed from the force. But now that I knew my father might have been being sought for murder, the police suddenly became off-limits.

Headed for the next encounter, I took my time, wending my way toward the Lincoln Tunnel. Driving, especially down Manhattan city streets, relaxed me. As a patrolman, back at the beginning of my law enforcement career, I had developed what I called the quasi-Zen practice of being aware of traffic and street life at the same time. In this way my awareness seemed at a peak while, almost coincidentally, I felt centered, even calm. After leaving the force I continued this routine, calling it my *motoring-meditation*.

But that day my reflections weren't of the transcendental variety. The word *murder* echoed like a jailhouse mantra in

51

my mind. It called up a hulking presence, both brooding and sweaty, in the nonexistent back seat of the tiny car. This imagined phantasm added the perils of prison into the mix of my mentality.

I might have gotten lost in the diversity of this inner logic if the cell phone had not sounded.

"Yeah?" I said, projecting my voice toward the smartphone stalk next to the clutch.

"Daddy?"

"Hey, honey."

"What's wrong?"

"Nothing. Why?"

"Your voice."

"What about it?"

"It's so low."

"Huh," I uttered. "Must be that I haven't talked for a while."

"Where are you?"

"Headed out to Newark."

"What for?"

"Nothing you need to know." These words usually meant that I was chasing some romantic interest and Aja never wanted to hear about that.

"You need me to do anything for you?" she offered.

"You remember that guy Anthony Orr?"

"That's the man who you were looking for his wife? From California?"

"Yeah. Because Glad brought me the job, I didn't do my due diligence. But, looking at it now, I'm thinking I should have done a deeper dive on the client."

"You want me to do it?"

"If you don't mind."

"It's my job."

"What else is goin' on with you?"

There was a pause before she asked, "Is something happening with Grandma B?"

"Why you ask that?"

"She never comes out to Brooklyn. She was asking me about how you go about finding people, and even though we had a good time, she was definitely there to talk to you about something."

"Just family stuff," I said, a shrug in my voice.

"You sure?"

"Absolutely. Didn't she seem fine?"

"Uh-huh, I guess. Okay. Talk to you later."

"Bye."

Through the Lincoln Tunnel to the 495 I went. From there to Newark and the Springfield-Belmont neighborhood. Gladstone's nighttime text told me that the man I was looking for lived on Kent Street, just off Eighteenth.

It was a four-story blue-violet plaster-slathered apartment building that came right up to the broken sidewalk. The double front doors of the tenement were open, and music of differing kinds sounded from windows and the hallway, down from the upper floors and maybe from a backyard.

The floor of the entrance was flush with the sidewalk. This was unsettling to me. I suppose in my mind, somewhere, was the conviction that a home should stand above the street, at least by a few inches.

"Can I help you?"

She stood in the open doorway of the first apartment, which was on the right as you entered the dowdy building.

Black, somewhere between the ages of thirty and fifty-five, she was wearing a much-worn dress, its hem to the knee, that was now gray but had once been a happier color. Little kids screamed with childish pleasure behind her and, oddly, Garth Brooks was singing from some kind of device hidden in the cluttered room.

"Hi," I said brightly, putting on my broadest smile. "My name is Joe Oliver."

I held out a hand for shaking.

She considered the offer, decided against taking me up on it, and said, "What do you want?"

Undaunted I replied, "Lookin' for a guy name of Gatormouth Williams."

My request stymied her. I was sure that she was sure that I was there about money. The only question was, was I there to collect or deliver?

While she deliberated on this important divide, a small girl, whose very existence was at odds with the background, skipped her way up to the woman's side.

She was dark brown, maybe four feet tall, and dressed in a pink dress that was recently ironed and spotless. There was a blue ribbon in her left pigtail and a yellow one binding the right.

"Hi," she said to me. "My name is Etta-Jane."

I nodded and said, "There was once a great singer named Etta James."

"Really?"

"Uh-huh."

The girl's smile revealed that she was missing one upper front tooth, making her just a little more perfect.

"What's your name?" she asked.

"Joe."

"It's nice to meet you, Mr. Joe," she said, and I almost forgot why I was there.

Looking up, I saw that the matriarch of apartment 1A had softened a little.

"What you want with Andrew?" she asked.

"He was my father's friend back in the day and I was wondering if he had seen him."

You could make out from her expression that she couldn't imagine how what I said was a lie.

"He up in 3E," she said.

"Thank you very much."

I turned toward the stairway.

"Mr. Joe," Etta-Jane called.

"Yes?"

"Do you think I could be singing?"

"Definitely," I said, earning myself a forward-thrusting shoulder and an unabashed gap-toothed grin.

Three-E's door was ajar but I knocked anyway.

"Who is it?"

"Joe."

"Joe who?"

"Joe Oliver."

The door swung open.

Andrew "Gatormouth" Williams looked almost exactly as I remembered him from childhood. His dark skin was still tight, and he was at least as slender as before. The only concession his body had made to the decades was that his hair had receded maybe four inches, and I realized then that the *chemical smell* he exuded was the same as that of my multivitamin tablets. He was wearing soft brown trousers and a turquoise T.

The look on his stark and slender face was both joy and surprise.

"King?"

"You look great, Gates."

"Black don't crack, now that's a fact. Come on in, son. Come on."

He backed away from the door gesturing me in with a flourish.

The living room I entered was very much a surprise. Each of the four walls was painted a different shade of blue. The carpet was woven from a bright yellow synthetic and there was a modernist wall-wide band of a window that looked down on Kent, allowing a generous swath of sunlight in.

There were four walnut chairs with yellow upholstered seats. These chairs were set as if at a dining table but there was no table between them.

"You want sumpin' to drink?" Gatormouth offered. "All I got is beer and cranberry juice."

"No water?"

"From the tap," he said with a sneer. "Sit, sit."

When I sat at the nonexistent table, my father's friend went through a doorway behind me. Soon after that came the clinking and gushing sounds of him preparing our drinks.

"What you doin' nowadays, Boy Oliver?" he called from the other room.

"Makin' a livin' in Brooklyn."

"You still out there in East New York?"

"No, uh-uh, Brooklyn Heights."

"Oh, fancy."

"If you say so."

"It's been so many years," he said, coming through the

door carrying a bottle of beer in one hand and a red plastic tumbler filled with ice cubes and water in the other.

He handed me my bland libation and then sat diagonally across.

"What you been doin' all these years?" he asked.

I gave him a five-minute synopsis. From college to the police, from the police to incarceration, from Rikers to private detecting. His face scrunched a bit when I mentioned being a cop, but then it smoothed out after I told him about doing my time on the island.

"How about you?" I asked.

"I got engaged," he said, making it sound like the saddest thing in the world. "Leaf Morton. Leaf Alyssandra Morton."

"Leaf like from a tree or the Vikings?"

"Tree," he said, smiling sadly.

I thought of asking where she was but decided not to because it felt like she might be dead, or worse, with another man.

"Why you here?" he asked, offering a reprieve.

"Lookin' for my father."

Andrew hadn't aged much, but he had changed. There was something weightier about him. He met my gaze and gave a curt nod, saying, without saying, that he understood.

"Life was never right to you, son. Your mama in the ground and Chief under the jail."

"I had my grandparents."

"Good people too." He nodded. "They saved my life."

"They did what?"

"You didn't know?"

"About what?"

"After Chief went away everything just fell apart for me. I was doin' all kindsa drugs and gettin' inta trouble with people who were afraid'a your father, but they didn't give a fuck about me. Not a half a fuck."

That was the first time I ever really thought about the broader impact of a prison sentence. I knew how much it hurt families but never thought about friends and acquaintances, people at the workplace and even neighbors who might only know the convict's first name.

Gatormouth needed a friend like Chief. He needed Chief.

"Your grandmother came over to my house one day. I had been up to see your father, and she wanted to hear about him. But I was so out of it I didn't even know that she was there, not really. I kinda remember her sittin' wit' me. And—and then your grandfather was there. He said that he was gonna take me up to a cabin in Maine and that either I was gonna kick or die. They didn't tell you about that?"

"I imagine they thought that that was your private business."

"Yeah, yeah, you prob'ly right. Them was some beautiful people."

"Brenda's still alive."

The joy that invaded that man's sadness was like a TV commercial where they'd pour a stain remover on a deeply soiled sheet and, like magic, that sheet was white again.

"She is?" he cried. "That's truly wonderful."

"What happened in Maine?"

The question caused my father's friend to look up into a vast area above my head.

"I never been so sick in my life," he said. "I didn't think I was gonna die—I knew it. And we were way out in the middle'a nowhere. Mr. Oliver th'owed the car keys in a pond down the dirt road. It was three weeks before I could breathe right."

58

"How long were you there?"

"Five weeks, two days."

"And you kicked?"

"Yeah...One night, just before we was gonna come back down, Mr. Oliver pulled out this mean-lookin' pistol. He said that I didn't need to worry a'cause he was gonna come see about me every now and then, and if I was back on the horse, he was gonna shoot me dead." When Andrew laughed you could see that he was missing the upper right canine. "That man cared about me that much."

The only furniture in the room was those four chairs. I placed my water glass on the seat next to me. Tears were cascading down Andrew's face. He wasn't blubbering or even sobbing, just allowing the tears to roll down.

I understood what he felt, but I was there for another reason.

"Mr. Williams."

"I got ya," he concurred. "You already know how beautiful yo' people is. You don't need me for that. What you wanna know about your daddy?"

"You knew he was out?"

"Not at first. A few years after, he got in touch. He had this girlfriend, Luwanda, that he was wit' down in Philly. I knew Luwanda some and she had this other friend that gave Chief a ride out to see me. That was Leaf Morton. It was great seein' your father and—and, I don't know, that Leaf was somethin' else. She saw sumpin' in me too. I tried my best to be what she saw." He laughed sadly. "Kept it up for a while too."

"That was a few years ago. What about now?"

"I don't know."

"Did he give you a phone number?"

"No."

"You ever see him face-to-face again?"

"One time him and Luwanda was up at this street fair in Brooklyn. They hold it under the Manhattan Bridge. They were sellin' sterling silver jewelry with amber jewels. Some other friend of Luwanda's was the jeweler.

"I guess Chief was missin' the old days, 'cause he called me and aksed to meet there. We had hot sausage-dogs at this street stand and talked about the way we used to did things."

"How was he?"

"Piss and vinegar."

"Did he tell you about Ira Gross?"

"Said he didn't kill the mothahfuckah."

"That's all?"

"One time, after me and Leaf split, he needed money. He told me to ask Felix Corn."

"You know where Corn is?"

"I got a number somewhere."

I waited in the avant-garde dining room while Gatormouth blundered through rooms I never saw. He finally came back with an old bright pink cell phone and read me the number from there.

"I need to get to my old man, Gates. It's for my grandmother."

He concentrated for some seconds, staring at the bright yellow rug.

"Luwanda prob'ly know where he at."

"You have her number?"

"Naw, but Leaf do."

"How do I get to her?"

"I'ont know exactly. That girl move around a lot. But I'll try an' send out a message."

7.

TRAVELING DUE SOUTH from Newark, I made my way to Goethals Bridge. From there I crossed over to New York, continuing my southern trek through Staten Island until just a mile or so outside Pleasant Plains. There I came to a deconsecrated church with high stone walls that I knew to be well fortified.

There was an outer stone postern that Melquarth Frost usually left open.

I drove up to a green iron gate, behind which five inquisitive Rottweilers came to investigate. I wondered where the sixth canine sentry was hiding.

"Hi, Joe," a woman's voice sounded over the speakerphone to the left.

"Olo."

"Mel's coming out to get you."

A few minutes later he emerged from the double doors that Pleasant Plains parishioners had passed through seeking penance until the congregation had donated enough money to build a grander edifice on the north side of the village.

Tall and lean, passionately insane Melquarth Frost—the patient watchmaker-assassin, philosopher–heist man, underworld bugaboo—passed through a shadow thrown by the church's highest tower. Wearing dark green military fatigues, he didn't have to speak for the dogs to disperse. He reached into a pocket and the iron gate rolled to the right.

I drove in and parked, climbed out of my toy car, and waited for the man named after Satan's uncle. When he walked up to me, I studied his face to gauge his mood the way prehistoric islanders must have studied the skies looking for signs of tsunami.

"Mel."

"Red," he hailed. "You look kinda beat."

"My grandmother has me looking for my father."

"Lookin' for him? I thought he was in Attica."

"So did I."

Mel was a darkly hued Caucasian, with a smile that was like a mischievous adolescent's grin.

"What does that have to do with Marigold and Antoinette?" he asked.

"Not a thing." I was relieved that he used my client's, and her daughter's, given names. This meant that they were *real people* in his eyes, and therefore worthy of respect and sanctuary.

"Then why you have them here?"

"The husband is rich, and he didn't want to go through proper channels to find them."

"I wouldn't either, if she took my child."

"In that case, I wouldn't tell you where she was if you asked me."

"Oh," he said. "It's like that."

Mel and I were of different spiritual species, but we were,

ofttimes, morally mutualistic. He turned back toward the entrance of the church, and I followed.

The nave of the church had twelve rows of pews separated by a threadbare carpeted aisle. Halfway down this walkway a little girl, seated on the floor, was laughing loudly as an eighty-pound Rottweiler bitch stood over her, licking her neck.

"Stop! Stop!" the child screamed in pleasure.

The guard dog gurgled in playful response.

Looking upon this scene, one might be appalled by a dog breed that had been trained since the days of the Roman legions to rip out men's throats and eat their livers, that dog standing over a defenseless child. But Melquarth, I knew, had set them together so, if it came to it, that dog would die for the child.

"Daisy," Mel said.

The Rottweiler stopped playing and turned her attention to my friend.

"Leave her alone."

Daisy ran to Mel's right side and sat.

Marigold and Oliya had been seated in a middle row. They had been watching the dog and child. When Mel interfered with the play, they stood and approached us.

Oliya was constructed from hardened muscle and girder-like bone. Past thirty but nowhere near forty, her hair was cut short and her hands reminiscent of small bear traps. She wore a uniform-like black culotte outfit that left her forearms and legs below the knee bare. She was even darker than Mel but could have been anything from a Pacific Islander to a Spaniard from the south of that country.

Oliya was a cross between a private detective and a merc.

She used to work for an international firm that offered protection for those who could afford it. But then Mel hired her to protect me, and they started a thing.

Now she lived in Brownsville, at an SRO informally called Mookie's Hotel. She worked either for me or for herself, plying the trade of a freebooter with a heart of cool platinum.

Marigold came up from behind Olo. Antoinette followed her mom.

The mercenary and I nodded a greeting, then the fugitive lady kissed my cheek.

"Thank you, Mr. Oliver," she said. "You know, I haven't felt this safe in well over a year."

"You can call me Joe."

"Joe."

My ex, Monica, née Lars, let me rot on Rikers Island because of my dalliances; that and the fact that she'd fallen in love with a cad named Coleman Tesserat. She was wrong to leave me in a place like Rikers. The stay there had nearly broken me. She was wrong about what she did, but she was right about my weakness for women. I wanted to be loved and adored, fucked, and clawed bloody, given everything I could manage by some woman, maybe any woman, but certainly a woman like Marigold Hart.

Since being released from Rikers, I'd been mostly able to keep my libidinous tendencies curbed. The memory of prison did that to me. I held back most of the time, but looking for my father opened a vein of insecurity that made me the moth, and Marigold an unchecked flame.

I think maybe she saw this weakness, this need in me. It had, after all, been her profession for at least a year to understand a man's needs, and to tend to them.

With Herculean effort I turned my attention to Olo and asked, "Everything go okay?"

"No one was watching," the lifelong soldier replied. "And no one saw us coming out here."

"Good."

"I'm going to go make dinner," Mel announced. "Any allergies?" There were none.

"You need me to stay here?" Olo asked after the master of the godless church had gone to the upper-floor kitchen.

"I thought that was what Mel needed."

"I don't think so," she said with a knowing sneer. "He loves the kid, and her mother doesn't bother him at all. Mel's not nearly as hard as he once was."

Taking in our words, Annie asked her mother, "Why are we here?"

"Because your father is looking for us and I need time to think."

"Am I going to school?"

"Not right now, honey."

"Good."

"Good?" That was me.

"Uh-huh," Antoinette said, defiantly.

"You don't like school?"

"I don't like *that* school."

"Why not?"

"They think their shit don't stink."

"Annie!" Marigold exclaimed.

"What?"

"Don't talk like that."

"You said it when Pava's mom said it was my fault Pava failed arithmetic."

It was fun to watch the changes the single mom had to go through to get to the place where she could say, "I'm sorry, sorry I said that. I was wrong."

Mel made hamburgers, French fries, and a salad. There was way more than enough for everybody, and he grilled the burgers to each diner's desired temperature. He seemed to be enjoying himself.

I spent a good deal of time explaining to Annie what I did for a living and how what I did was good for them.

"Your daddy's mad that you and your mom left Santa Barbara, and before they can talk, she needs me to explain to him why you aren't doing anything wrong."

The little white girl's severe expression reminded me of deep brown Etta-Jane out in Newark.

"So," she ventured, "if you talk to him and then he talks to us, does that mean we have to go back to Santa Barbara?"

"Do you want to go back?"

"No." The word coming out of her mouth was so small it could barely be heard.

"Why not?"

"Because you know when I have dinner with Mommy now, we're always laughing and talking about things that make us feel good. But when we were in Santa Barbara nobody hardly ever laughed. Everybody only ever said mean things."

Marigold turned her head away while Oliya's eyes passed silent judgment, and Mel gave a little nod that made my shoulders go cold.

At the very back of the church there was a third-floor dormitory that held twelve cells. These were rooms that had once been occupied by deacons, attendants, and sometimes, Mel said, by elder members of the church who needed a helping hand. Each one-room apartment had a simple writing table, two wall hooks for a clothes closet, and a single cot for the temporary tenant-penitent to rest.

That night only two rooms were occupied: one for Marigold and her daughter and one for me.

I stayed because it was late, and I wanted to be there if Marigold needed anything—at least that's what I told myself.

Sitting at the foot of the cot, my only light was a flickering candle. Through the small window, recessed in the thick stone wall, I could see the three-quarters moon. I wanted to think but all I could do was feel. My grandmother was sick. My father was on the run, had been for years. It was as if I had been asleep for all that time. I wanted to save both, but there I was, in lambent darkness, and all I could think about was Marigold Hart.

She and Annie were asleep at the other end of Penitents' Hall, as Mel called it. When I inhaled, I could almost taste the scent that woman wore at the Versailles when I was stalking her, working to bring her down.

I was a brooding beast, my unsuspecting prey down the cave-like hall and my hope of salvation residing in that moon, which so much seemed like a free-floating soul. I wanted to sleep. I needed the rest. But all I could do was sit there holding back from dogging down that stone corridor.

Then there came a gentle knock on the unpainted oaken door.

"Yeah?" I spoke aloud.

"Joe?"

"Come on in."

And there she was, the penitent's prayer, wearing a pale pink silken slip under a turquoise kimono that came down to the middle of her thighs.

"Were you asleep?"

"No. Just thinkin' about things I have to do."

Closing the door behind her, Hart, as I came to call her, walked over to the blocky chair set at my writing table.

Her feet were bare.

"What things?" she asked.

"I need to make plans, but I can't seem to think like that right now."

"Maybe you should sleep," she suggested.

"Can't."

"Why not?"

"I can't get my head to accept that I have to rest, I guess."

"What do you need?"

You. That's what I wanted to say. Not love or forever, not even sex, not really. I was hungry for something while in the process of losing and having lost everything.

When it became obvious that I couldn't answer her question, she said, "Tell me what it is that you have to do."

"The only thing I can do. I haven't seen my father in thirty years, but now I—I need him."

"Is he lost or . . ."

"He went to prison for aggravated assault and attempted murder when I was thirteen. I haven't heard from or spoken to him since then."

"He didn't write?"

"He did. But I was a child and so angry that I didn't read the letters until now. And I never knew when he got out of Attica."

"And now you're looking for him."

"Because his mother, my grandmother, has a tumor and is gonna go under the knife."

"Oh my God."

The emotion coming from her brought me, unexpectedly, to the verge of tears.

She rose from the chair and alighted next to me on the cot.

"Do you know where to look for him?" she asked.

"It'll be hard because the police are after him, so he's in hiding. He might be in New York, Philly, or anywhere else in the world."

She put a hand on my shoulder. I shuddered in response.

We sat like that for a few long minutes.

"You can't do anything about that right now, Joe."

"I know."

"Lie down."

"I will, right after I walk you to your room."

"You don't have to."

I gave a harrumph-like laugh and said, "I surely don't want to. But that would be best for both of us, I think."

I kissed her good night outside the far cell. She kissed me back and I thought of my mother and father in shadow on the outer edges of my hungry heart.

Back in my room, laid up on that cot, I realized that I'd been having trouble breathing before M. Hart came to my room. Her gentle offers and ardent kisses were enough, more than enough, for me to believe that there was some chance that Brenda would survive and so would her son. All I had to do was be true to myself and that bright moon.

Sleep overcame me within minutes.

8.

THE STONE WINDOW was filled with sunlight.

Usually, I knew within a quarter hour what time it was when I awoke. But that morning, in that primitive cell, I had no inkling of the time. I couldn't even have said what day it was. It might have been Sunday afternoon in some Dutch hamlet, the year 1159.

I breathed in deeply this possible present. That felt good.

The good night kiss from the evening before was what I needed. Not love or forever.

"Hi, Joe!" Antoinette called brightly from the dining table set off from the kitchen. She and her mother, Melquarth, and Oliya were all seated. They seemed almost like a normal family before going off to school and work.

"Hi, Annie, everybody," I hailed. "What's for breakfast?"

"Smoked trout hash," Mel said. "Also, sourdough toast with goat's butter and homemade blueberry jam."

We mostly talked about silly things and some sensible ones. Mel was thinking of having the church painted bright lemon yellow. This made Antoinette laugh uncontrollably. Oliya told a joke about a hundred-year-old woman and her older sister. Hart smiled at me — twice.

The other adults at the table decided that it would be a good thing to go to the Bronx Zoo. I was invited, but everyone knew that I had work to accomplish.

I had called the number for Felix Corn the afternoon before. The person answering the call said, "Christian Charities."

After a few words my next morning was planned.

Christian Charities and Hope appeared to be little more than a storefront on Bowery a few blocks south of Delancey. The entire facade was made from windows that surrounded a door that was also crafted from glass. Three desks lined up across the front of the room, like the first line of defense in some modern war that was to be fought sitting down, and at a great distance. Behind the desks was a door that led to a private office. I was pretty sure that that room was my goal.

The front line consisted of a triumvirate of bureaucratic guards. The first was an older white gentleman on my far left. He was short and still exhibited vestiges of the powerful frame of youth. He was scowling at a paper spreadsheet that he seemed to think was lying to him. The man had on a worn red-and-black work shirt. His horn-rimmed glasses frame was thick and chipped here and there.

At the center desk sat a middle-aged white woman wearing a powder-blue Versace suit. Her necklace was composed of about a dozen pink quarter-carat diamonds. She was on the phone.

"Yes, Mr. Carlyle, I am Dorothy Ridges…Yes…I don't know of any other women by that name, but there might be…" she said, then patiently listened to his suspicions. "Well then, I suggest you ask your friend to ask me if I am me and so worthy of your donation. Good-bye."

Ms. Ridges, whoever she was, then looked up at me and smiled.

"Yes?"

"Hi. My name is Joe Oliver, and I was hoping to see Mr. Corn."

The strength of her smile waned a little.

Jutting her head forward a few centimeters, she asked, "What is it you want with him?"

"It's a private matter."

"He's a busy man."

"And you are one of many possible Dorothy Ridges. So?"

"There's no reason to be rude," she said.

I had a reply for this observation but decided to keep it to myself.

"Padma," Ms. Ridges said.

"Yes?" answered the young brown woman seated at the desk to my right.

"Would you please go ask Mr. Corn if he'd like to speak to a Mr. Joe Oliver on a private matter?"

"Sure," Padma said, though her tone didn't sound agreeable.

The young, maybe Hindu, woman stood in brown silk splendor. The loosely form-fitting sari she wore did not belong in that room, under the name of Christianity, or behind that desk.

Confidently she made her way to and through the door at the back of the room.

"Have a seat, Mr. Oliver," Dorothy Ridges requested, gesturing toward the two straight-back chairs that flanked the front door.

"I prefer to stand." Anything to be at odds with her.

She weighed the value of arguing with me, finally deciding that it would do no good.

I moved down to stand in front of Padma's desk so as not to get blamed for hovering.

Five or six minutes passed before the slumming Indian princess reentered through the back door.

She walked up to me and asked, "Are you related to Chief Oliver?"

"He's my father."

She looked up at me and smiled with real pleasure showing through, happy that I gave the right answer.

"Come with me," she said.

I expected to find Mr. Felix Corn somewhere near the back door of the storefront charity, but instead there were four more desks around which eight more young people, seated and moving around, were busy accomplishing many tasks. Lots of telephone talking, computer entry, and paper files being shuffled from one pair of hands to the next.

Padma led me to the left, where there rose a corkscrew-shaped ladder-like stairway.

She went up first and I followed.

"That Ms. Ridges is certainly in charge," I said.

Padma stopped and turned, looking down on me.

"She thinks that she's everybody's boss," the young woman agreed. "I don't have to report to her but she's always telling me what to do."

"And you show her respect because of her age," I said. "Not her money. But she'll never understand that."

Padma smiled, squared her shoulders, and continued the climb.

There was a round hole in the ceiling above. Passing through this portal, holding on to the spiral banister, we came into a lovely old-fashioned office. The ceiling was twelve feet high, and the walls were all bookshelves containing a whole lifetime's worth of reading. There were no windows but still there was a feeling of airiness.

In the northeast corner of the spacious room stood a behemoth of a desk made of dark wood.

"King," a man said. He was standing up from behind the desk. Barrel-shaped and white, he had generous gray eyebrows giving a feral cast to his otherwise friendly face.

This impressive older man came around the desk and strode toward me in an aggressively friendly manner.

Taking both my hands, he held them close to his chest with true primitive sophistication. Even though he was near eighty, there was still some muscle to his grip.

"I am so happy to meet you, son. Your father never stopped talking about you."

"The only time I ever heard about you," I replied, "my father was indicted for attempted murder. You were the victim, testifying against him."

The older man nodded slightly, released my hands, then turned to usher Padma.

"You can go now, my dear," he said.

She made eye contact with each of us, one after the other, and then headed for the circular stairway.

"Have a seat, King," Felix said when her head bobbed down and away.

There was a chair in front of the table-wide desk. It was substantial and walnut brown, lacquered and designed for comfort.

"You remind me of him," Felix said, making it back to his equally impressive throne of a chair. "He always said exactly what he thought, never considered any other way."

"Uh-huh." I was wondering if Corn had a gun somewhere below the green blotter before him.

"I'm looking for Chief."

Corn considered my request.

"You ever been in prison?" he asked.

"Spent a while at Rikers." Just speaking these words caused a little gasp in my chest.

"Ever get raped in there?"

"No. You?"

Those feral eyes lost their friendliness, for only a moment.

"Chief's been out a long time," he said.

"That's what they tell me."

"I haven't seen him for a good while."

"But you've heard from him. You sent him money."

This assertion aroused suspicion in the octogenarian.

"How do I know you're his son?"

"All you got to do is look at me." It was true. I looked a lot like the old man. Brenda often commented on it.

Felix Corn allowed a momentary smile out from under his gray and tawny mustache.

"Did you make it all the way out of Rikers?" he asked.

I understood the question. You could take the man out

of the prison but not the prison out of him, that's what they said. Letting go of the fear and humiliation, the rage and the feeling of abject defeat, was by far the most difficult part of rehabilitation.

"What do you do here, Mr. Corn?" I asked instead of giving an answer to his question.

He clasped his hands before his face as if in prayer, the forefingers coming together, pointing upward. This pose made it seem like he was considering the question for the first time.

"I've been out for years," he said. "I found Christ in there. Not the spiritual savior but the saved man. A man who endured all kinds of suffering and poverty and accepted that as his lot, his destiny. Can you understand that?"

I could.

"Most prison salaries are pretty low," he continued. "Twelve cents an hour, forty at most. I bought up whole big lots of hours, made deals with the gangs and the guards, then sold it to corporations all over the world; a united, contained workforce cheaper than anywhere in the so-called third world."

"Sounds a little like slavery," I commented.

"Yeah."

"Lotta money in that?"

"Yeah."

"And so, what does that have to do with charity and hope?"

"We use most of the profit to help the families of the incarcerated," he said. "The rest goes toward getting the ex-cons meaningful employment once they're out."

"That all?" I asked, suggesting with my tone that there might be a darker side to the business.

"No," he acknowledged. "But you must understand something, son. This business exists only to give the poor convicts and their families some hope. Anything we do under the table will one day set some poor soul free."

Switching it up again, I said, "About my father."

"I honestly don't know where he is, King. Every once in a great while he gets word to Andrew Williams and Andy comes to me. But that's it. If he does that again I'll send him a note."

"What about Ira Gross?"

"He's dead."

"And they want my father for it."

Felix gazed down upon the concentrated green of his blotter. He sighed, reminding me of when I was a child and my little lungs couldn't manage to contain a yawn.

"Did you kill him?" I asked.

"No."

"Did my father?"

Shaking his head in a dug-in sort of way, he said, "I don't think so."

"Do you think you know who did?"

"No. No, I don't."

"How about why," I said. "What was he into?"

"We lost touch after I was convicted. The only thing I know for sure is that Ira never stopped buying and selling stolen goods."

"You know to who, uh, to whom?"

We both smiled at the corrective of proper grammar.

"I didn't wanna know," he said.

"It's important that I get to Chief. Is there anything I should be asking you that I'm not?"

The question, its meaning, tickled my father's victim-cum-friend.

"Maybe Ruby Lee," he proposed.

"His old girlfriend?"

"Yeah. Her."

"What about her?"

"They were close—real close."

"What's that supposed to mean?"

"It means you should find Ruby and ask her the questions you're asking me."

"You know where she's at?"

"I don't know anything."

I doubted that.

Across the street from Christian Charities and Hope was a gritty coffee shop called the Daily Grind. They didn't serve lattes or cappuccinos, no espresso-based drinks at all. But the coffee was strong and cheap. I like cheap. Not that long before, I came upon a potential windfall of nearly seventy-five million dollars' worth of emeralds. That said, I should have been living on the coast of St. Lucia, eating green figs and salt fish along with beluga caviar and Dom Pérignon.

The problem was that the emeralds, given to me by the wife of a dead man, were connected to what I can only call . . . a database of evil. Intelligence so disturbing and fundamentally wrong that I couldn't bear to hold on to it.

So, I found someone to take the database and the gems off my hands.

Broke once more, I searched out cheap coffee in open-air cafés, sitting upon wobbly metal chairs at small round tables that were wiped clean once a day.

There were only four tables on the inside of the Grind. Across from my little counter sat a young Black woman with a body so impossible that it could only truly exist in the sweaty dreams of a thirteen-year-old boy. Lips, legs, and extra-long lashes were so outsize, and yet so perfectly proportioned, that I kept glancing at her, again an effect of my anguish over my father and his mother.

"What you lookin' at?" the young woman asked. There was no perturbation in her tone.

"You."

"Sumpin' wrong with me?"

"Not unless there's somethin' wrong with God to be teasin' me with heaven before my time."

I knew I'd hit the right note when it became obvious that she could not add to the banter.

She let all of fifteen seconds pass, rose from that lucky chair, and walked out, smiling and shaking her head.

I was thankful for that woman, because she reminded me of another woman, a woman named Tita. Marguerita Fordham, daughter of Ilse Fordham, aka Ruby Lee.

9.

"HELLO."

"Gates?" I asked, using the name my father had always called him.

"Hey, King," answered Andrew "Gatormouth" Williams.

"I wanted to ask you somethin'."

"Anything outside'a money, and it's yours."

"Do you know how I could get in touch with Ruby Lee?"

"Your father's old girlfriend?"

"Yeah."

"I know her, but I haven't seen her in twenty years. Your daddy didn't talk about her when we got together either."

"How about Marguerita Fordham?"

"You mean Tita Lee?"

I'd liked that man since I was a child.

"Yes. That's exactly what I mean."

"Gimme fifteen, and I'll call you back."

I was seated on a bench in Washington Square Park, enjoying the dappled sunlight through the covering canopy of leaves. When the cell phone sounded a few minutes later, I answered without checking to see who it was.

"Yeah?"

"That's how you answer the phone?" Gladstone Palmer lilted.

"Sorry, Glad," I replied. "Thought it was a unwanted booty call."

"And who'd be pesterin' you that way?"

"Nova Jennings." I liked making up names on the fly. "She good-lookin', so when she started talkin' 'bout havin' kids, I had to go cold turkey."

Glad was a scalawag but not only that. For all his selfish, shallow egotism, Sergeant Palmer's mind was sharp as a razor. I had to mislead him or he'd have all my secrets.

"That's the only way, me boy," he assured me. "Woman needs to live in a castle, and property values are too dear."

"So, what is it you want, Glad?"

"Been gettin' calls from out west."

"I should have something soon, supposed to be meeting with my helper tonight."

"That's that Ruez girl?"

"It is."

"You ever hear of a company named Int-Op?"

"The International Operatives Agency."

"So, you know who she worked for before coming here."

"I do. Girl's gotta rep."

A double beep sounded on the line.

"I got another call comin' in, Glad. I'll call you in the morning. All right?"

"Okay. Try and leave Miss Nova alone till then."

I accepted the new call while canceling the good and bad cop.

"Gates?"

"I got what you need, Joe."

Two blocks from the intersection of Main Street and Roosevelt Avenue, on Union Street in Flushing, Queens, is an upscale curio store named Kao's Jade Imports. From the display window it seemed as if Kao specialized in white jadeite sculptures and jewelry. If I hadn't been on the job, I might have gone in there to look for something for Aja.

Instead, I entered the vestibule to the left of the entrance of the jade shop.

Therein I found a list of names correlating with apartment numbers.

Gregory Xú was in apartment 33.

Up the slender staircase, on my way to the third floor, I passed a diminutive late-middle-age Chinese woman in a gray skirt and green top. She looked up at me with wonder but no concern in her eyes.

"You going to three-three?" she asked.

"Got it on the first try."

She gave me a grin and I gave it right back.

The door to 33 would have been a blue sapphire had it been made from crystal. Even as painted wood it was stunning. It had an old-fashioned brass knocker that I employed, sparingly.

A minute later a tall and elegant Asian man opened the beautiful door. He wore a sleek business suit over a buttoned-up white shirt that sported no tie. Behind him was the entrance hallway of a small apartment that seemed to go up rather than out. Stacks of boxes and newspapers stood in front of shelves that held everything from books to canned goods.

"Yes?" he asked.

His hair, once jet, now streaked with gray, looked more like a lion's mane than a human scalp. He was maybe ten years older than I, but his life force was immortal, that's what I thought.

"Greg Xú?"

"Who's asking?" He had no discernible accent.

"Joe Oliver."

"And what is a Joe Oliver?"

"A man looking for a woman named Ruby Lee."

"There's no one by that name here," he informed me, but his eyes said something else.

"Come on, Gee," a Black woman's voice called from somewhere within the warren-apartment. "I'm back here, Joe."

Fastidious and uber-human Gregory Xú tilted his head to the left and backed away sideways, allowing me into the tall hall.

I walked past him, going twelve paces down the jam-packed hallway, where I entered a nearly perfectly round room that was maybe fourteen feet in diameter. There were three padded chairs set in an arc against the far wall, across from the entryway. Seated in the middle chair was Marguerita Fordham, Tita Lee, daughter of Molen Jarman, who, the rumor mill said, had impregnated but never married her mother, Ruby Lee.

She was sitting back on the roundish mini settee with the sole of her left foot lifted to the seat. She wore a green robe that was rich and evocative of some long-ago and faraway time, and her demeanor was fresher than country milk.

Tita was long and lean, Black in the extreme, with outsize

features that would have seemed just right to any portrait artist worth his salt. Her smile was infectious.

Gregory came in around me and sat down to the right of the youngish-looking woman, who was in her mid-thirties.

"Sit, Joe," she said, patting the seat of the chair to her left.

I followed this instruction.

"What are you doing here?" she asked me. "You plain-clothes now?"

"I was bounced out ten years ago."

"You? You the straightest arrow they ever made."

"That's what they tell me."

Gregory had been looking at me a little harder since hearing that I might have been a cop.

"So, you're not police?" Tita asked.

"Not for ten years. I'm here because a man told me that if I want my questions answered I'd have to go to Ruby Lee."

"What questions?"

"I'm looking for my father."

The flickering humor of a woman in charge faded away. Tita put her foot on the floor and watched me.

"Gee," she said.

"Yeah?" her man replied.

"Can you go down to the store and get me a forty?"

"Why?"

"Joe's an old friend of my people, and we need to talk some family business."

Not liking being ejected from the apartment that bore his name, Gregory X got up out of the padded seat, stared at Tita for a whole ten seconds, and then walked off down the hall.

When we heard the front door close, I asked, "He your sugar daddy?"

"You got the sugah part right."

I smiled, appreciating the intentional haziness of her answer.

"What you lookin' for my mother for?" she asked.

"I told you."

"But you might not be sayin' all that you mean. From what I heard, you a detective now, private."

"Then why you call me a cop?"

Offering an enigmatic smile, she repeated, "What you lookin' for my mother for?"

"My grandmother, Chief's mother, is real sick. She wants to see her son, and I heard that Ruby might know how to get her there. That's all there is to it."

Tita turned a little more in my direction, looking for something in me.

"I know where Ruby at," she said at last.

I skipped the where and asked her, "How much?"

"I look broke to you?" she mocked. "Shit. I don't need no man's money."

"My grandmother always says, 'Trouble or money, either one, you get what you pay for.'"

"Ain't that the truth."

"Come on, Tita, I need to find my dad."

"I need to get away from here," she said, looking around as if the silo of a room was her own private prison.

Not wanting to drag out the conversation, I asked, "You got a specific place you need to be?"

"You mean other than not here?"

"I mean that it don't do no good to run if you don't know where you runnin' to." I liked speaking the language of our upbringing; it felt just that much closer to truth.

"Charleston. I got friends down there."

"That's a good start. Now all I need to know is what you're running from."

"Why you need to know that?"

"Because, if you know where Ruby is, then somebody else does too. And if what you're runnin' from means katanas and guns, then maybe I should ask somebody else."

"What's a katana?"

"Cutter," I said, crossing my throat with a point-finger nail.

When Tita gulped, I knew we were going to do some business.

"Where's Ruby?" I asked again.

"After you help me," she stipulated.

"No. Gettin' you out of whatever you in and then all the way down to South Carolina, that's heavy liftin'. All you got to do is give me an address."

"How can I trust you, Joe? I mean, you might not be a cop, but you was one."

"You can trust me because you know you can," I said. "Otherwise, you wouldn't have asked for my help in the first place."

She knew I was right.

"Okay. All right. So how does this work?"

"Write down Ruby's address and your phone number. I'll go to Ruby and the minute we talk I'm'a call this man named Rags. Rags will come and get you and make sure there's a seat on a plane to take you down Charleston."

Tita did not like the offer. She wanted to force me to make a different deal. A transaction that she'd be more in charge of. I could see the furious plotting going on behind her eyes. But everything I'd said was true. She had no one and nothing else.

So she pulled a semitranslucent purple plastic purse from the side of her chair and rummaged through it until coming out with an ink pen and simple pad of paper.

"So, you goin' to my mom's and then this Rags man gonna call me?"

"First you tell me what you runnin' from."

Tita was a perfect example of the contradictions created by industrial-strength poverty. She was an extraordinary human being but didn't know it. She could have had a PhD in philosophy or maybe German literature. She could have carved out a place for herself on Wall Street or even in Hollywood. She was that smart, that charismatic. But she was also a hood rat, brought up worrying about last month's rent, her next meal, and how to get over on those who only knew violence, inebriation, and death. For her, survival was rarely a plan and, more often, just the luck of the draw.

"Gregory a piece'a work," she said. "He makes his money in what they call human trafficking."

"Prostitutes?"

"It don't stop there. He makes his mules carry whatever the market want. Drugs, jewels, guns. I told him that I didn't wanna be around that shit and he told me that there was only two ways I could get out: my death or his pardon."

"His pardon?"

"That's what he said. So, um, I been goin' in these big envelopes that they bring him sometimes. When they's money in 'em, I peel me off a little. I got almost ten thousand dollars. I got money, so all I need is to get away clean."

"Who brings the envelopes to Greg?"

"Men," she said, sneering and shaking her head to impart her ignorance about these men's identities.

"Tita."

"What?"

"What you need me for? I mean, why don't you just pick up that purple purse and take the subway to Port Authority?"

"I'm too scared, Joe," she said, holding up fists that writhed like balls of mating snakes. "Greg got people everywhere. I'm afraid they might see me."

"Couldn't you just find a peaceful gangbanger to hang wit'?"

She laughed, showing her teeth.

"Don't call your mother," I said. "Because if she ain't around when I get there, you are shit outta luck."

"You not gonna get her inta nuthin', right?"

"No. I just need to find my father."

I'd taken three steps on the sidewalk when Gregory Xú confronted me. He presented a bit of a conundrum in that he was carrying a translucent plastic bag containing two over-large cans of beer. This was an offering to Tita. Maybe he loved her. Maybe he'd cry after cutting her throat.

"What did she want?" he asked me.

"It's what I wanted."

"What's that?"

"She's my people, brother, but I don't know you. So, if you need to know somethin', then you'd do well to ask her."

"Don't fuck with me," he said. For the first time I thought I might have caught a hint of an accent.

"Wouldn't think of it," I replied jauntily, and then I walked away.

10.

THE ADDRESS TITA gave me was on 138th Street down the hill from CCNY, once called the workingman's Harvard.

The front doors of the huge apartment complex weren't locked and there was, of course, no doorman. I made my way up to apartment 8G with no problem.

My luck ran out there.

I was just about to knock on 8G's door when, "Hey, man, who the fuck are you?" a young man's voice both questioned and declared.

The youth was tall and heavy, strong, and ready to fight. His eyes looked as if he were crazy or high—maybe both.

"What the fuck is it to you?" I replied.

In other circumstances I might have given my name, but on that floor, at that moment, capitulation would have been the admission of weakness. And in that particular situation weakness was akin to guilt.

"What?" he sputtered.

"Is this here your fuckin' door?"

He looked at the door, maybe a little confused.

"You shittin' me, man?" he asked.

"If I was, you would smell it."

My back was maybe six inches from the doorjamb and my hope was that I was faster than the angry young man.

I didn't have to wait long to find out. The man, who I thought of as *Tiny,* dipped a little to his right and so broadcast the right cross. I waited until the blow was launched before ducking down and to my left.

Tiny yelled in pain when his fist broke against hard wood.

The ensuing ballet couldn't have been presented at Lincoln Center, but there's a whole world of men, and some sisters, that would have been entertained and enlightened by the performance.

The angry man was an inch or three taller than I, and four stone heavier. Definitely in a higher weight class, he was limited by an injured hand. So, when he moved to hit me with a left, I grabbed onto his right shoulder to get myself out of range. Even just the tug on his right side brought pain to his hand.

He hollered and tried to ram me against the wall with his bulk. I moved to the side, got around behind him, and pushed him hard against that wall. He turned quickly but was still holding the wrist of his right hand with his left.

I decided that this would be a good time to test Tiny's chin.

Hitting flesh and bone with a bare fist is always going to hurt. But sometimes it's the only answer. I had to do something, Tiny was dangerous, and he might have had a knife or even a pistol in his pocket. So I threw a punch that landed on the hinge of the left side of his jaw. This blow stalled him for two seconds before he leapt at me. I just barely got out of the way. He belly flopped on the tile floor and slid about a yard, slamming his head against the wall. This fall hurt him more than half a dozen of my fists could hope to.

I could have kicked and stomped him while he was down.

I should have kicked and stomped him, because in a street fight your life and continued well-being depended not only on winning but on winning quickly.

Tiny got up on his left knee and started pushing his pained right hand against the far wall.

I cursed myself for not ending the fight with my heel.

"Jules Harvey!" a woman yelled.

Tiny had made it to his feet. His white T-shirt had flecks of blood from a gash that the wall had inflicted on his scalp.

"I'm'a kill you!" he shouted.

"Step back, Jules!" the woman warned.

I turned to see that the speaker was Ruby Lee from the old neighborhood.

Tiny took a step toward me, and Ruby produced a dangerous-looking revolver from the apron she wore.

"Bettah step away, son," she advised.

She pulled back the hammer.

The stunned look on Tiny's face was almost funny.

"Go clean yourself up, boy," Ruby said. "You bleedin'."

When she called him boy, I realized that my attacker wasn't more than sixteen.

"Joe."

"Yeah, Ruby?"

"Give the man twenty dollars."

I reached into my pocket and came out with some bills. These I handed to Jules Harvey. He took them with his left hand. The right had swollen to twice its normal size. He brought the good hand, money and all, to his bleeding scalp. Then he turned away and staggered back down the hall toward whatever door was open to him.

I took a deep breath. I would have won that fight, but not without some scars. I wasn't ruthless enough to stomp him.

That was not good.

"What you doin' here, Joe?" Ruby Lee asked.

"Can I come in, Rube?"

Her apartment had a familiar feel to it. The sofa and its matching chair were swirls of white and blue fabric. The coffee table was low with curvy and strong maple legs.

"You need a drink?" she asked.

"Absolutely."

"I ain't got no vodka," she said.

I wondered if that was a play on the word *absolute*.

"Whatever you got."

She left the room, and I lowered onto the chair heavily. There was a feeling of elation glimmering around the folds of my brain — that's what it felt like. To get into a fight and come out of it alive was a major feat in the streets I'd come from.

She came back with a squat glass filled with a clear liquid.

"Tequila."

"To you," I said and downed the draft.

Ruby sat, saying, "Joe, how in the world am I gonna open my door and see you fightin' a man twice your size?"

"Looking for Chief."

Ruby was an older version of her daughter — Tita. She was around fifty years of age and beautiful, deadly as a viper and captivating as an eclipse of the sun. And she was thin, almost preternaturally so. Where Tita relied on the kindness of strangers, self-assured Ruby was a predator in all situations.

But every predator has a heart. Her lean face softened at the mention of my father.

"You look like him," she said.

"You know where he's at, Ruby?"

"They say you became a cop," was her answer.

"That was a long time ago, and even if I was still on the force, I wouldn't turn that shit on my own father."

Ruby studied me. Her face was serious. The room was as still as a mausoleum.

Then she grinned.

"You shocked the shit outta Jules," she said. "He been jumpin' on folks all ovah around heah. Think 'cause he so big that smaller men got to bow down. Shit. You prob'ly saved that fool's life. Next time he see some smaller man like a victim he gonna remember you."

"That's silk right outta the sow's ear," I said, and she laughed again.

"How you find me?" she asked.

"Tita."

"She just give me up like that?" Ruby asked, but she wasn't bothered by her daughter's indiscretion.

"She knew I was smart enough not to try and do nuthin' to you," I said. "And on top of that, she got a problem with her man."

"Gregory Xú." Ruby's grimace was designed to scare small children and wild animals.

"You know him?"

"He sells children."

That was a showstopper.

"That reminds me," I said after maybe half a minute. "I need to make a call."

I took out my phone and entered a number.

"King," Rags answered on the first ring.

I told him about Tita and her troubles.

"You need me to get her out of there?" he asked.

"I do indeed."

"This for Grandma B?"

"It is."

"Okay. Text me her number. If it's easy enough, I'll just take care of it on my own. If there's a kink, I'll call you back."

When I disconnected the call, I looked up to see Ruby staring at me, an indecipherable expression on her face.

"Yeah?" I inquired.

She didn't answer right away. Instead, she sat back, pulling her left foot up on the sofa just as Tita had had her foot on the chair in her prisoner's apartment.

"I love that girl," she said at last. "She no end'a trouble an' got sass up the ass, but when she was a li'l girl she'd look up at me when my heart was 'bout to bust an' say, 'It's all right, Mama, it's all right.'"

Now and again, when I'm with people I've known since I was a pup, it feels as if we were creatures of some kind, animals that don't need domestication or laws. Just the blood in our veins and the language of our actions proved to be enough to guide us.

"I cain't say for sure where Chief's at," Ruby said. "But there's some people that might know."

"Who's that?"

"A man named Carney is one."

"Where can I find him?"

"You cain't. Carney stays away from most people. That's why Chief trust 'im, he moves in places where most people cain't get to."

"Can you get there?"

"I think so."

"What's the magic word?"

"What you want wit' Chief?"

"Grandma B got a tumor and she wanna see him fore she goes under the knife."

"Lemme go make a call."

It was evening before I got my little car down east of Sheepshead Bay.

"This is the most uncomfortable car I ever rode in," Ruby complained. "Why you drive a old hunk a junk like this?"

"Gets me where I'm goin' and I can always find a place to park it . . . I think it's that place up there."

On the border of the beach and the Atlantic Ocean was a small warehouse, three tall stories high. It was well maintained and protected with cameras, steel bars, signs that warned you to keep out; all that added in with a certain somber mood.

I parked out front.

"Looks spooky," Ruby said.

"You never been here before?"

Moving her head from side to side, she said, "Never even met the man. Years ago, Chief give me a number and a name and said to call if I really needed him bad."

There was a small door over which hung a sign that read INTERNATIONAL OPTIONS, INTERNATIONAL.

"This is the place," Ruby said.

There was no ringer and it seemed silly to knock on the door because even that small warehouse was pretty big. I didn't have to worry about knocking, however, because the door came open as we arrived, revealing an unexpected host.

He was seven feet tall, at least, and no less than sixty years of age. His gray hair was a little too long and his white skin seemed, somehow, drab. Even though he had no facial hair, you wouldn't have called him clean-shaven. The only thing about him that glimmered with life was his light topaz, nearly lemon-colored eyes.

He wore a tan shirt and pants of the same color and material. Oddly the clothes seemed to belong on a smaller frame.

"Joe Oliver?" he asked, a hint of threat in the tone.

"Yeah. Carney?"

"Come on in."

Ruby and I entered the behemoth's warehouse. Behind him was a huge room, two stories in height, that was brightly lit and unique in my experience. Along the walls were piles of boxes, racks of tools, and various barrel-like canisters painted garish colors. The center of the space was a perfectly laid-out fifteen-hundred-square-foot apartment. Bedroom, kitchen, living room, and den. The showroom-like apartment didn't contain a toilet because there were no walls to provide privacy.

Carney led us into the living quarters.

"Drink?" he offered.

"You got orange juice?" Ruby asked.

"In the icebox," he replied, nodding toward the kitchen section.

She headed for the refrigerator.

"What about you, Joe?" the titan asked.

"I'm okay."

He smiled at this answer.

"Ruby," Carney called into the kitchen.

"Yeah?"

"I'm gonna go upstairs with Joe and talk to him for a minute. The stereo, TV, and telephone all work. We'll be back down soon."

"Okay."

The elevator was built for two and so we were a little crowded in there. Carney had to bow his head and I was pressed into a corner. But we made it. The next flight up was the actual third floor. It was also one big room. In a far corner stood a big white desk, a bookcase, and a padded chair for visitors.

Once installed behind the desk, Carney said, "So, Ruby says that you're looking for Chief."

"And what does that have to do with you?"

"Chief and I are very good friends."

"How did that come about?" My decision to question the big man was more instinct than design.

"I was in Attica with him for two and a half years."

"In Attica for what?"

"Murder."

"First degree?"

He nodded.

"Then why you out?"

"My son," he said and then halted. "My son killed my wife's lover. I was charged and pleaded innocent, but I didn't really challenge the prosecutor. Chief came up to me my first day on the yard and we struck up a friendship."

"What kinda friendship?"

"The kind that protected me."

"What he get out of it? Money?"

"No. Chief collected people around him for what he called self-defense and civility. He had every race, religion, and crime—except for sex crimes and unnecessary brutality. I think maybe he thought I could handle myself because I didn't act scared, and I didn't take shit. I mean, they could'a cut me down to size but I would'a made 'em work for it."

"How'd you get out?"

"That's where the money came in," he said. "Your dad talked to me up in Attica. He told me that I was depressed."

"You didn't know that already?"

The big shaggy man looked up at me, an expression of bewilderment on his rough-hewn face.

"No," he said. "No. I felt that I deserved what had happened; that I really was the criminal; that I belonged in there."

Carney shivered violently, reminding me of a man I once saw electrocute himself by grabbing a downed power line. He wasn't trying to commit suicide, just didn't understand the danger. It was the most useless death I'd ever seen.

"Okay. So, my father diagnosed you. What next?"

"He got me to hire this lawyer, and the lawyer, James Roll, applied for me to get psychiatric treatment. While I took the pills, Roll came up with evidence that the prosecutor had withheld. By the time he was ready to go to trial, I was too. Now I'm out, and my son is dead."

Carney looked me in the eye when uttering the last five words, almost begging me to ask what had happened to his son. But I didn't bite.

Thinking that Carney needed a little more psychiatric treatment, I asked, "So can you get me to my father?"

"That depends."

"On what?"

"If you let me take a cell phone picture of you, I'll see that Chief gets it. He can decide from there."

After going through the picture-taking procedure I asked, "How long will it take you to get to him?"

"It's not a straight shot," he said. "Maybe a day, maybe a week, maybe never."

11.

"YOU ARE ONE tall drink'a watah," Ruby said to Carney. We were eating Greek salad and garlic-pepperoni pizza that a local place delivered.

Sitting there, at a small table in the kitchenette of the display apartment, we tried in our ways to be courteous. I could have just as well been on the road home, but Ruby was hungry, and Carney offered.

"My parents were both normal size," he said. "But me and my brother came out like this. I had a sister too, but she was just small."

"You live here full-time?" I asked the big Boy Scout–clad man.

He looked down and nodded before saying, "Yeah."

"Needed somethin' a little bigger after a prison cell, huh?" Ruby joked.

"All my people are dead," he said. "Only ones left are me and my ex. And we both feel so guilty about Teddy that we can't bear each other's company."

"Teddy your son?" I asked.

"Yeah." He shrugged. "My mother was the last of our blood to die. I got everything after that. Not much really. This building and some investments that just about pay for it."

After the feasting was over, Carney brought out the wine.

Intending to go home that night, I abstained.

"Your wife did you dirt, huh, Big C?" Ruby asked.

They were three-quarters of the way through a second bottle of Chianti.

"I couldn't blame her, Rube," he said as if they'd been friends for years.

"No?" my father's girlfriend said. "How you gonna forgive sumpin' like that?"

"I was...I don't know. I was shy and I was rude, bad-tempered too. Not that I'd hit Felicia or Teddy, but I'd walk away, stay away sometimes for days. I didn't know how good I had it and she needed more."

There were a thousand questions to ask and no reason to ask them. So, "I think it's about time to get you home, Ruby," I said.

"You go on," she told me. "Maybe I'll stay here a little longer."

"How you gonna get back?"

"I got my subway card."

I hesitated, feeling a little like dead Teddy, trying to do right in a situation that had nothing to do with me.

On my way home I changed directions and headed for Pleasant Plains.

I knocked on her penitent's cell door.

She opened up, this time clad in only the slip.

"Hi," she said.

"Hey."

"Let's go down to your room."

"What about Annie?"

"I got a little mike on her, connected to an app on my phone."

It had been a while since I'd spent any real time with a woman. Hart was so sophisticated and well put together that it was a surprise how down and dirty she could get. Even though I didn't realize it at the time, she taught me things that would change me for the rest of my life.

After many hours of love-sex, and a few false alarms about Annie, we were lying naked in the bed made for one. If I lost my edge, she'd get me aroused again. If I started to drowse, she'd pinch my face.

I was wondering if Ruby and Carney were having the same kind of time we were when Hart said, "I never even heard of people like your friends."

"They're just people."

"Melquarth . . ." she said, and then interrupted the thought. "What kind of name is that, anyway?"

"Pre-Catholic." That was the truth.

"Anyway. Mel said that him and a man named Mingati spent a whole season hunting in lion country."

"Hunting lions?" This was a surprise.

"No. Hunting lion hunters and poachers. He told Annie that and she laughed. But it felt like he was telling the truth. He said that after a few weeks in the bush the number of dead lions fell appreciably. That's what he said.

"And Olo is just amazing. She pressed a hundred and fifty pounds like it was nothing down in the gym."

"A gym rat and a raconteur," I said. "Quirky but not out of the norm."

"And then there's you," she disagreed, tugging gently on my half erection.

"Me?"

"I doubt if it's normal for a man in your business to just take a mother and her child out of their lives...just because they might need to be saved."

"Yeah," I said. "We need to talk about that."

"About what?"

"What to do about your husband."

The next morning, we were sitting at the breakfast table again.

"How was the zoo?" I asked Annie.

"I liked the monkeys."

"How come?"

"They looked like old men who know things."

"What kind of things?"

"Special things."

"Like what?"

"Like my grandfather," she said, a little sadly. "He would show me how to fly kites and do science projects with just things around the house."

"My father was always very playful," Hart said.

"But then he died," Annie put in.

"Your mother and Joe have some boring things to do today," Oliya said to Annie. "They thought that you might want to come swimming with me."

"Can I, Mom?"

"Do you want to?"

"Yeah."

"After you guys finish with that," Mel said, "maybe you wanna come down to my repair shop in the Village."

"Hi, Dad," Aja greeted when I arrived at the office with Hart in tow.

"Hi, honey. Aja, this is Marigold Orr, and, Mrs. Orr, this is my daughter, Aja Oliver."

After the ladies shook hands, I walked Hart into my office. Between a few errant kisses I told my client that I had to talk to Aja about another case.

"Can you entertain yourself for a few minutes?" I asked her, pulling away.

"Sure. I just love this window. People watching is one of my most favorite things."

"She's pretty," Aja said when I was back at her desk. "That's Mr. Orr's runaway wife?"

"What you got on him?"

"Plenty."

"Dígame."

"Anthony Orr was arrested for manslaughter when he was nineteen in Columbus, Ohio," Aja reported. "That's where he was born and raised. The victim was a Black kid named Motie, a teenager that sold weed."

"Shot him?"

"Bludgeoned him with a brick."

"It come to trial?" I asked.

"Uh-uh. His lawyers told the prosecutor that Motie thought Tony had money and tried to steal it. They said Motie had a knife that the cops found on the scene. Report says that the cops had proof that Tony's father owned the knife, but the prosecutors dropped the case anyway."

"How long ago was that?"

"Thirty years."

"Orr comes from money?"

"On his father's side. The family owned an iron fabrication business. And the grandfather was a judge."

"What about the first wife?" I asked.

"You know about that?"

"His wife heard something."

"Natalia Henly. She was killed in their home when Orr was out of town. The SBPD was pretty sure that he paid for it but there was no proof and, once again, he had friends in high places."

"Where you get all this? Glad wouldn't have told you. He probably wouldn't have even looked it up."

"You said not to go to him anyway."

"So?"

"There's a hacking major at Beckton. They call themselves the Digital Path."

Beckton University was a low-residency leftward-leaning school that worked out of Detroit. That was the only college I could convince her to attend.

"So they hacked into official records?" I speculated.

"No. Of course not."

"Your innocent face needs some work, honey."

"If you turn Mrs. Orr over to that man, he will kill her."

After that Aja gave me all the contact information she'd gathered on Orr.

*   *   *

Hart was perched on top of the desk looking out the window when I returned to the little office.

"You like Montague Street?" I asked, sitting down next to her.

"It's like being away on an extended vacation."

Our sides touching, I asked, "What kind of work did you do in California?"

"Same thing I did here."

"Escorting?" I asked, wondering if maybe she meant something else.

She smiled. "That's how I met Tony. His VP in charge of operations brought me to a company picnic. Tony didn't talk to me there but later on he asked the VP about me. When he found out that the guy was just trying to impress an ex who was at the barbecue, he made a plan.

"Tony took me out fifteen times before he asked if he could see me more normally. I should have known then what it was going to be like."

"You mean men who hire women for their, um, their charms always want to own them?"

"No. Not really. I mean, sometimes you hire someone for a service, it doesn't matter what that service is, hairstyling or a blow job, but if you're asking for what you want, then it's honest. Tony acted like he just needed company for functions. He was lying and I should have treated him as a liar."

"You are an amazing woman."

"That's a high compliment coming from you, Mr. Oliver."

"Thank you," I said. And then: "I tell you what. Why don't we call your husband?"

"What?"

"I have to talk to him, to tell him why I haven't located you yet. And because you know him so well, I was thinking that maybe you could help me understand his, um, his subtleties."

Shaking her head and grinning she said, "Do you usually have your clients help you with an investigation?"

"I don't usually do anything."

She laughed. "Okay, so how does this work?"

"Holoman Construction," a woman said over the loudspeaker of my office phone. "How can I help you?"

"Hi, my name is Joe Oliver. I'm working, tangentially, on a job that Jason Manheim suggested."

"Um, I don't really understand what you're saying, Mr. Oliver."

"That's okay. Just tell your boss that it's Joe Oliver, a man working on the job that Jason Manheim farmed out."

"Hold on."

Hart covered her mouth to stifle the giggles. It might have been the first time ever that she had a leg up on that man.

"Hello? Who is this?" demanded Billy Goat Gruff.

"Mr. Orr?" I asked in as servile a manner as I could muster.

"Who is this?"

"My name is Joe Oliver, sir. I have been tasked with locating a Mrs. Marigold Orr."

"Say what?"

"I'm a private detective and have been asked to find Marigold Orr."

"I don't know what you're talking about." That was a good place for him to hang up, but he didn't.

"A guy that I've never met, a Jason Manheim, asked somebody I know in the NYPD to locate your wife, sir. That individual tapped me."

This claim brought us to a gulf of silence.

107

"Mr. Orr?"

"What did you say your name was?"

"Oliver, sir, Joe Oliver."

"And somebody asked you to find my wife?"

"Marigold and Antoinette."

"And why are you calling me now?"

"In a delicate operation like this, sir, I like to talk to the primary client when I start getting close to the goal."

"Have you found them?"

"One of my operatives thinks that he's got a strong lead."

"What does that mean?"

"I gave him the pictures you sent, and he found someone that has seen them on the Upper West Side."

"Where on the Upper West?"

"I don't have the exact location yet, but my operative will investigate, and he'll follow until we have an address."

"Have they located both my wife and daughter?"

"I think so."

"You think so, or you know so?"

I didn't answer that question. I might have been subservient, but I wasn't going to play the role of his bitch.

"When will you know for sure?" he said.

"I'll call at the latest by day after tomorrow."

"Why not tomorrow?"

"I'll call tomorrow if I know by then, but I don't want to make promises I can't keep."

"What if I add another twenty-five thousand?"

"That wouldn't speed things up, and I took the job for twenty-five. I don't need any more."

"Okay. I appreciate your professionalism. I'm just, um, you know, eager to see my daughter again."

"That's what I want too."

"Um, do you think your operative could maybe get hold of my daughter and put her on a plane?"

"What about your wife?"

"I just need to know where she's living."

I looked up at Hart then. She nodded solemnly.

"I don't want you to take this the wrong way, sir. I want to do what you're asking for, but . . . at the same time I need to protect myself."

"You're not doing anything wrong."

"Is there paper out on your wife for kidnapping?"

"Listen, Mr. Oliver, my wife is a whore and a cunt. She took my daughter away in the middle of the night while I was out of town. There's no cop or court in the world would go after you over that."

"Uh-huh, okay. But what about your wife?"

"What about her?"

"Why do you need her address?"

"Because I want the police to arrest her and put her away."

"I see. Would you like me to call the NYPD and have them bring her in?"

"Maybe. But first I want to know where she is, and, if you manage it, I'd like to have my daughter too."

"Umm." I hesitated. "I guess that sounds doable. Just let me get out there with my operative and see what's what."

"You do that," he said in a commanding voice. "And the sooner, the better."

12.

HART AND I sat in silence for quite a few minutes after that bicoastal conversation. The man I spoke to, and whom she spied upon, was ready to kidnap and murder, maybe so, most probably so.

When a car horn sounded on the street she asked, "Did you record that?"

"No." I was hoping that my innocent face was better than Aja's.

"What can I do?"

I'm an old-fashioned kind of guy. When I share a bed with a woman, when we've breathed the same air—I feel at least partly indebted. This brand of obligation is not a clear plan of action, not an ironclad contract. But, that said, there was a debt in there somewhere.

"There's nothing you should have to do," I said. "He's the one that owes you. He's the one that should pay."

"But back down here in reality..."

"You know how you said that me and my friends were different?"

"Yeah?"

"And how I said that we were mostly the same as every-body else?"

"Uh-huh."

"The only real difference is that we believe that we can cre-ate our own reality; hunting the hunters, expecting a woman to be able to match most men in combat, blow for blow."

"I don't know what that means." She was nearly in tears.

"Would you like to hire me to get you out of this mess?"

She looked at me for one beat and then for another. Inquis-itiveness turned to wonder; wonder became a smile.

"Yes," she said.

"So," Aja said when Hart and I were once again at her desk. "I have to go stay with Granny B, and Mrs. Orr——"

"Hart," my new client amended, "Miss Marigold Hart."

"Miss Hart," Aja corrected, "is going to stay with Mel out on Staten Island. And you, Daddy, you're gonna what?"

"After Oliya comes to spirit you away, I'm going upstairs to think."

"Shouldn't you have done that before you called Santa Barbara?"

"It's only TV cop shows where the detective can work to solve the crime like it was nine to five. A job like this is round-the-clock."

My daughter reluctantly acquiesced with a weak nod and, "Okay."

I ordered a fish dinner from an upscale Greek place a few blocks from my apartment. The halibut was superior to Dover sole. The gigante lima beans were better than their dwarf relatives.

I was prepared for anything, at least that's what I told myself.

At a few minutes past midnight, I was sitting in the big window of the third-floor studio apartment; just sitting there. I wasn't reading or listening to music, jotting down incriminating notes, or thinking about how Hart dug her nails into my butt to increase the force of our thrusts. When my cell phone sounded, I was as far away from material thought as I could get.

The caller's number did not appear.

"Mel?"

"How'd you know it was me?" the sometime repentant killer asked.

"Timing."

"I usually call around midnight?"

"In situations like this you do."

"Situations like what?"

"When you want to go out there and wage war."

"Don't you think Marigold can use some help?"

"I got it covered, man."

"You need me for anything?"

"Not right now, Mel. Right now, it's a light touch that's warranted."

Mel's call started my conscious mind up again.

I wanted to figure out how to get Hart and her daughter out of trouble, but the only things that came to mind were memories of my father.

In my eyes he was the heavyweight champion, the Lone Ranger, and Louis Armstrong all rolled up into one. He was a gentle man with a terrible temper, a friend to everybody with an answer to any problem you might have.

I remembered one time when I was no more than six. Two men were fighting on the sidewalk in front of our East New York house. They looked like giants with curse words in their mouths and blood on their faces. I was so afraid of the violence they unleashed that I hid my face and covered my ears.

"Chief Odin, don't you go out there!" my mother yelled into my self-imposed darkness.

Her cry opened my eyes to see my father walk right out into the buzz saw of those men's battle. He grabbed them both by their shirts and shook them.

"All right, now!" he commanded and, to my surprise, the men unballed their fists.

Chief said something to them, I couldn't make out what, and the three of them walked off down the street together.

"Where they goin', Mama?" I asked.

She was crying too hard to answer.

Chief Odin came home late that night. My mother had drunk herself to sleep on the couch and I was sitting next to her, waiting.

Chief lifted my mother in his arms and carried her to bed. I tagged along.

"You have dinner, King?" he asked me.

"Not yet."

"Not yet? It's after ten."

"Mama was scared," I explained.

He made me a crunchy peanut butter and grape jelly sandwich with bacon on the side. Then he sat next to me while I ate.

"What happened with those men, Daddy?"

"You mean them fools fightin' out in the street?"

"Uh-huh."

"I told 'em that they was just idiots and then I bought 'em some beer. When I asked 'em why they was fightin' one of 'em said that the other one owed him a quarter and the other one said he didn't. That's when I asked 'em if a quarter was worth a life. Then I give 'em fi'e dollars each and sent 'em on their way."

"How come you did that?"

"Because they were fightin' 'cause they were hurtin', not because they wanted to hurt."

I understood what my father said because I believed everything he ever told me.

"Come on, now, King, time for you to go to bed. Me too. I got things to do tomorrow."

"What kinda things?"

"Got to go out and make me ten dollars."

I was hip-deep in memory when the intercom buzzed. My smartphone said 2:37. The intercom sounded again.

"Yes?"

"King?" Her soft voice had a ring of steel just below the surface.

"Yes."

"My name is Leaf, Leaf Alyssandra Morton."

"Of course you are," I said while pressing the entry button. "My door is the white one at the end of the hall on the third floor."

Waiting by the open door with one foot in the hall, I could hear the step and slide of her backless shoes on the stairs until she stood at the far end of the darkened corridor. Her silhouette was lean and somewhat tall.

Half the way to my door I could distinguish the dark skin of her face, arms, and legs against the lighter color of her dress. When she drew near, her features began to emerge.

Being a man in his forties, having been raised in the most populous city in the United States, I have seen and even studied tens of thousands of faces. Men and women, living and dying, of all ages and in hundreds of fleshly hues, from the very old to the newborn, with cultural baggage that informed the subtlest nuances of character; I have seen the entire world in the many faces of humanity on the streets of New York. I have seen the faces of people that I knew long ago on those I had just met; therefore, I've had potent emotional responses to persons unknown to me. I have seen hatred, love, and confusion in the eyes of strangers.

I thought I had seen it all until Leaf walked down that hall.

The prominent skull under her berry-black skin bore a face that was handsome, assured, and beautiful. This face was contradictorily lean and yet substantial. Her eyes were dispassionate, nearly disarming my tendency to distrust.

Her dress was the color of Meyer lemons, with a rounded white, maybe ivory sculpture of a moon face pinned between her left shoulder and breast.

Leaf Alyssandra Morton walked right up to my door and gave me the slightest of smiles.

"Mr. Oliver?"

"What happened to King?" I asked, and that faint grin gained heat.

"Mr. Oliver?" she insisted.

"Yes. Come in."

*   *   *

I offered her coffee and she demurred.

"Tea?"

"What kind?" she asked.

"Malawi white."

That got me her biggest smile yet.

I have a red table for two set at the window wall of my apartment. From there I had the same view as my office, just below. I bade her sit and went about making her tea and my coffee.

"Luwanda send you?" I asked from the hot plate maybe five steps away.

"How you know that name?"

"Gatormouth."

Her head rose slowly to regard me. There was a hint of anger in her eyes. She didn't seem to be upset with me but with something outside.

"He told me that you two were engaged and that you were his connection to Luwanda and Chief," I said, carrying the two mugs to the table.

"Oh."

"Cream?" I asked.

"No, thank you."

"Sugar?"

"No. What else did Andrew say?"

I sat before answering. "That he was sad that he couldn't have been a better man."

"There's nothing wrong with him."

"How old are you?"

The question sat her back on the fancy red folding chair.

"Thirty-one. You?"

"Forty-four."

"What does my age have to do with Andrew?"

"Nothing."

"If it's nuthin', then why you ask?"

"You said that there was nothing wrong with him," I replied, hoping to change the trajectory of the conversation. "I agree. I do because I've known him since I was a small child. Thinking that, I wondered how old you were."

"Luwanda said that Chief Odin said that you were slick."

Leaf's coif was spiky; formed from differing lengths and thicknesses of braided hair, it could almost be seen as being weaponized.

Completely without context, I wanted to ask her if I could get to know her, but between the annoyance her eyes exhibited when I mentioned Gatormouth and the posture of that hairdo, I suspected that she wouldn't have been receptive.

"Which one sent you?" I asked instead.

"Is Brenda Naples really dying?" was her answer.

"I never said she was."

She leaned her head back the way some Caribbean women do to show appreciation.

"Okay," she said. "What is going on with her?"

"Brenda's sick and about to be operated on. She hasn't heard from her son in more than thirty years and wants to see him before she dies."

"And what do you have to do with that?"

"What do you think?"

When I expected them to be angry, Leaf's eyes took on an engaging aspect.

"I think that I'm not your enemy here," she said.

"Maybe not, but it's like you're testing me, and I don't like it."

Leaf seemed to study these words, then she nodded.

"I understand," she said. "You don't know me and here I am, in the middle of the night, questioning you about things you said and people you love."

There wasn't anything to add to that, and so I didn't.

"But what you have to know is that I'm not here for myself," she lectured. "Your father is in trouble, and you were a cop."

"So? He doesn't have to go through all these somersaults. Just call Brenda and be done with it. I don't need nuthin' from the motherfucker at all."

My anger made her grin.

"I get it," she empathized. "Here he wants you jumpin' through hoops, and he won't even call. But you have to see it from his side. They are blamin' him for murder, and he's got to be careful."

"So? Just leave me out the fuckin' equation, then."

"What if somebody set the trap with his mother as the bait?"

"Look here, I don't have nuthin' for you or him. I passed on the message, and he's got it. Now I'm gonna get back to my life."

"But—"

"Finish your tea an' get your narrow ass out my house." This sentiment surprised both me and my late-night guest.

"I know you're upset, King—"

"Mr. Oliver," I corrected.

I might as well have slapped her. She levered up from the chair and then made for the door.

Leaf Alyssandra Morton left my early morning home without another word from either of us.

I didn't want to be at odds with that woman. She came to me as a lifeline. She knew about my father. She was someone I wanted to get to know. But I wouldn't be fooled with, not by my father and not by her.

So I sent texts to Oliya, Aja, and Sergeant Gladstone Palmer, finished my coffee, and went to bed with a book about the nature of inhumanity — *The Painted Bird*.

13.

BETWEEN MY THIRD-FLOOR apartment and second-floor office there were days on end when I didn't get outside at all.

That morning I did a modified version of the RCMP exercise program. Forty-five minutes of cardio and weight resistance and I felt that I might be able to defeat another misguided youth like the one outside Ruby Lee's door.

By the time I got downstairs it was 10:15 and Aja was at the front desk. She was salting something away in the pink filing cabinet, which we used for new business. She wore a knee-length dark blue and light gray business suit that I had not seen before. It was a close-fitting ensemble but also very conservative.

"Hi, Daddy." She looked up at me and smiled.

"I never seen this suit before."

"I bought it last winter for when you ever finally let me work on a case."

"I'm not sending you out in the field."

"But I'll be doing things for Miss Hart, right?"

"We'll see. You want coffee and a croissant?"

"Maybe just the coffee," she said. "This jacket's feelin' a little tight."

Manzo's was a bakery and coffee shop owned and run by Manzo Watanabe and his ex-wife, Edith Lorne. Manzo was from Japan. He left Sapporo when he was seventeen to come to Brooklyn to go to school. Mr. Watanabe studied to become a machinist, met Edith, they fell in love, got married, and took over the bakery that Edith's aunt owned. It turned out that Manzo was a great baker, so they were happy—and successful. Then, six years into the marriage, Edith fell in love with a woman named Barber. She left Manzo, moved in with Ms. Barber, realized that she didn't like that either, and now lives alone somewhere in Queens.

The marriage was over, but the bakery was going great guns. For whatever reason, Edith and Manzo were never at odds, maybe that's why their passion took a back seat and also why they could work together.

You could see Manzo's from my office and apartment windows. Aja and I took turns going there for coffee and pastries on the mornings that we were both in the office.

Manzo was maybe five-four with dark ocher skin. His expression was that of bemused indifference and his forearms were the strongest thing about him. His English was perfect, which was odd for someone who learned a new language after the age of twelve, and he worked like a dog.

"Hey, Manzo," I said upon entering the shallow storefront café.

"Mr. Oliver." His voice was gruff and also warm. "Your turn today?"

"I guess. She only wants coffee. I'll take the regular, and

can I get a few buttermilk doughnuts with matcha tea and an Irish breakfast too?"

As he set about preparing the order, I observed, "Not so busy today."

"Morning rush is over. The bankers don't come in again till afternoon."

Manzo's was wedged in between two national banks.

"It's a wonder that they haven't tried to push you outta here," I said.

"Oh, they have. Edith wants to sell but we both have to agree, and I like this place."

"Think you'll ever sell?"

"I want to get married again," he said, almost wistfully. "If I have children, it's something I could leave for them."

I remember him looking me in the eye with sincerity. Impossibly, I imagined he knew my plans and agreed with them.

By the time I made it back to the office, both Oliya and Gladstone were there. Olo was wearing her usual culottes uniform, this time in dark brown. Glad had on a lime-colored sports jacket and golden slacks. His shirt was midnight blue. She was short and inscrutable, and he, tall, brandishing an unextinguishable smile.

I put down the breakfast fare and we all sat around Aja's desk.

"It's a nice place you got here, my friend," Glad said.

"You been comin' here over ten years and you just noticed that?" I complained.

"I don't know..." He shrugged. "Maybe it's the mornin' sun or the lovely company."

Even Oliya, the dour killer, smiled at the cop's heartfelt love of life, which seemed, somehow, to include her.

For close to a quarter hour, we ate, drank, and talked about the weather and how Aja's online education worked.

Then I changed tones.

"We got a problem, Sergeant Palmer."

"Oh?"

"It's this job you got me on."

"And what job is that?"

"Orr."

I knew that Gladstone would resist admitting to any extra-curricular activity with a dishonorably discharged New York cop, but we had to start somewhere.

"Play him the tape, honey," I said to my daughter.

It was the entire conversation I'd had with Anthony Orr.

After hearing this, Glad's smile slimmed down to the razor's edge of a crescent moon. His eyes dulled a bit. He glanced at the ladies and then turned to me.

"That was him?"

"Yeah," I said. "Called him at his office in Isla Vista."

"Fiddlesticks."

"And a big bass drum," I added.

"You have her?"

I nodded ever so slightly.

"What tipped you off?"

"Oliya followed her a bit. She's got good instincts."

"Strong hands too," the cop observed.

He nodded at her in a friendly manner, and I wondered what a showdown between him and Melquarth would be like.

After a moment's reflection he put out his hands, palms up, grinned, and said, "So, we dodged a bullet."

"We did, yeah, but what about her?"

"She's safe," he assured me.

"For now."

"Oh, come on, boyo. You can't save everybody all the time."

"I can try."

His Irish eyes inquired into my soul for a minute or so.

"Why don't we take this back to your office and palaver a bit more?"

"I don't know, Joe. I hand ya a pot of gold and when you pour it out there's nothing but shite."

He took the seat behind my desk, and I leaned against the window.

"Come on, Glad, you can't blame this one on me."

"And why not? If I had asked anybody else, we'd both have pockets full of money by now."

"And an innocent woman would be dead."

"But not because'a malice."

"Not malice . . . greed."

"She's not even a Black woman. Her great-great-grandparents probably owned yours."

I laughed out loud at that. Glad's people, like my own, had come from hard times. He didn't really see himself as a white man. In his mind it was the English who were whites.

"I have to think about this mess," he said.

"I know. But you also have to know one thing."

"What's that?"

"Regardless of what you decide, I have to help her."

"Don't you have enough trouble already?"

Something about his tone derailed me.

"What's that supposed to mean?" I asked.

"This thing with your father."

Once, when I was fourteen years old, my grandparents took me down to the Florida Keys. We ate Jamaican food, fished off an old rickety pier, and one day we went scuba diving. My strongest memory was putting on goggles and snorkel, then diving below the surface of the water. It was a completely different world. Alien and magical, filled with life. It was the greatest lesson I ever learned: that at any moment life might change so utterly that you could lose all sense of what was real.

That was Gladstone Palmer just mentioning my father.

"What about him?" I asked.

"The state police are looking for him and so are you."

"How you know that?"

"They called me."

"The state police did?"

He nodded like a bouncer granting a pretty girl entrée to the VIP area of the club.

"And said what?" I asked.

"That someone had told them that you were looking for your father."

"Who?"

"A woman named Ridges."

This brought to my mind a golden string of quarter-carat pink diamonds.

"Dorothy Ridges?" I asked.

"They didn't give me a first name and I didn't ask."

"What did they say about my father?"

"What I already knew. That he was being sought on a charge of murder."

"You knew that?"

"Of course. They told me when it happened. They asked me for the best way to get at you and I told them that you hadn't talked to your father since you were a boy."

"And they just backed off?"

"Well, they did after I told them that I'd keep an eye on you."

"Why didn't you tell me?"

"What good would it have done?"

I wanted to hit him, I did. I might have done it if the phone hadn't rung. It was only one ring and then someone, Aja, answered in the outer office. I heard her muted voice, probably saying, "King Detective Service."

A moment after this, over the intercom: "For you, Dad. A woman named Leaf."

"Give me twenty-four hours," Glad said while climbing to his feet.

I nodded. He left. And I picked up the receiver.

"Hello?"

"I'm sorry for running out on you like that."

"That's okay. Half the conversations I've ever had I wanted to do the same."

"It doesn't seem like you run from anything."

The wonderful thing about beginnings between people who don't really know each other is that they project whatever it is they want, or need, one upon the other. Leaf was someone I wanted to get to know, and I was something to her, something that had yet to be revealed.

"I run," I disagreed. "Run like a dog in the night if the odds are bad enough."

"That's not running. It's surviving."

"Where you from, girl?"

"I'm a woman," she said, "straight outta Tennessee."

"They make 'em tough down there?"

"Have you ever heard of Tennessee pig iron?"

"Not before. But I guess I have now."

"Luwanda wants to meet with you."

"I told you I was outta this shit."

"You didn't mean it," she pronounced.

And she was right. This was my family. My blood.

"Where?" I asked her.

"I'll pick you up in front of your office at nine tonight."

"Can we make that tomorrow night?" I tested.

"It would be better tonight."

"Not for me."

"What do you think Glad'll do, Pop?" my daughter asked.

She, Oliya, and I were back at her desk.

"Whatever's best for the Gladstone clan," I said.

"We could go out to Santa Barbara," Oliya offered. "I know people in the mountains around there."

Olo's size and strength were reminiscent of modern poetry—extreme power in a small package. Her suggestion was chock-full of metaphor and innuendo.

"You're such a romantic," I replied.

"I believe in direct action."

"Like your boyfriend?"

"He's not," she said, as if it were a full sentence.

"What we need is subtlety. It's not just bodyguarding.

There are civilians involved, people that need to come out of this with their innocence intact."

"Whatever you say . . . boss."

"What does all that mean?" Aja wanted to know.

"We have to make sure that the Misses Hart are safe while not being implicated in something criminal."

"And how do we do that?"

"I'm not sure yet. But, because we gave Mr. Orr my name and profession, you're going to have to go stay with your grandmother and work remotely for a while."

"For how long?"

"No more than a week, probably only a few days."

"Can my boyfriend come visit at Silbrig Haus?"

"As long as you pay close attention to Grandma B."

"I thought you said she was fine."

I shook my head.

"She's sick?"

"Yeah."

Oliya drove Aja out to Roger Ferris's house and then, she said, she was going back out to Staten Island.

I sat at my desk trying to unravel the Gordian knot in my mind. I had a sword, Oliya, but that wasn't the answer. Three hours later the knot was still firmly bound, and I was very, very tired.

I climbed the rope ladder to my apartment, fell into bed, and from there into sleep.

I was sitting at a table with two women. Hart and Leaf.

"So, what is your decision?" Hart asked.

"Which way are you going to go?" asked Leaf.

"Um," I said.

The room was circular with the outer wall and ceiling made from glass. It must have been a high floor because it felt as if we were sitting in the sky.

"Nobody's ever going to give you what you want," Leaf told me. She sounded angry.

"And what about your mother?" Hart added. "You're always talking about your father as if your mom was just some trash to be thrown away."

"My mother's dead."

"Did you go to a funeral?" Leaf asked.

"I can't help how I feel," I told them both. "It's like you're blaming me for wanting pistachio ice cream just because somebody said that certain cannibals also eat it. I'm not a cannibal, I'm a man."

"What are you talking about?" Hart demanded. She leaned over the round table in the round room and slapped me.

I had never experienced such pain in a dream. I brought my hands to my jaw and the pain was so intense, so jagged, that I could hear it.

The women were talking but I couldn't hear them over the din of the agony.

The pain got louder and louder until I realized that it was my phone ringing.

I picked up the cell phone, but my eyesight had gone the way of the dream and refused to pass the screen readout to my mind.

"Who is this?"

"Rags."

"Who?"

"Your cousin, Joe. Rags."

"Rags. Rags, why—why are you calling me?"

"I told you I would if I ran into a problem."

It was almost as if he were speaking a foreign language, no, not another tongue but English if a hundred years had passed and the dialect was beyond me.

"Joe!"

"What?"

"You okay?"

"Yeah. Yeah. What's up, cousin?"

"I talked to Tita."

Tita. She was—she was the daughter of Ruby Lee from the old neighborhood. Ruby was my father's girlfriend in the day. These two barely connected facts pushed me to wonder, could Tita have been his?

"What did she say?" I asked, feeling helpless.

"That ever since you were at her place her boyfriend has brought in protection."

"Oh. So, you need some help getting to her," I reasoned.

"That's about it. It's two guys watching from up and down the street. I scoped it out already."

"When we goin'?"

"Tita says that somewhere around eleven's the best time. She's gonna call back in an hour or so and we'll nail the exact time down then."

"What time is it right now?"

"A little after four."

"A.m.?"

"No."

"Oh, okay. I'll meet you at the subway stop at nine thirty."

"See you there."

14.

JASON MANHEIM WAS an art curator for one of Manhattan's premier museums, but he maintained private headquarters a few blocks away on the Upper East Side. This office space was on the third floor of a three-story building located on Madison Avenue.

I pressed the button labeled JASON AND THE ARTONAUTS and a woman answered, "Manheim and Associates."

I guessed that she was embarrassed by the faux Greek reference.

"Joe Oliver for Mr. Manheim."

"Do you have an appointment?" the squawk box inquired.

There was a camera lens next to the intercom, which meant she was probably trying to match this request with my appearance. I wasn't looking bad. My one-button jacket was light blue, and the shirt was of the same color but dark. The black pants were cotton, and I don't think she could see the bone shoes.

"No, I don't. But I have an urgent need to talk to him about Anthony Orr."

"What about him?"

"That's between me and your boss."

"I can't just give him a name."

"Yes, you can."

There came a pause that stretched out into a wait.

This didn't bother me. I was still pondering the dream of Hart and Leaf. What was I thinking? What did I want?

"Hello?" the intercom said in a tenor male tone.

"Mr. Manheim?"

"Yes."

"Hi. My name is Joe Oliver and I'd like to speak to you, sir, about Anthony Orr."

"What is it you want to say?"

"What I want, what I need is a conversation."

"So, talk."

"Face-to-face."

"I'm a very busy man, Mr. Oliver."

"Tell me about it. This inflation got us all workin' overtime."

"What do you want?"

"Asked and answered, sir."

Another pause. Another wait.

"Mr. Oliver, if you don't leave now, I'm going to have my receptionist call the police."

"Okay," I said. "Maybe they can help me figure out about Marigold Hart."

Magically, the buzzer in the door lock sounded.

I took the stairs rather than the elevator because I once saw a spy movie where the protagonist had gotten into an elevator and his nemesis shut the lift down between floors.

It felt silly, but still . . .

*   *   *

The stairway led to the northeast corner of the third floor, all of which was Jason and his Artonauts. A young high yellow and freckled Black woman sitting behind a smoke-dark glass reception desk tried, and failed, to keep distaste for me off her face.

"Mr. Oliver," a man said.

I turned to see the face I'd spied on Google when looking for images of the fancy upscale art dealer.

He wore a pale pink T-shirt under a brocade sports jacket of silver, gold, bloodred, and white thread. One side of the blazer, his left, contained the likeness of a stemmed red rose that came up to his breast. The other side encompassed a white stallion rearing up in equine ecstasy. I got the feeling that the basic material for this jacket was torn from some original museum-quality piece. His pants were skinny blue jeans and his shoes of the tennis variety.

"Mr. Manheim." I held out a hand.

Instead of shaking the hand he said, "Shall we go to my office?"

The office was neither modern nor special. No seventeenth-century French furnishings or ancient Tibetan carpets. His desk was made from pressboard, covered with, top and bottom, white linoleum sheeting. The chairs were of the passable folding kind and there was no art on the walls at all.

He sat on his white folding chair and I on mine.

"Okay," he said. "What do you want?"

"This office is amazing," I replied. "Here you're wearin' a blazer probably cost eighty thousand dollars and you got an office come with a price tag under eight hundred."

"My father was a salesman," he allowed. "This was his stuff. When he retired, he gave it all to me because, he said, I'd need it when I had an office of my own."

My respect for the man grew then. This admission of love and fealty for his father gave him an aspect of uprightness and truth. Don't get me wrong, he was still a poseur and a liar, but he wore it well.

"Now," he said. His face was round, almost moonlike. "What about Anthony and Marigold?"

"You know them because they buy art from you?"

"I know *him* because he's a client."

"But you recognized her after seeing her from far enough away that you couldn't get there before she was gone."

"How do you know that?"

"You saw Marigold, called Tony, and he asked you to call the cops, on the sly. You did call them—Gladstone Palmer, to be specific. Glad tapped me to find the lady."

"I've never heard of this Palmer."

"Of course not, it's your contact in city hall that talked to him."

The specificity of my knowledge darkened the art dealer's visage.

"What does any of that have to do with you needing to talk to me?" he asked.

"Have you ever met Mrs. Orr?"

"Of course. Her husband took her to quite a few of our sponsored events on the West Coast. What of it?"

"I'm looking for the lady right now, and I'm very close to finding her."

"Then call your policeman and tell him that."

"Yes. Of course. I intend to do just that. But first I'd like to ask you something."

"What?"

"Do you think..." I said and then hesitated, or at least pretended to hesitate. "Do you think that Marigold would be safe if I told her husband where she was?"

"Of course she'd be safe," he said with no hesitation whatsoever. "Why wouldn't she be safe? He's her husband, the father of her child."

"She also ran away, taking Antoinette with her."

"Well, I mean, if you don't trust in her safety, then why not drop the matter?"

"My question exactly."

"I can't help your paranoia, sir. You have a good man trying to get back with his family. That's all there is to it."

"That's your final word on it, Mr. Manheim?"

"Yes. Certainly."

He must have been a wonderful salesman. He looked into my eyes with not even a hint of duplicity. No nervous blinking, no sweat on the upper lip. I gazed back searching my mind for anything else this inveterate liar could help me with.

I came up blank.

Back on Madison Avenue I had to admit to myself that I'd just wasted a couple of hours. That's the way it is with investigating; half the time you follow up leads that take you nowhere.

The next stop after the Artonauts was a bench, half the way across Central Park, going toward the West Side. I was close enough to walk all the way to Silbrig Haus, where my grand-mother and daughter were keeping company. I wanted to see them both, while at the same time wondering if maybe that would be the best way to spend my energies. I had work to do, a job or two that needed attention. But maybe I could get them over with easily. I could dispatch Oliya to Santa Barbara or send Hart and Antoinette to Perth. I had a phone number for the down-home enchantress, Leaf. All I had to do was give that to Grandma B and she could call.

Neat and simple.

I imagined what the great twentieth-century preacher Tina Turner would have to say about my internal negotiations. Maybe something like, *We don't do nuthin' neat and simple.*

My next stop was a twenty-by-twenty-five-foot storage space in a facility once called Save-it that had changed its name to Shove-it. My stowage room had a fifteen-foot ceiling and was located on the thirteenth floor, though the elevator marked it as level 14. There all my serious tools and belongings were stacked in huge plastic trunks.

Placed dead center in the solitary space was a cushy sofa-chair where I liked to imagine myself an interplanetary astronaut delivering provisions and tools to faraway colonies of Earth's new breed of settler.

There I took out the weathered paperback of Kosiński's *The Painted Bird* and read its grim pages until I fell asleep. I awoke somewhere between seven thirty and eight. There was only one red trunk in the storage space, this I rummaged through until finding an item I'd put away seven or eight years before: a black plastic tube nine inches long and three inches in diameter. I'd gotten the device from Melquarth.

He'd told me that this was Russia's ultimate weapon against terrorists that they wanted to stop without killing—at least not immediately.

I donned a black suit along with a dark, dark green T-shirt, took out another, smaller, nonfatal device from the red trunk, and trundled down the dozen flights of stairs to the first floor and the street. From there I walked three blocks to the subway.

The people closest to you are always the most dangerous. This motto is true both spatially and emotionally; maybe even genetically too.

Around a decade before, Gladstone Palmer had been given hints that I was going to be killed because I had, unknowingly, crossed certain elements of the department that had dipped their beaks into the drug trade. Glad didn't tell me about the conspiracy; instead, he set me up to be arrested and bunged into Rikers Island, a medieval prison masquerading as a modern-day jail. I hadn't been there for two days when I was slashed by a shiv made from the jagged metal lid of a tin can. I still carry the scar on my right cheek. It has been there so long that I think of it as part of my identity.

After the attack, Glad reached out to help again and had me transferred to solitary confinement. I tried to get in touch with my wife at the time, Monica Lars. But part of the plan to put me in stir was to set me up for a false rape charge—with video and everything. Monica refused to go my bail, leaving me, I feared, to spend the rest of my life locked away.

That experience broke me, for at least a while. Since then, I've mended and healed, but the break will always be there, along with the scar.

Every time I have to go down into the underground rail system of New York I remember solitary and the fever of the American incarceration system. For a long time, I couldn't sit or stand anywhere but next to an exit. I was always ready to fight and, once or twice, when some young thug offered to hand me my head, I obliged with a severe beating that no one could possibly deserve.

After a while I had a client who was being held informally at Rikers. I visited him a couple of times and abject terror softened to mere fear. Nowadays I can survive any subway journey by simply reading a book between stations.

Queens was busy but not quite crowded. Mostly Asians out and about. Probably most of them were Chinese.

"Joe."

He was standing right behind me, next to a recessed tobacco store door. I'd scanned that door but hadn't seen him, but this was no surprise. Rags could blend into any environment better than a polar bear in a snowstorm.

"Hey, cuz. What's up?"

"I called Tita," he said, getting right down to business. "She said that you put a bug up Xú's ass. Like I told you before, he got two guys watchin' the place. She also said that he's carrying a pistol, somethin' she says he never does.

"There's a coffee shop one block up from his place. We could go there and work through a plan."

Hun Lo's wasn't really a coffee shop in that they didn't serve coffee. I had jasmine tea, Rags ordered milk, and we shared a pastry platter. As soon as our server, an extremely old gentleman with a sparse but longish mustache and a blue silk tam, had served us and gone, Rags took out a mini iPad and began flipping through pictures he'd taken of Gregory Xú's block.

"The first guy," Rags was saying, "is up here next to the furniture store. See him?"

"Yeah," I said.

On the small side, the young man wore clothes that came out a yellowish gray through the device's digital lens.

"Your guy is across the street watching these dudes playin' mah-jongg."

He was taller and more substantial, dressed in loose, dark clothing.

"So, you give me the bigger guy 'cause you know how good I am," I said, wheedling my merc blood relative.

"I'm givin' you that one 'cause he's older, slower, and the other dude walks like kung fu."

"I wouldn't have it any other way. What else you got?"

"Tita's coming down at as close to 11:51 as she can. The minute she comes outta that door we put these guys down, take her to my car in the alley three doors up. From there we head out to a private airport twenty miles or so past Elizabeth."

"New Jersey?"

"Yeah."

"That's Roger's airport."

"I told him that it was for Grandma B. I'm right, right?"

"Yeah. Eleven fifty-one?"

"That's it."

I went around the alley where Rags had parked his car. It was a brown Dodge, Rags' preferred auto for anonymity.

There I took out my phone and sent an e-mail to Detective First-Grade Henri Tourneau. Henri was my one solid contact on the force.

After that I took a long walk looking through the various shop windows of the second largest Chinatown in the U.S.

I got back to the alley at 11:39. I didn't walk past Thug Number Two until just a minute before Tita was supposed to appear. Eleven fifty-one came and went, as did I, past the big goon, and down the street.

I got a pretty good look at the sentry. He was maybe an inch shorter than I, five-ten, and his shoulders were certainly brawny. But his eyes were rheumy, and his focus was questionable.

I pulled the black plastic tube out of my shoulder bag and turned to make another pass. I'd made it to eight or nine paces away from the big thug when Tita came running out the front door of her building.

Glancing over my shoulder, I saw Rags engaging his man. It wasn't going to be a long fight. As the *kung fu walker* ran toward Tita, Rags shoved something like a broom handle between his legs. The man tripped and then my cousin fell upon him.

"Hah!" Thug Number Two exhorted.

I turned just as he was reaching my vector. Pointing the black tube at him, I slammed my palm into the base. The resultant cloud of dusty steam hit him directly in the face. He went to his knees, grabbing at his throat. When he fell, face down, I turned to see if Rags needed help.

He didn't, of course. His chosen victim lay motionless while Rags had already gotten to Tita and was hurrying her toward the alley.

I was going after them when someone shouted, "Hey!"

That's when a police siren burped. Three squad cars squealed onto the scene, surrounding Gregory Xú, who stood there in red silk pajamas, an automatic pistol in hand.

After rounding the corner, I stopped to glance at the melee in the street. The unconscious bodyguards were being handcuffed where they lay. Gregory Xú was disarmed and cuffed too. And, wearing a tan-and-black checkered suit, young Detective First-Grade Henri Tourneau hurried up, barking orders at his seasoned NYPD legionnaires.

15.

WE TOOK THE Lincoln Tunnel to New Jersey.

Tita was in the back seat, crying and laughing in turns.

"It was so crazy," she said. "Like a madhouse. I couldn't take it no more. I just couldn't."

She went on like that for a while.

"What was he doin' up in there, Tita?" Rags asked when there was a lull in her litany.

"Sometimes he'd bring li'l chirren up there, tie 'em up, an' put 'em in a closet. I mean, he was nice when I met 'im and then he was doin' that shit..."

That's when she started crying in earnest.

She was still bawling when we were coming near the guarded gate of the private airport. It was pretty much undeveloped countryside out there, so we were free from detection, more or less.

Rags pulled off to the side of the road and cut the headlights. I understood why. Tita did too.

"I can get myself together," she vowed. "I can do it."

"That's okay," Rags assured her. "I got a tranquilizer if you need."

"No, honey. I wanna keep my eyes open."

"How come he kept such a tight hold on you?" I asked, hoping to connect with her objective mind.

After three snorting breaths, she said, "One night he had this lovely li'l girl, no more'n 'leven years old, tied up behind the door. I put a pill in his tea and set her free. She dint talk English but I was sure she could find somebody'd unner-stand her. In the mornin' I acted just as surprised as he was. But after that he was just more an' more suspicious. I could tell that he'd end up killin' me one day. I knew it."

Her breathing was jittery but at least she'd stopped crying.

"And that's why," I said, "you jumped at the first chance outta there—me."

Tita had a toothy grin.

"I sure'n hell did. You promised that Rags'd call an' he did. He said 'leven fi'ty-one an' we was gone. Shit. This ole beat-up car like Cinderella's pumpkin carriage an' you two my mouse footmen."

"You know once in Charleston you can't be talkin' to nobody you know back here," I said, intent on spoiling the fairy tale.

"I know."

"How 'bout the people you goin' to see? Can you trust them?"

"They don't know my fam'ly."

"Where you know 'em from, then?"

"Hunter College. I did one semester there and Angelique an' me made friends."

We got her to the six-seater private jet. Roger's pilot was stone-faced and silent. You could tell that he knew how to keep quiet.

*　*　*

"Where to now, Joe?" Rags asked as we were driving away.

"If you could take me home, I'd appreciate it."

"No problem, cousin. You know I needed this. I mean, it's a real treat to be out in the street, raisin' hell."

"Glad you havin' yourself a good time."

"You are too. I could tell. What was that shit you used on the big dude?"

"The guy gave it to me said that it was a Russian deterrent for terrorists and insurgents in general. You know, in 2002 they had the Moscow theater hostage crisis. They used an earlier iteration of this gas to pacify the radicals and the hostages, but about twenty percent of them died. After that they went back to the drawing board and came up with this shit."

"I never heard of it," Rags admitted. "You got some ex–Russian spy you workin' with?"

"You don't wanna know."

Home again, home again…Lying abed, watching shadows roil across the ceiling in secondhand ambient light, I realized that I was at that middle place that I often came to in a case. This time I had two commissions: my grandmother's and Hart. Inside of those two jobs I had passions, one for my lost childhood and the other for a woman I hardly even knew.

I drowsed under these mantles of responsibility, feeling, somehow, connected to the world in such a way as to allow me to feel like there was possibility, even hope.

This cracked optimism in mind, my heart responded buoyantly when the phone rang.

"Hello?"

"Hey, Joe," Henri Tourneau said.

"Hey, son, how you doin'?"

"All I know is the NYPD gave up a great cop when they allowed you to get away."

"You get somethin' outta that bust?"

"Gregory Xú had an unlicensed pistol, so we got a warrant to search his apartment. He had a book with pictures of children he was selling. Babies."

"He talkin'?"

"Naw. And his two guards were also armed. I think they might get deported. Who was the girl?" the NYPD detective asked.

"What girl?"

"The black one."

"A family friend."

"She in the business too?"

"No."

"Okay, Joe. You probably got me a promotion with this, so I owe ya."

"There's no such a thing as debt between friends," I said, wondering if I'd read that adage somewhere.

At seven thirty the next morning I was seated behind my desk, thinking about my resources and those of my enemies. I was a lifelong cop but the police, on the whole, were not my friends. I had spent the first twelve years of my adulthood standing against criminal activity, but nowadays my best friends were crooks. I treated my father as if he were culpable for his dignity. I was a fool and I'd probably continue to be one for the rest of my life.

That's when the phone rang.

"Hello."

"Joe Oliver?"

"Yes, Mr. Orr, it's me."

"It's been two days."

"That it has."

"Well?"

"My associate staked out the school your daughter's going to. Your wife came to pick her up. She took an Uber but Max, my operative, lost her at a tricky intersection. He was going to break into the school last night and get her address that way."

"And did he get it?"

"I'm slated to talk to him at 10:00 a.m."

"Call me on this number as soon as you know something."

"Yes, sir."

"You only have to remember one thing in this life, King," my father had said to me one Saturday afternoon. I was standing by his side while he was using a slender grass-green hose to sprinkle water on tomato bushes in the backyard.

"What's that, Daddy?"

"That it's at least three times harder to get outta trouble than it is gettin' in."

He wasn't saying that I should stay out of trouble, only that I had to know the cost.

What would the trouble be to get Hart out of Dutch? What would be the cost for me to go up against Gregory Xú and his slavery ring?

But, then again, what would be the buildup of rot in my soul if I hadn't done what I knew to be right?

Those questions led me to an unconscious truth: I loved my father even while hating him. He formed my life by giving me somewhat objective realities with which to evaluate my own worth.

As I arrived at that realization, it seemed right and proper that the office doorbell should ring.

One of the pillars of my life was the door to my office. It had cost me ten thousand dollars with not one cent wasted.

To anyone looking at or knocking upon the door, it was a simple wooden plank, like any other, but little did they suspect its stainless steel heart would turn away any bullet. The steel bolts anchoring it into the wall would stand up to a rhino's charge.

I strode up to that portal with not the slightest fear.

"Who is it?" I asked through the speaker.

"Glad."

He was sitting behind Aja's desk, and I before it.

"You had me goin' last night, acushla. I mean, in my veins," Glad regaled me. "Ya know, I look out for me, my blood, and me mates. That's what I do. I got a cold heart when it comes to business, and I shut both my eyes when it's needed. But ... after you played me that recording, I felt somethin' else."

"And what was that, Sergeant?" I asked lightly. The corrupt cop's often unexpected innocence amused me.

"That I'd closed my eyes when they should'a been open wide. Like you said, I let my greed do the thinkin'. What kind of man would I be if I let that mother die?"

"I'm glad you feel like that, because I got to do something about it."

"But there's a catch."

"Yeah," I agreed. "You're too deep into this to be involved in any bust."

"I could survive his day in court if you could snag Mr. Orr, but..."

"I just need you to stay out of the way, and I'll get something going."

"With one'a yer bad seeds?"

I laughed and he did too.

I made some calls after Glad had gone his way. It was going to be a delicate procedure, like grooming a fancy doll with razor blades in her hair.

After all that I rang Ogre Orr, as I had begun to think of him.

"I got the address," I told him.

"What is it?"

"We'll get to that," I said, "but first we have to set some ground rules."

"Listen, brother, you don't make rules for me."

The use of the colloquial term used among Black people, *brother,* probably meant that he'd looked me up. Good.

"Either you hear me out or start over," I said.

"Do you know who I am?"

"I don't care who you are. I might be a tool, but I'm on loan, not the payroll. Hear me?"

There was a wait and then: "What do you need?"

"That's my question for you," I said.

"What's that supposed to mean?"

"I got addresses for the school and the apartment. Which do you want?"

"Both."

"Why not just the school? Why not just call the police and have them do the job?"

"What do you care?"

"Just coverin' my ass, man."

"What kind of trouble could you be in?"

"What if somebody comes after her at the top of the stairs and she trips and breaks her neck? What if the cops find out who went there after her and they say that I sent 'em there? What if you get to them and then forget to pay me?"

"You just a pussy, huh?"

"Just a businessman, in need of payment and insurance."

"I'll send you the money."

"Great. As soon as I get it, I'll send you the addresses."

"That won't work," he said. "How am I to know that my wife doesn't suspect something? No, too much time would pass."

"Not for me."

"Okay. If you can't have any trust, I'll send some people to New York. They'll have the check—"

"They'll have the cash," I corrected.

"Okay. They'll have the cash. You get the money and give them the addresses."

"Now, that's a plan I can live with."

"Yeah, but what if you give me a bad address? What if you don't even know where they are?"

"To begin with, I take it you've looked me up. You know where my office is at, and you realize that it's not worth twenty-five thousand for me to move. Secondly, I might be givin' you grief but I'm not squeezin'. I'm just bein' careful. And as far as me lying, I'll have Max take a picture of them and I'll send it on to you."

That bought me a whole raft of silence.

"Okay. All right. You get me the photograph and I'll go along."

"Max is on another job right now, but I'll talk to him tonight. You get data across this line?"

"I do."

"Be on the lookout for your precious proof."

I hung up then, wanting to underscore the fact that I did not need his leave.

"Hello?" she said on the third ring.

"Hey, Olo."

"Joe."

"I need you to do something with Hart and Antoinette."

"Of course."

I spoke to Oliya and then to Melquarth. After that Hart got on the line.

"Hi," she said in an upbeat tone.

"Hey. How you guys doin'?"

Skipping over my almost meaningless query, she said, "You don't have to worry about me, Joe. I was already tough when I met Anthony; he only made me stronger. When you want to see me, I'm here, but you don't owe me a thing."

Her read of me was bull's-eye accurate. Henri didn't owe me, and I had no debt to Hart. We were all equals.

Later that night I was lying on my bed, again staring at the ceiling, when the cell phone sounded.

"Hello?" I asked whoever it might be.

"Are you ready?" asked Leaf.

"Ready for what?"

"I'm parked in a car out in front'a your place."

16.

THERE WAS A two-tone lavender-and-cream 1955 Buick
Century parked out on Montague Street. It looked like a
dream.

I love old cars. All the way back to the Duryea Motor
Wagon I know their power, their specifications, and their
provenances. I didn't need to own one or even drive one.
For me classic cars are like prehistoric bison running free. It
soothes my heart to know that they once existed in the same
world that I do.

Leaf Alyssandra Morton was standing in the street next to
the driver's door. She wore a designer shift that revealed the
left knee but not quite the right, had a strap across only the
left shoulder, and was cut from a silken fabric the color of a
fresh red rose underlain by hints of pink, coral, and lemon.

I crossed the street to meet her, shedding any bad feelings
I had about our altercation upstairs and hoping that she had
forgiven me.

"Hey," I said. "You look great."

I had on a straw-colored jacket, stark brown pants, and a

T-shirt with the barest green tint. I also was carrying a Walther PPK that was permitted a carry license in my name.

I ran my hand along the smooth mauve fender of the Buick thinking about the curves of my driver.

"Thank you," she said, acknowledging my compliment, simultaneously proving that she was a modern woman as well as an unfettered spirit.

"You gonna take me for a ride?" I asked.

"That's the idea."

"Where to?"

"You'll see when we get there."

She stared me in the eye, daring me to walk away.

"Okay," I said, and then went around to the passenger's door.

Leaf negotiated our way onto the Brooklyn Bridge with no trouble at all. Considering the manual transmission and her comparative youth, she drove like a seasoned pro.

Traffic was moderate and the going across the span was slow.

"So, what was it about you and Gatormouth?" I shouldn't have asked. Even as I thought of the question, I knew it would cause friction. But this was not a date, dammit, and I didn't want to seduce myself over this unique woman.

"What about him?" she replied, an edge to her tone.

"When he talked to me about you it sounded like the first time he had felt like that for a woman, ever."

"It did, huh?"

"Yes, ma'am. He said that you two were engaged but that he couldn't come up to the mark."

"He's a good man on the inside," she said, almost to herself. "He just couldn't bring it out."

"I hadn't seen him since I was thirteen. But I got to say that he seems to have come pretty far since then. That's not enough for you?"

"You got that backwards; it wasn't enough for him."

"But I thought you were the one that broke it off."

"Oh? What else he tell you?"

"It's not so much what he said, but what he showed."

"And what was that?" she demanded.

"It was like he had a stone pressin' down on his heart. Like he saw the promised land but couldn't take one more step."

She took the curving exit off the bridge leading to the FDR.

We were silent there for a while driving past the Manhattan projects that lined the river; huge brick structures that housed the working minions of the city. Places where men like my father went to die.

"I didn't care what he did," she said out of nowhere. "I mean, I don't let no man nor woman tell me who I got to be, what I got to do. And I don't make those demands on anybody else. But his heart was like you said, always heavy and sad. He'd look at me and see what he could never be and then blamed himself for that. I couldn't take the guilt."

Stunned by the clarity of her words, I went silent. This was why I was drawn to Leaf. She was so certain about the space she occupied that there was no gainsaying her position.

"Well?" she demanded as we traveled down the Forty-Second Street exit.

"Well, what?"

"There you are diggin' all through my personal life, and then when I give you a answer you go quiet."

"Yeah. I mean, what you said, I could tell it was the truth. All I have to do is remember what Andy was sayin' and I could see it. He always needed somebody to lean on. My father, then my grandfather, and finally, you."

She turned right on First Avenue and drove past the United Nations building, up to Forty-Ninth. There she took a right turn into a slender one-lane-wide driveway until we came to a long, low structure, three stories high. No one questioned us but I got the feeling that we were being watched.

Leaf pulled up in front of a door and disengaged the engine.

She turned to me and said, "I'm what the old heads call a natural woman, Mr. Oliver. I don't fuck around."

I leaned over and kissed her on the corner of her mouth.

She accepted the osculation, then opened her door. I did the same. We walked up to apartment 4; she pressed the buzzer and then moved back a few steps, leaving me to stand dead center.

I tried to imagine whom I'd see there. I knew that her name was supposed to be Luwanda, but would it just be her? I doubted if my father would be in a locale under official international authority. So it would most likely be another step on the long road I had to travel, getting to him.

All that knowledge and still I felt butterflies as the door came open.

Whatever I expected, it was not Ruby Lee.

"Hey, baby," she said. "Come on in."

"What?"

"You don't understand English?"

"Ruby?"

She reached out for my hand and pulled me through the doorway.

It was a generous apartment with low ceilings and furniture

from the fifties, all sleek and dark wood along with a sofa and two matching chairs upholstered in light blue fabric. There was a coffee table behind which Bernadette Broadman sat next to another woman, about the age of the other two.

Bernadette stood and came toward me. She took both my hands and said, "Surprise."

"What are you doing here?" I asked my father's existentialist prison teacher.

"I work for a Turtle Bay realty company, in the back office..."

While Bernadette spoke, the other woman seated upon the sofa rose and came up to us.

"...so usually I just work with application forms," Bernadette continued. "But one day, when I was there alone, the assistant to the undersecretary of the Polish embassy came to talk about finding a new residence for the undersecretary's son and his wife. Foreign trade is a big part of our business..."

The woman from the sofa had middle-brown skin with a reddish undertone. She was studying me.

"...when I found him a few options," Bernadette continued, "we started to talk about how the current residents of this apartment hadn't spent much time here in the past few years. It wasn't optimal for their purposes. I offered to find temporary residents until they wanted to get rid of it."

Leaf came up to us and so did Ruby.

"I dipped into a fund that we three girls have and leased the place last year."

"You sublet an official embassy apartment?"

"Yes."

"That has diplomatic immunity?"

"More or less."

"Hello, King," the reddish-brown woman said.

"Hi," I replied, holding out a hand.

She smiled and accepted the clasp. Up close she radiated confidence and physical strength.

"I'm Luwanda."

"I've heard the name."

Not letting go of my hand, she asked, "Why don't you have a seat?"

I allowed her to pull me toward the sofa.

Luwanda sat at one end with Leaf on the other and me in the middle. Bernadette and Ruby took up the matching chairs that sat across from us, looking over the low oak coffee table that stood on two oaken L-shaped legs.

"Well," Bernadette said, "we're all in the same place at last."

"Amen," chimed Ruby Lee.

"But what are you doing here?" I asked. "How do you people even know each other?"

"I got in touch with them after the police framed your father for murder," Luwanda said.

Even just the sound of her voice was imbued with strength.

"Why?" I wanted to know.

"So, we could help him if he needed," Bernadette said.

"But, Ruby, why'd you take me out to Carney when you already knew where Chief was?"

"Chief wanted Big C to take a look at you before lettin' you get this far."

"So you did already know him," I conjectured.

"I knew who he was, but we never met, no."

"Okay. I surrender. What do you ladies want?"

"First," said Luwanda. "Why are you lookin' for Chief?"

"I already told all y'all. Grandma B is real sick, and she wants to see her son."

"She definitely gonna die?" Leaf asked.

"No, not definitely, but she's ninety-four, so, better safe than sorry. Anything else?"

"Are you armed?" Bernadette asked.

"Yes, I am."

They exchanged glances over that intelligence.

"Are you working with the police?" Luwanda added.

"I talk to cops all the time. Right now, I have a sergeant helping me with a case got nuthin' to do with Chief. But to be clear, I don't need to go through all this agitation. I assume you have gotten the message to my dad. So, if he's too chickenshit to talk to his own son, then fuck it."

That complaint rolled out a few yards of silence.

"Now I've answered your questions," I said. "Maybe you could speak to a few of mine."

"What you need to know, King?" That was Luwanda.

"Why you women huddled round my dad?"

"We love him," said Bernadette Broadman.

"Odin always been there when we needed him," Ruby agreed. "I was havin' a problem when he was still at Attica, and he solved it from his prison cell."

"Is Marguerita my sister?" I asked Ruby. As long as we were plumbing truth I figured — what the hell?

She winced and said, "Half sister, yeah."

"And what about my mother?"

"What about her?"

"Did you go to her funeral?"

She froze up, staring at me. Then there must have been a motion to her left because she turned to look.

I turned in the same direction.

It was as if he were carved from a log of ebony wood. His hair and beard were like white lichen and his eyes were clear and luminous. When he took the three steps into the retro living room, I could see the slightest limp in his left leg.

Chief Odin Oliver carried his years the way a tree might: strong and erect until some inner rot, centuries on, knocks it down.

I was on my feet, but I didn't remember standing.

"Dad."

He wore a medium-gray dress shirt with tails hanging out over black trousers, fit for a party. His feet were bare. I remembered all the way from boyhood how big my father's feet were.

His smile made me wonder how a tree would show joy. Maybe a deep, rumbling kind of laughter that carried notes of flowing water and chittering insect wings.

"Come here," the old man commanded, and I lurched toward him, a child for just that moment.

"I ain't no chickenshit," he whispered in my ear.

"Have a seat, Chief," Ruby offered.

I noted that he had to hold on to the backrest to lower himself. This brought my grandmother to mind.

Ruby settled on the edge of the oak coffee table, and I went back to my center seat.

We had a quorum.

Chief Odin might have actually been the king of the gods, he sat so erect and regal. The women all looked at him, waiting for his pronouncement.

"King," he said.

"That's the name you gave me."

"Tell me about your grandmother."

"Look, man," I answered. "You done already heard about it from at least five different people. I think that's enough, don't you?"

My father looked a little thrown by his child's impudence.

"Where'd you get that scar?" he asked.

Lifting fingers to my right cheek I said, "I was in Rikers for a month or so. This was my welcome gift. Did you kill Ira Gross?"

"No."

"For real now, Chief. I am not a cop, and I would never testify against you, regardless."

"No."

"Then why they think you did?"

"They got a witness."

"Who?"

"No one knows."

"Somebody does," I said. "At least they think they do."

My father smiled and, despite my ambivalence, a wave of pleasure ran through my core.

"The district attorney," he said on a shrug.

I took a few seconds to mull. Then: "Grandma B wants to see you."

"I know where's she's at," he said. "But I don't have a number and those gates locked tighter than a rooster's butt."

"I could get you in there."

"Don't, baby," Ruby said to my father. "Don't take the chance. She need to come to you."

"You want dinner, boy?" was his answer to Rube.

"What you got?" I replied.

17.

DOWN A LONG hall and through an unexpected door in the deceptively large apartment, there was a dining room large enough for the whole tribe.

Somebody must have been cooking all day for the quintessentially American feast that was served.

Cheese enchiladas and blue crab gumbo, with long-grain white rice and collard greens, were set out in fancy serving china. There was tart lemonade, with and without bourbon, and biscuits short enough to dry out your tongue. The corn bread wasn't sweetened. And the hot peppers knew their job.

I was very hungry.

The three older ladies chattered among themselves, talking about things they loved and hated about New York, men in general, and nuances to the day-to-day that made life bearable.

I was seated at one end of the table and Chief at the other. Leaf sat at my right. This made me happy. I needed something to assuage the sour feelings at the end of my search. Finding my father was more bitter than sweet. He was lost to and abandoned by me for too long. Sitting at that down-home feast, I realized that I'd probably never recover from the loss.

"What you thinkin', King?" Ruby asked me.

We were three-quarters of the way through the meal, and I'd managed to stay mostly quiet while fighting down the feelings rising in my craw.

"We got to talk," I said to Chief rather than Ruby.

"Talk," he offered.

"Got to be just you an' me."

"We all family here, son."

"You people are family. I'm a man with a job."

"And just what job is that?" he asked, as beneficent as I remembered when I was a child in trouble.

"Maybe two jobs," I conceded. "Okay. Let's talk about one right now and the other alone together."

Chief Odin nodded.

"All right, then," I began. "Grandma B got a boyfriend name of Roger Ferris."

"The man owns all the silver in the ground everywhere?" Bernadette wondered.

"Yeah. That house she's in is owned by him. It's guarded by a dozen mercenaries and is fortified in other ways. Rags is B's personal bodyguard."

"Who?" Chief asked.

"Oh, right," I said. "You remember Richard Naples? Yvonne's child?"

"Snot-nosed runt?"

"That's what you called him."

"He's a bodyguard?"

"A merc, with serious skills."

"Damn."

"I could take you to Roger's place and you will be safe with your mother by your side."

"I'm comin' with," Luwanda decreed.

"Me too," said both Ruby and Bernadette.

"No," I replied to all three. "Roger's one of the richest men in the world and needs a modicum of protection. His security would never allow it. I'm pushin' it with a man wanted for murder."

"How would we know if he's safe in there?" Ruby asked.

"That's not your call, mama," Chief said. And then to me: "You tellin' me that the police couldn't get to me in there?"

"You be better protected than even in an apartment with diplomatic immunity."

"B's there?"

"Yeah."

The big man leaned forward and laced his fingers before his mouth.

"With a white man?" he asked, incredulous.

"It's a new world, Pops."

"And she asked for me?"

"That's why I'm here."

"And you say I'd be safe?"

"Only thing could catch you in there would be a heart attack."

Luwanda crossed herself, Catholic style.

Chief nodded at me.

"Come on, son," he said. "Let's go outside."

Walking back down the hall leading from the dining room, I asked my father, "You actually go outside with the police after you?"

"It's a patio out the window-door to my bedroom."

The opposite end of the hall brought us to a set of double doors that opened onto the master bedroom of the diplomatic retreat. The lights snapped on automatically when we walked in.

It was a large room without much, if any, personality. The bed was a double king, the desktop empty except for an electric typewriter that must have been at least fifty years old. The carpet was blue like a late-day matte azure sky and the walls rendered a washed-out yellow.

The wall on the opposite side from the entrance was glass with a glass door carved into it. Chief went to that door and, when he opened it, light came up on a lovely patio.

Lovely, that was the only word for it. The courtyard was paved with rough-cut but finished marble bricks that contained a little man-made pond, home to a school of a kind of shimmering blue ornamental fish that I'd never seen before. There was a dwarf mandarin orange tree in a half-barrel planter next to a raised dais on which stood two blocky wooden chairs that faced each other. The armrests of the chairs were thick enough for drinking glasses and even dinner plates.

"Have a seat," Chief offered.

"Wow," I said.

"Yeah, boy," my father agreed. "First time I ever stepped out here I knew how to get ninety percent of convicts to go straight."

"How's that?" The furred cushion of my chair felt like a giant's palm holding me up.

"If I had something like this outside my cell at Attica, I would have known that I was forgiven and never had another bad thought again."

He lowered onto the chair, took out a cigarette that looked a bit thicker than most, and lit up. The smoke was acrid but, somehow, not unpleasant.

"Okay, King. What we got to talk about?"

"Ira Gross."

"He's dead."

"And you didn't kill him?"

"No, I did not."

"You realize that I would never turn you in, no matter what you did."

"And I would not lie to you."

"So, why do they think you killed him?"

"Just the cops needin' to kill two birds with one stone."

"Cut that shit out, Chief."

"What you say to me?"

"I said, cut that shit out. You and me both know that even if they wanted to frame you, they'd have to come up with an explanation."

"So?"

My father's angry stare invigorated me. As a child I could never dispute him or his word. But it was a new day, and he was the one who had to swallow his pique.

"What was the frame they had for you?" I asked.

"I went to see Gross one day," my father capitulated. "And that night he was killed."

"What you go to see him for?"

"He was tryin' to horn in on Felix's prison labor business and I wasn't havin' it."

"You argue with him?"

"Some voices were raised."

"You threaten him?"

"I might'a said that his ass needed my foot."

"You say you was gonna kill him?"

"No. You never threaten a man's life unless you ready to act on it."

"Felix know who might'a done it?"

"Maybe. I haven't talked to Felix since before Ira was kilt. You know, a man in my position can't be travelin' on familiar ground."

He took a drag on that strong cigarette, and I sat back, relaxing for the first time since my grandmother told me she was sick. From her admission to that fancy patio my mind had been a pinwheel of obsessive sex, violence, deep loneliness, and childlike fears.

After banishing him from my mind three decades before, I was sitting across from my father in the open night air of New York. It was a desire I had that was so powerful, I wasn't even aware of it. Wanting to be with my dad was like wanting to look into the sun.

"I never even knew how much I missed you, Pops."

"I know."

"Everything I did from then to now was about fillin' up that hole."

"You had to let me go," he said.

That was my judgment day. I was my father's Judas, whom only he had the power to forgive. I was the last member of a lost tribe, having wandered in the wilderness so long that I'd forgotten that there was ever a home to go back to.

Only saints and psychotics could hold on to feelings like that for very long.

"Tell me something," I said.

"What's that, son?"

Son.

"How does it work with you and three women in the same house?"

He laughed long and hard. The only thing that stopped him was the cough all that mirth brought up.

"You know I was never bound down by what people say you got to do. I love each and every one'a them and the children they give me."

"Children? Like more'n two?"

"No. Just you and Tita."

"Tita knows you're her dad?"

"Naw. She calls me uncle and that seems to work good enough."

"What about Mom?"

I regretted the question inasmuch as it brought pain to Chief's mien. I regretted the question, but it had to be asked, had to.

"Your mother paid the price for what I tried to do. I mean, prison wasn't nearly as rough on me as it was on her."

"I don't even know where she's buried," I complained.

"When this is all ovah I'll make sure that you do."

"When what's all over?"

"I got to get outta the country, King."

"Where to?"

"I got people in West Africa. All I need to do is get some serious money and find a way to cross the borders."

And there it was, my lifeline.

"None'a that's a problem," I said.

"What you mean not a problem? I need money and papers, a safe way to travel, and a way to get away if somebody catch on."

"You got your needs, and Grandma B got Roger."

"He could do all that?"

"In less than forty-eight hours . . . over a Sunday."

"Damn."

"But I don't think you should do it," I said.

"Why not?"

"Because instead'a bein' worried 'bout yourself, you need to be here for your blood."

That sat Chief Odin up in his plush chair. Maybe for the first time I wasn't an overgrown child in his eyes.

"What the fuck that s'posed t'mean?"

"It means you been runnin' an' hidin' long enough. It's time you concentrate on fixin' shit."

He stood up out of that chair, ready to fight.

"What the fuck you know?" he challenged. "You got thirty days in jail and a scratch on your cheek an' you think you understand me?"

I stood up too.

"Yeah, mothahfuckah, that's exactly what I think. You left me an orphan and Mama to die. You went out armed against two men owed you some chump change, got in a gunfight, and then said it was your pride made you do it. All I could say is, fuck that. You just another niggah runnin' the street, makin' a mess wherever he go."

"Sit down or I'm'a put you down," he promised.

"Even if you could it wouldn't make no difference. You are wrong. You been wrong so long it feels like right to you. Right that your own daughter don't know who you are. Right that your wife drank herself crazy and then into an early grave. Right that your own mother haven't seen you for thirty years."

Chief Odin was trembling with rage. For most of his life he would never allow a man or a woman to talk to him like that. Now he had to decide whether or not to beat me down.

I would have liked to see him try.

That was the worst of it. His hot rage and my steely anger subsided together.

He sat back down first.

"What—what you want me to do?" This question housed the conviction that there was nothing he could accomplish.

"You don't have to do a thing," I answered, lowering into my chair. "I'm'a go out there and figure out who it was killed that man. And after I do, I'll take it to the police."

"What if they don't listen?"

"I know how to make 'em listen."

"What if you can't find the killer?"

"The only question is, what if I don't try?"

That stopped the juggernaut of my father's overweening pride in its tracks. He stared at me, wide-eyed and mute.

"Okay," I said. "This is what's gonna happen. I'm gonna call Rags and he will have Roger's chief of security send over a limo to bring you to Silbrig Haus—"

"Where?"

"That's the mansion where Grandma B stays at. While you're there I will be out tryin' to find out who killed Ira Gross. After I do that, we'll get you down to where Tita's at and you will tell her that you're her father. You will give her that."

I don't know how Chief responded to my commands because, upon completion of these marching orders, I stood up and walked out.

*   *   *

The four women were in the living room when I blundered in.

"Can you give me a ride home?" I asked Leaf.

"Sure." She stood and headed for the front door. "Just let me get the car."

"It's not at the door?"

"I parked it in the garage after you left with Chief."

While Leaf and I spoke, the other three rose and headed for the back rooms. Maybe they thought I'd hurt their man.

I was soon alone in the living room. There I took out my phone, called Rags, and told him what I said to my father.

"You're quiet," Leaf commented.

We were on the FDR headed back to the Brooklyn Bridge.

"I guess so."

"You want me to come stay with you tonight?"

I heard her clearly, but for some reason it felt like she must have meant something else.

"Come again?"

She smiled as if I had just made a joke.

"I said, do you want me to come stay with you tonight?"

"Really?"

"Mm-hmm." Her chin nodded.

"I—I—I thought that that road was up on the top of a mountain, somewhere that I might never get to."

Teeth showed in her smile.

"It was when you said, *You people are family. I'm a man with a job.* When you said that you were speaking my heart."

18.

LEAF WAS A different woman in bed. Friendly, full of laughter, and engaging; her dour manner was submerged, even gone.

"It's like you haven't been with a woman for a long time," she was saying in the early morning.

The sun was coming up somewhere near but hadn't made an appearance in the sky as yet.

"Hasn't been that long," I said. "I think the difference is you."

Our reclining bodies were parallel to each other, our heads, both propped up on elbow-elevated fists, facing each other's feet. We were wrung out but not tired.

"I can tell that you like women," she said, looking me up and down.

"I can tell the same thing about you."

Where there might have been anger, she grinned.

"How'd you get mixed up with my father and his harem?"

She moved easily from prone to half lotus and said, "Luwanda was a friend'a my mother. After Mama died, she took me in."

"That's Luwanda," I said. "What do you think of Chief?"

The question furrowed her brow. She moved her head this way and that before saying, "He's like the cornerstone at the bottom of the pyramid. I mean, he's smart and funny, kinda cute for a man so old, but what makes him special is that he can take all the punishment you have to give and never even break a sweat."

After that pronouncement, she moved back to lying across from my feet.

"That's my dad," I agreed.

"You see?" she observed.

"What?"

"Almost any man I evah been wit' wanna know what I see when I look at him. They might not ask or nuthin', but I could be sure they're looking for their face in my eye. Not you, though; you studyin' the world around what most people lookin' at. The spaces in between. I—I like that."

I reached out and tugged on the big toe of her right foot. Then I pulled the foot over to kiss that toe.

"Bite it," she ordered.

By 8:00 a.m. we'd climbed down the rope ladder to my office.

"You got a nice little life," Leaf said. "It's kinda like you live on a houseboat in a marina somewhere."

"You ever lived on a houseboat?"

Shaking her head she said, "Stayed on one, once or twice."

"You want coffee?"

"Tea."

"I know just the place."

We sat at a round table made for two in the front window of Manzo's bakery. She had white tea and I a triple latte. We were pretty much isolated from the coffee-to-go crowd or any other table, so I felt free to talk.

"You ever met Felix Corn?"

"A couple'a times."

"What do you think of him?"

"Like any other pimp or plantation owner, white or Black. He owns how people make their money and so he owns them."

"If that's so, why did King take money from him?"

"What else could he do? The cops wanna put him behind bars forever and Felix owe him."

"You ever meet Ira Gross?" I asked.

"Just the one time when I drove Chief over to talk with him."

"Where was that at?"

"One of those workspaces where you rent a desk by the month. Out in Queens."

"Did you hear them argue?"

"Yeah. Chief told him that he better lay off Felix, else he was gonna have to answer to him."

"And what did Ira say?"

"He said he wasn't scared of Chief. But he was."

"Were there lots of people around?"

"Yeah. It was in the middle'a the day an' everybody was workin'."

"And you say you remember where these workspaces were?"

"Yeah, like I said, out in Queens. Want me to take you there?"

"Maybe in a little bit. Any of the ladies at the embassy apartment know Ira or ever seen him?"

"Not that I know."

"Did Chief say anything about him?"

She was watching the pedestrian traffic on Montague, reminding me of a playful cat looking for something to kill.

"He said that somebody needed to put him in the ground."

"He did?"

"Yeah. But you know him. He talks like that."

"Where'd you go after seein' Gross?"

"Back to Luwanda's down Philly. No, no, I'm'a lie. We went ovah to see Andrew. That was the first time him and me met."

"What Chief want with Gatormouth?"

"Just to talk."

"About what?"

"I'ont know. I was readin' a book for this class I was takin' an' they was in another room. All I remember is that they was like Black men I known all my life. Talkin' shit an' havin' a good time."

The Working Circle occupied the first four floors of an eight-story office building on Thirty-Fifth Avenue in the Ditmars neighborhood. Leaf walked me to a far corner of the second floor.

There were at least fourteen temporary renters in that section, sitting in cubicles that came in a variety of sizes.

"That one down at the end was where Gross worked," Leaf told me, pointing.

"You recognize anybody from that day?" I asked her.

"That man there was here," she told me, indicating a tiny compartment that housed a large metal desk painted green, behind which sat an even larger white man. I went over to the space while Leaf sat down on a bench at the window in the common area.

*   *   *

"Hi, Carlton," I greeted the blubbery man as I passed through the gap of the wall into his office.

"I know you?" he asked, his face seeming to scrunch down on the question.

"No," I said as friendly as I could manage. "Your nameplate says Carlton Rob."

"Oh, yeah," he said behind a forced smile. "I forget about that sometimes. Can I help you?"

Parking on the chair in front of his desk, I handed Carlton my private investigator's business card.

He read the information closely, then raised his head as I said, "I'm here investigating the murder of your old cubicle buddy, Ira Gross."

"That was a long time ago."

"I know, but the insurance company is about to pay off to his silent business partner and they asked me to nose around."

"For what?"

"They want me to find out if he seemed iffy."

"Iffy?"

"You know, was he crooked. It seems that there's a clause in the life policy that can refuse payment if either one of the partners was engaged in criminal activity. I guess they think that because he was shot that maybe it was a falling-out among thieves."

The fat man sat back in his office chair and stared.

"So, you're trying to cheat some poor schmoe out of his money."

Hunching my shoulders, I said, "I'm just tryin' to make enough money to feed my kids."

That got me a measure of understanding from Mr. Rob.

"I don't know much," he said. "The day before the night he got killed, another white-haired guy came in and they had an argument. The cops showed me a picture of the guy and I identified him. They never told me his name."

"Did this white-haired man threaten to kill Mr. Gross?"

"Not in so many words, but he was really mad."

"Did he have a beard?"

"Yes, he did."

"That was white too?"

Mr. Rob nodded.

"Did Mr. Gross talk to you after the argument?" I asked.

"Yes. He said that the man was an ex-con who was trying to tell him how to do his business."

"What was his business?"

"They didn't tell you?"

"No."

"Why not?" Suspicion laced his question.

"I suppose if whatever I dug up went to court, they didn't want to say that they prejudiced my investigation."

"Oh. Okay. I don't really know that much, but he was a salesman of sorts."

"What did he sell?"

"The closest I could tell was that he bought large lots of products that out-of-state companies couldn't move and then he'd sell those goods to a consortium of distributors he worked through."

"Did he say anything else about the guy he argued with?"

"He used a couple of derogatory terms and then called him a coward."

"The gray-haired visitor, was he Black?"

Carlton nodded.

"And Gross was shot there?" I asked, pointing at the cubicle Leaf had identified.

"Yeah, but late at night. Only ones here were Ira in his office and the security guard downstairs."

"What was the security guard's name?"

"I don't think I ever knew it."

"Huh. And the only people who saw anything were like you? Ones that saw him having the argument?"

"The security guard ran up from the ground floor, saw Ira, and then went down the back stairs after the shooter. I don't understand that. If I knew a man with a gun was headed east, I'd sure the fuck haul my ass west."

"Did the security guard see the killer?"

"That's what the rental agent said. I never talked to the guy myself."

It was a great deal of information. I sat there trying to envision how any of it might help my father.

"Tell me something, Mr. Oliver."

"What's that, Mr. Rob?"

"How's any of this going to make Ira look mobbed up?"

"Insurance is one of the best ideas money ever had," I opined. "And insurance companies are the greatest evil. They send out a dozen guys to gather information and then they sit down in a pit under the insurance office and try to make it look like what they wanna see. They get it just right and the insured is shit outta luck."

Carlton nodded. I was speaking his language and, on top of that, I was telling the truth.

Leaf and I walked out to her classic car. Every time I saw that car it made me glad.

"Is this yours?" I just had to know.

"I wondered when you were gonna ask."

"Looks expensive."

"Used to belong to my daddy before he died. When Mama passed, it came to me. I work on it at a garage on the weekends up in the Bronx. This here Buick is my pet project."

"Huh."

"You don't think a woman could be a mechanic?"

"Do you think that even if I didn't think so I would tell you?"

Her smile was worth my tongue-twisting work. But this mirth quickly faded.

"I can't go with you to the next stop," she said.

"He don't seem mad."

"Not mad," she said. "Sad. Andrew see me an' he spend the next week beatin' himself up ovah what he cain't do right."

"How about if you let me off a block away and then pick me up at the same place when I call?"

The door to Etta-Jane's guardian's apartment was closed, but through it I could hear Johnny Cash singing, "A Boy Named Sue," live at San Quentin.

I jogged up to the third floor and knocked on Gatormouth Williams's door.

"Who is it?"

"Me again."

He pulled open the door grinning shyly. Giving me a quick bro hug, he moved back, a quizzical look on his face.

"New cologne?" he asked.

That's what threw me off. The scent of my skin and the impossible question in his eye.

"Just what I found in the medicine cabinet this mornin'. Might'a been something my daughter put in there."

"You got a daughter?"

"Yeah."

"How old?"

"Nineteen."

"That's nice," he said as if my words were the window of a clothes store showing a shirt he might like to try on.

"The light of my life."

"Hey, what we standin' here at the door for? Come on in, boy."

Back at the nonexistent dining table, seated across from each other and both drinking ice water, Andrew and I were set for our next meeting.

"How's it goin' lookin' for Chief?" he asked.

"Gettin' closer."

"Talkin' to his girlfriends?"

"Ruby and a white lady named Bernadette."

"How about Luwanda?"

"She called me," I lied. "Said that she heard somewhere that Chief was tryin' to get to Africa."

"Yeah, yeah. He got people in Accra, that's what he said. You gonna go over there lookin' for him?"

"Maybe later. Right now, I'm tryin' to see what this murder charge is all about."

"Oh yeah. I guess if you could pry that off'a him, then he could climb outta that hole they got him in. How's that goin'?"

"Talkin' to Luwanda helped. She told me that Chief went to see Gross the day before the night he was killed. She said that they argued and then he came to see you."

"Yeah." He was staring at me, his eyes just a bit glassy. "That was the first time I met Leaf. She liked my setup here. Said she never saw anything like it before."

"It is pretty wild," I said, agreeing with the woman I was pretending never to have met. "How you come up with this design?"

Gates grinned at my attention. "It come to me in pieces. I decided on one color blue, painted one wall, but I hadn't bought enough for any more. When I went to the store there was this other blue I liked. I painted the wall next to the other one and damn, if they didn't look good like that."

"Okay. But what about this place where the table should be?"

"I like the chairs," he said, a satisfied growl in his throat. "Bought 'em and put 'em where the table should be. Ain't nevah fount the right board to put between 'em."

He was gazing around the room like some Renaissance master appreciating the discovery of form.

"What did Chief have to say?" I asked.

"Huh?"

"When him and your future fiancée come by after seein' Ira Gross."

"Not too much. Ira was threatenin' Felix's prison work business. He said he wanted in and that they could expand to a big contraband operation. Felix said no but Ira was pushin' hard."

"You think Chief went back there and killed him?"

Andrew twisted up his mouth as if trying to disgorge a bad taste and said, "Nah."

"Why not?"

He started rocking back and forth in his chair.

"I don't know," he said. "He just wasn't talkin' like that. I mean, he might'a gone there an' kicked the shit outta that son, but I don't think he would'a kilt him. It wasn't like that."

"What was it like?"

"Chief wanted to protect the friend that got him outta prison, but he didn't wanna go back in. I think he would'a told Felix to cut bait or make some kind'a deal. You know, big money bring out the big guns."

"You think one'a those guns got Ira?"

"I really don't know."

"Maybe I need to go ask Felix about that."

"You could, I guess," Andrew said reluctantly, "but you know Felix is born-again. I think the Bible frowns on murder."

I remember thinking that that was a perfectly good answer.

"But even still," I said. "Felix is involved with all the players."

Andrew nodded and then asked, "You gonna talk to Luwanda again?"

"I don't know. I expect that at least one of Chief's girl-friends could get in touch with him. If she's the one, we might talk."

"Did she say anything about Leaf?"

"Your ex?"

"Uh-huh."

"No."

"She didn't say she was here with Chief?"

"No, why you ask?"

"I didn't want you stalkin' her, that's all."

"I bet ya Luwanda thought the same thing."

Andrew could see the sense in that.

"If you talk to Luwanda again, could you tell her that I was thinkin' about Leaf, her and Leaf?"

"Sure."

He smiled sadly.

"I just can't get that girl out my mind," he said.

"She all that?"

"And more, a lot more."

"I'll try to get word to Luwanda," I promised.

I was almost out the front door of the building when she cried, "Mr. Joe!"

I squatted down and Etta-Jane ran into my arms, her guardian watching closely from the doorway.

"Hi!" I said to both.

"Mr. Joe, I got in the church choir. I went to sing for them, and they liked it so much that they said they were gonna put me up front."

"That's wonderful."

"Uh-huh. That's what they said. And Mama Beah says that she don't mind bringin' me on Wednesdays."

"You'll be just like Etta James."

"Yeah!"

19.

LEAF WAS A trifle subdued on the drive back to Brooklyn. I thought that she was feeling something about Gatormouth. I was feeling something too. Gates could smell the slightest scent of her on my skin. I'd taken a shower and changed clothes, but he could still smell her. That was animal love. The kind of love that was beyond most adult human beings.

I didn't want to think it right then, but Andy's potent feelings drove me even closer to his ex.

"You want to go out tonight?" I asked as we exited the BQE.

The question prompted a smile.

"What?" I asked.

"Nuthin'. I mean, I know you must feel somethin' 'bout your daddy's friend and me, but you still wanna find out what this all about. I like that."

"You like a lotta things."

"About you."

"You'd like dinner tonight, then?"

"I would, but I cain't. Luwanda needs me to help her."

182

"She still at the UN apartment?"

"Uh-uh. She back down Philly now that your father is at your gram's."

"Oh, right. I almost forgot about that. When can I see you again?"

"Whenever you want."

My cellphone chimed as I was walking up the stairs to the office.

"Hey, Olo, what's up?"

"I got what you asked me for. You at work?"

"Yes, I am," I said while pressing the cylindrical key into the specialized lock of the armored front door.

"I'll be there in ten minutes."

Hunger gnawed at my stomach as I sat there behind Aja's receptionist's desk. That's why I'd asked Leaf if she wanted to go out; I was hungry—body and soul. This craving made me both restless and inquisitive. In my mind I was looking for something like those elephants in East Africa that dig cave-size holes in the ground in search of salt.

The door buzzer sounded, and, psychically, I morphed back to human form, walked to the entryway, and let in the onetime International Operative.

The little black dress looked odd on her long-muscled physique, like maybe the garment was a tattered cocoon almost completely ripped apart in the process of her becoming her true self. She had a ten-by-fifteen-inch manila envelope under her arm and, as usual, she carried no purse or pocketbook.

"Hi," she said happily.

Olo and I never hugged and rarely even shook hands or slapped shoulders.

She handed me the envelope and I gestured toward the front desk.

On the way there I said, "That's a different look for you."

"An old client paid me to follow her to high tea. She said that some guy was pestering her, but he didn't do it today."

"Oh."

Olo was not one to indulge in small talk, so I got to look through the photographs with complete focus.

There were a dozen or so nonglossy nine-by-twelve photos of Hart and Bernadette. Some with just one and about half with them together. I imagined that Oliya had snapped hundreds of pictures and that these were the best of the crop. There were none that revealed the ladies' home or Annie's school. If anyone knew New York well, they might have recognized the neighborhoods. But there was nothing to do about that.

One photo had them playing and laughing together under a tree with no building or structure to be seen.

"Where'd you take this one?" I asked Olo.

"In the park."

"Central Park?"

"Yeah. They walked over there instead of taking a car right off. You can see how much older Annie looks than in the old photos he sent, and they look so happy together."

I dithered a bit over which photos gave the least away, but in the end, I took the park picture because I liked it so much.

"Wanna make a bet?" I asked my overqualified passe-partout.

"On what?"

"On how long it'll take for Hart's husband to call."

Her smile told me that she would not play the game but that she understood my need to understand my enemy.

The office printer did triple duty as a copier and a fax. With no written word I sent the picture to Ogre Orr's number. As soon as it was off, I felt relief. We were moving forward. That's always a good thing.

"What do you think about our clients now?" I asked Oliya.

"The mother's tough and her daughter has picked it up."

"You know I spent the night with Hart, right?"

"Seemed like that."

"You have any criticism?"

"I never criticize the people I work for."

"What if you disagree with what they're doing?"

"Then I quit."

Before I could respond, the phone rang.

"Hello."

"Where was this taken?" Tony Orr managed to ask the question as if it was a command.

"Outside."

He needed a moment to swallow and then said, "I got two guys will come out there day after tomorrow. When I have the flight number, I'll send it along with the time. You meet them and we'll complete the transaction."

"Whatever you say."

"Somethin' wrong, Oliver?"

"Not at all. I'm eager to finish it."

"Good." He hung up in response, I felt, to our last conversation, where I abruptly ended the call.

"There's something wrong with that man," Olo said.

I'd had the call on speakerphone.

"How you see that?" I asked.

"He sounds rotten," she said, giving a rare frown. "But there's something else."

"What?"

"I don't know, but you better be careful with him, it's like he's a rat with a permanent case of rabies."

Alone in my little office I spent the time trying to understand something that I couldn't articulate. It had to do with how Oliya interpreted the trace notes in Ogre Orr's voice. I heard the madness there too, but that hadn't warned me enough to reconsider my approach.

I was reminded of my tenure as a police detective. We were always setting criminals up to be arrested, through either undercover agents, false promises in newspaper ads, or almost continual surveillance. I would relish the surprised look on perps' faces when we'd come busting into places where they believed that they were safe.

My problem, I decided, was that I didn't believe it could happen to me.

"Hello?" she said. "Daddy?"

"Hey, girl," I said to my daughter.

"Granddad is here," she said on an audible grin.

It hadn't dawned on me that Aja would think of my father as what he is to her. Their meeting was a major moment in her life.

"How'd that feel?" I asked her.

"Like magic, I guess. I never thought I'd ever see him."

Her tone didn't carry anger or hurt. I'd always told Aja that her grandfather was a bad man who had run out on me and my mother. It was such an easy lie to tell.

"I'm sorry, baby," I whispered. "I should'a told you about him. I should have said that he was incarcerated. You deserved to know."

"It doesn't matter. I knew anyway."

"You did?"

"Mama told me when I was twelve. She wanted me to think you were awful. But the way she said it made me understand how hurt you had to be. I don't think she could see how you felt. She only ever cares about her and Coleman."

Coleman Tesserat. He was the motherfucker who took up with my wife, Monica, while I was out running the streets with half a dozen different women. Of course Monica told Aja about Chief. Of course she did. She was always confusing her hatred for me with her love of Aja.

"Well, anyway," I said. "I was wrong, and I apologize."

"Okay. When you comin' over?"

"Now, I guess. Tell Forthright I'm on the way."

The gates of Silbrig Haus opened to me without any trouble.

Once more Rags opened the fancy double doors of the city estate. He brought me to the library, a generously rendered room that had three small tables, one settee that was done up in red fabrics that mimicked the dance of flames, a computer nook for research, and a chessboard of black and white stone set into a table built for two.

Roger and Chief were at the chess table, hunkered over the board. I could tell that Roger was taking the game seriously because his left eye was nictating, almost closed. Silently, I pulled up a chair and watched.

I'm a decent player, but I could see by the splay of pieces that both these men were above me in ability. Because of the nature of the game, I couldn't tell whose move it was.

The silence deepened.

Chief's right hand rose, making a gesture that made you think he was about to tap someone on the shoulder. Then his left hand came up to touch his lower lip. He stayed like that for long seconds. Then he moved a pawn from its original position on the far right to one square beyond.

Roger nodded, telling me that Chief had thrown a monkey wrench into King Silver's machinations.

"Hello, son."

"Dad. Roger."

"You brought me a worthy opponent," Roger replied.

"I guess prison's good for somethin'."

Roger smiled at my words and said, "I need a little time to think about your move, Chief. How about a break?"

"Fine with me."

"Good. I'll go round up the family. Joe can show you to the dining room."

The nonagenarian rose from his chair without the use of his hands, stood still a moment, to achieve balance, and then headed for the door.

When he was gone Chief asked, "How's it goin', son?"

"There's a witness that saw a Black man running from the place where Ira was shot."

"Lotta Black men in New York."

"True."

"The girls told me that you left with Leaf."

"You not gonna tell me she's my sister, are you?"

He laughed.

"No, son. But she did get with Gates for a while."

"So?"

"You right," he said and then he stood. "Every man gotta carry his own water."

"What about you?" I asked.

"What about me?"

"You like it here?" I stood too.

"I missed Mama more than I thought. When I saw her, I cried. It's been so long that I forgot."

"Forgot what?"

"That there's a reason for this loneliness."

"This is one mothahfuckah of a house, man," my father proclaimed as we moved from one chamber to the next. "Sixty-three rooms not countin' toilets, hallways, and basements."

"Yeah. And my science class in high school didn't have one microscope."

Chief stopped in his tracks. "You not complainin', are you?" It almost sounded like a threat.

"No," I said, stopping too. "Just injecting a little truth into wonder." This was an aphorism that my grandfather, Chief's father, used to explain his off-the-cuff critiques.

Chief smiled while taking me in.

"You really turned into a man, didn't you?"

"I do my best."

We continued our walk.

The dining room was a broad chamber that could seat twenty-four guests and accommodate well over a hundred people. The far wall was made of bulletproof, concussion-proof glass that looked out onto New Jersey.

Roger, Grandma B, Rags, and Aja were sitting at the far end of the table talking at a normal volume and seeming convivial.

Roger rose when Chief and I approached.

"We were about to send out a search party," the rich man said.

"Tried to make a break for it," my father answered, "but the moat was too wide."

The waitstaff brought platters of cheese, breads, and dried fruit. I had a cognac and Roger an aged port.

"I've always been afraid of prison," Roger said out of nowhere.

"Me too," Chief and I said together.

We laughed.

"You see," Brenda Naples said to Aja. "That's what the men think. They afraid about what's gonna happen to them and there us women is, scared about what's gonna happen to 'em too."

"You not scared'a prison, Grandma B?" Aja asked.

"Nah."

"Why not? Black women get convicted of crimes too."

"Yeah, but we got sumpin' men don't know."

"What's that?"

"Love."

"You mean you love the men, but they don't love you?"

"The love I'm talkin' 'bout don't have nuthin' to do with the men. Us girls know how to bring together and be together and only fight when we got to. Men so scared they only know how to fight."

"How's Tita?" Rags asked me, wanting, I think, to derail the conversation.

190

"I don't know," I said to my cousin. "But if somethin' went wrong on the way, Roger's pilot would have said."

"You talkin' 'bout Ilse's girl?" Grandma B asked. "What about her?"

"She needed to get outta town," I said. "And I was looking for Chief. This and that got together and here we are."

"What she have to get outta town for?"

"Why any woman have to change the numbers on her door?" I did and did not ask.

"She okay?" Grandma B wanted to know.

"Did you know that she was your granddaughter?" I asked Brenda. I probably shouldn't've, but there it was.

Brenda's sharp eyes turned to my father. He looked like a street mime who'd suddenly forgotten what to do with his hands.

"Chief Odin," she said.

"It was a mixed-up time, Mama. We did what we thought was right."

"She Ruby's child?"

"Can we talk about this later?"

That put a chill on our little get-together. After about twenty minutes I was headed for the door.

20.

I'D MADE IT all the way to the foyer before Aja caught up with me.

"Daddy."

I didn't want to stop, but I'd learned a long time before that parenting was not about choice.

"Yeah, honey?"

She hugged me, kissed my scarred cheek, then hugged me again.

"Thank you," she said.

It would have been disingenuous of me to ask, *for what*, so I said, "Sorry 'bout all that mess in there. Chief and me got some issues, I guess."

"Are you okay, Daddy?"

"'Course I am. Why you ask?"

"You haven't told me I could go back home, or to the office."

"I wanna make sure about Hart before we go back to normal."

"You bein' careful?"

"Yeah," I said with two-syllable emphasis. "I'm in the catbird seat with this one. It'll be like setting up dominoes before tippin' the last one back."

She studied my eyes while I spoke. I could feel her great-grandmother in that stare.

"Okay," she said. "Call me."

I couldn't bear to read *The Painted Bird* anymore, and so I dug out a seventy-five-year-old paperback inherited from my grandfather called *For Love of Imabelle,* by Chester Himes. It was an extremely dark but still very funny rendition of Black people in the mid-twentieth century. The story could have come from the ancient Greeks or even war-torn China from millennia ago. This universal story was that love doesn't so much conquer poverty as assuage it. This was, in the author's opinion, why money and love so often run afoul of each other.

I needed that story and so skipped that night of sleep.

In my office the next morning, I was hunkered over an extra-dark paper cup of Manzo's coffee when my cell phone sounded.

"Yeah?"

"Your girl took off."

"What?"

"Marigold," Melquarth said. "She asked Oliya to watch Bernadette for a couple'a days and then she was gone."

"Where?"

"I didn't talk to her and Olo says she didn't say."

"Damn."

"Yeah."

"Did she have a car?"

"I think somebody came and picked her up."

"So, whoever it is knows about your place."

"Maybe." Mel was unconcerned. "I wouldn't mind a good shoot-out, not at all."

"Damn. Oliya there?"

"She's out with Annie somewhere."

I called Oliya's cell, but she didn't answer.

I tried Hart's number but that went to voicemail too.

"Hey, girl, it's me," I said to her automated answering service. "I don't know if it's such a good idea with you runnin' around without protection. Call me and we'll talk."

Christian Charities and Hope's door was open for business.

I walked in and the same three guardians awaited. Dorothy Ridges stared daggers into my eyes. You could see that she was preparing a stern rebuff for any request that I might have. So I veered right, to Padma's station.

"Padma, right?"

She gave a meaningful smile and said, "How can I help you, Mr. Oliver?"

"Lookin' for Felix again."

"Padma—" Dorothy began.

"Excuse me, Dot, but I'm talking to somebody right now."

Dot. Damn!

Then the young woman said to me, "I'm sorry, Mr. Oliver, but Mr. Corn hasn't been in since lunchtime yesterday."

"Did he say he was going to be out?"

"Mr. Oliver," Dorothy Ridges said.

"Excuse me, Dot," I replied, "but I don't give a damn."

"He's missed three meetings," a grinning Padma was saying.

"Have you called him?"

"All his numbers. No answer or callback."

This was not acceptable. I'd finally found my father again and I would not have him taken from me by a frightened ex-con shoving his head in the sand.

"I'm gonna go across the street to the Daily Grind," I said to my young confidante. "If you can, why don't you come over there and we could talk...in private."

Glancing at Dot, she understood me and gave me a quick nod.

I ordered and received my daily grind and then went to a small table in a forward corner.

The impossibly beautiful Black woman from before was sitting there with a friend, another young woman with similar attributes only she was Hispanic and even more glamorous. The woman I'd spoken to about God and fate two days earlier smiled at me.

There was so much information packed into that smirk. It said that she expected me to come back, that if I could come correct, she might even talk to me—until I got to be a bore. She crossed those big legs jutting out from that extra-mini skirt, crossing them to indicate how difficult that trek would be.

I was trying to be a better man, had been striving to achieve a more stable state of being, but I was still the man my grandmother talked about the night before, living through my nose without the slightest hope of deliverance.

Three minutes later the beautiful, sophisticated, well-educated, and probably even innocent Padma walked in wearing a sari that was saffron and indigo. Looking around for a moment or two, she caught sight of me and then walked up to my little table. The two beauties stared at her brazenly.

I couldn't help but smile.

Taking the seat across from me, Padma asked, "What can I do for you, Mr. Oliver?"

"Have you heard about Felix's ex-friend Ira Gross?"

"The man that got murdered a few years ago?"

I took a business card out of my shirt pocket and handed it to her.

"Yeah," I said while she read. "I've taken on a client who wants me to find out who committed the murder."

"And you think Mr. Corn knows something about that?"

"I know that I have to ask him about it."

"Didn't you do that the other day?"

"I did. Since then, however, I've come across more information. But that doesn't matter. If he's missing, he might be in trouble, and him and my father, Chief Oliver, are friends."

"So, what do you want from me?"

"Do you know where he lives?"

"Yes. Of course. When he works at home, I deliver files over there."

"I'd really appreciate it if you'd give me his address."

Padma studied me closely.

What made con men so successful was convincing people that they were trustworthy. This one simple human twist had cost many people their life savings, even their lives.

The only thing that separated me from a con man was that I hadn't lied to the young Indian woman.

"I can take you there," she proposed.

It was a meaningful offer. The pros were all mine while

the cons clustered around her head: unseen and mostly evil spirits. Her dark eyes were vulnerable, thinking they were strong. Hart was in a place I couldn't imagine. My father was, once again, about to disappear from my life, and my grandmother was going to die on a surgeon's table.

"Okay," I said, accepting both inescapable fate and Padma's offer.

Gramercy Park is one of the two private parks in New York. Between Twenty-First and Twentieth Streets, east of Park Avenue South, it's a posh neighborhood lined by expensive old brick apartment buildings and some offices that were once the homes of the ultrarich.

Padma walked through a wrought-iron gate and up a dozen blue-and-white marble stairs to a set of very nice copper doors that, due to oxidation, had turned a costly-looking green. Carrying a box of folders that Padma had picked up from CCH, I followed the young woman. She pulled the doors open revealing a portly young man with pink skin who sat behind a dented-up dark-wood desk.

"Hi, Malcolm," Padma said.

The big man struggled to his feet, smiling and giving a slanted nod.

"Hey, Padma. You comin' to see Mr. Corn?"

"Yes. Is he in?"

"I guess so," he said, looking at me. "I been here since six and he haven't showed yet."

Noticing the suspicion in Malcolm's stare, Padma said, "This is Oliver. He's helping us out today."

"Okay, go on."

* * *

Felix's apartment was on the fourth floor. The box wasn't heavy, and the span between each stair and the next was short, designed with senior citizens and children in mind. On the way we passed an older gentleman in a three-piece walnut-brown suit, a derby of the same color, and carrying a cane, which was black. After him came a young woman who was leading a cat on a leash down the stairs.

Felix's door was across from a sunny window, its deep red turned lustrous under the solar light.

She knocked.

I bit my lower lip.

She pressed the doorbell.

I bit harder.

"You got a key?" I asked.

She knocked louder.

We waited.

After the appropriate number of seconds I said, "You should call the police and ask for a wellness check."

She looked up at me, her eyes pleading.

"What?" I asked.

"I—I have a key."

The apartment ceilings were at least eighteen feet high. The living room was furnished with solid old furniture and had recently been gussied by a professional housecleaner, probably a weekly maid. There was an oil painting on the wall that looked great. It was a young woman, wearing a windblown cream-colored gown, communing with a black stallion. They were standing in a clearing next to a stream, surrounded by a dark forest.

"Mr. Oliver," Padma said.

"Yes?"

"We should look in his bedroom."

I imagined Roger and my dad poring over their chess pieces, knowing that the slightest error would mean defeat.

"Yeah. Okay."

I suppose the most surprising thing was that Padma didn't scream.

Clad in cotton pajamas and a royal blue robe, he was lying on his back on a creamy white comforter atop the bed. Both bed and blanket were covered in his blood. His eyes were open, and the jutting eyebrows gave some semblance of a time when he was alive. We stood in the doorway, staring for a short span that felt very long. Finally, at the same time, we both moved forward. Upon reaching the body, Padma took my hand.

At that moment Felix Corn's head turned toward us and he uttered, "King."

I nearly lost control of my bowels.

It was then I noticed that Felix's neck and head were making a throbbing, syncopated gesture every few seconds or so. I figured this metered spasm was following the beat of his dying heart.

"Call 911," I said to Padma. "Use his landline if he got one."

She moved quickly and I was impressed.

"What should I say?" she asked, receiver in hand.

"That a man has been shot and he's alive. He's lost a lot of blood."

"Should I ask for the police?"

"They'll take care of that."

* * *

I was sitting next to my father's onetime friend, onetime enemy, and then friend again, holding his left hand with mine while using the other hand to press a throw pillow down on the wound. He was steady talking, making dis-jointed claims about my father and me.

"Chief told me that you would be a better man than he was," Felix said. "'King will take my place and push it, push it.' That's what he used to say."

"Who shot you?" I asked.

"He forgave me. He forgave you."

"Was it somebody trying to get the business?"

"There's nothing to do."

"Was it a Black man?" I asked.

"No . . . white, white man."

When the paramedics arrived, they put him in an inflat-able bodysuit designed to keep his blood pressure up. They gave him oxygen and two injections.

Padma and I sat in the living room. We could have run but I figured it would be pretty easy to prove we didn't do it. I had a gun, but it was licensed and hadn't been fired in more than three months.

When the police came, they didn't even put us in chains.

21.

"WHAT WERE YOU doing in Mr. Corn's apartment?" Detective Ralph Lewis asked for the fourth or fifth time.

"Like I said before, I had come by Christian Charities to ask him about his old partner Ira Gross. But when I found out he wasn't there I asked Padma—"

"Miss Vyas?" Lewis asked.

"I guess. We didn't get to last names. I asked her where he lived, and she said that she'd take me to his condo."

"Why would she do that?"

"Because I'd come there a few days before and she knew that me and Felix were talking. She was also worried about her boss because he hadn't been to work, and he wasn't answering his phone."

"What would you say if I told you that she claims you had forced her to go to the house and then you shot him and threatened to kill her if she didn't alibi you?"

"That depends."

"On what?"

"Is it against the law for me to call you a liar?"

"Come on now, Oliver. You know we got you."

"Okay. All right. But first, could you tell me what gun I shot him with?"

"We haven't found it yet."

"Then what say we wait until that momentous discovery?"

"I know you used to be a hotshot detective," Lewis said. "But that was a long time ago. Right now, you're just a piece'a shit."

This cross-examination went on for a couple of hours. I had to urinate but didn't ask for a toilet because I knew that it was part of the technique of interrogation to put the suspect into a weakened position. If it came to it, I'd go to a corner and piss there before asking anybody's leave.

"Explain to me," Detective Lewis said, "how you think anybody else could have gotten in there and shot the victim."

"Why don't you ask the victim?"

"I'm asking you."

There was no reason to say anything and so I didn't.

"I'm tryin' to help you, Oliver." Lewis was around my age, thin, and what America calls white, with intelligent green eyes. He was doing his job, and I was doing mine.

"The fuck you are," I said, with emphasis.

Those four words were a gauntlet between cops.

"Don't use that language with me," he warned.

"You mean *fuck*, Detective? Because you know I will call you a fuckin' son of a bitch from here to election day."

That got him on his feet.

I tried my best to hide the grin wanting to come out.

It was fifty-fifty that he was going to hit me, not so much because of my language but because of my calm. I wasn't worried and so there was no need to crack. I had places to be, but that was okay; the key to my liberation was already in the lock.

"Nigger, I will fuck you up."

He put the *r* in the word and everything. This was a whole new wrinkle. Actually, it was an old one that didn't rear its ugly head nearly as much as in years gone past. Sometimes, for weeks at a time, I even forgot about the great divide between our so-called races.

I wasn't physically restrained and, due to protocol, he was not armed. On top of that, Lewis had figured out how to get under my skin.

My parry to his thrust was imagining jumping up, getting my hands around his throat, and choking until he no longer could draw breath.

After seeing that in my mind I said, "Congratulations, Detective, you just made it so that I will never help your sorry ass."

"Why, you goddamned—"

The door to the shallow but wide interrogation room came open before Lewis could finish his sentence.

Gladstone Palmer waltzed in, all smiles and light hands.

"Sergeant Palmer," Lewis uttered, showing one thing an inquisitor never should—surprise.

"Hey, Lew."

"What are you doing here?"

"Come to make sure that you don't get sent down to HR for reeducation."

Lewis wanted to argue but didn't. There were deputy commissioners who wouldn't attempt to gainsay Gladstone. He knew where the bodies were buried. Literally.

* * *

Another coffee shop across another city street. Glad and I were at his special corner table where no one could overhear our conversation. There was a rumor that the dispatch sergeant also carried a device that could detect and disable any type of bug. This gossip is unsubstantiated.

"This is about your father?" he asked me after a little light banter.

"I'm going on the assumption that Chief did not kill Gross and so someone else must've done it."

"What does he say?"

"Who say?" I asked.

"Chief."

"Haven't talked to him. I'm doing this for my grandmother."

The most distinctive thing about Glad was the color of his eyes, along with the eyes themselves. They were emerald green and almost always alight.

"Corn came out of surgery," Glad said. "He passed the word down through his doctor that you were not the one who shot him."

"Who did?"

"He said he didn't know the guy. But that he was white."

"They question the doorman?"

"No doorman after ten. From that time on you have to be buzzed in."

"And that's what Felix did?"

"Called him a pizza man."

"Huh," I grunted. "No cameras?"

"I guess the residents don't want to keep tabs on each other."

"That's too bad."

"Yeah. What about our other thing?"

"Orr's sending two goons who're gonna trade my fee for her address."

"When?"

"Sometime tomorrow."

"You want protection?"

"Whatever I do, you need to be out of it."

"You gonna use that young'un, Tourneau?"

"Maybe." It was useless trying to keep police secrets from Glad. "If we can catch the guys Orr sends, then maybe we could turn 'em."

Those flexible eyes were studying me doubtfully.

"What?" I asked.

"There's somethin' with ya," he determined. "It's like you're not in balance. Like with Detective Lewis. The way you were needlin' him might'a pushed him over that razor's edge."

"I wasn't worried. I knew you'd get there about then."

"So what? I know when my gun is unloaded but still, I check it every time I pick it up."

Being susceptible to gun metaphors, I said, "Can't argue with you there, my friend. But listen, I got sumpin' else."

"Okay."

"I know you don't do investigations, but can you have somebody compare the bullet used to shoot Felix with the one in Gross?"

That request got me a smile and a nod.

I called Christian Charities and Hope from the street.

"CCH," a man answered.

"Yes. May I speak to Miss Vyas, please."

"Who may I say is calling?"

"Frank Bold." That sounded to me like a good alias.

"And what is it you want with Padma, Mr. Bold?"

"I'm a criminal lawyer. I was given her name because our firm is considering making a donation to your fund."

"Hello?" Padma said a few moments later.

"Hey, Padma, it's Joe Oliver."

"Oh. Hi. Did they let you out?"

"Yeah. After a few hours of telling me that you claimed that you saw me shoot Felix."

"I didn't say anything like that."

"That's what I told them. It's just the way they try and get confessions."

"But it was a lie."

"Lying is permissible in the execution of justice," I quoted from the grand compendium of common street knowledge.

"Have you heard anything about Mr. Corn?"

"He's doing well. Talking and everything."

"That's a relief. There was so much blood that I was sure he was dead."

"You are one brave woman, Miss Vyas."

"Oh, no. Not me. But thank you for being there."

We shared a few more niceties before hanging up.

The number of my next call, I knew by heart.

"Hello? Joe?"

"Hey, Olo. You hear from Hart?"

"No and that worries me. I think she would have gotten in touch by now to check up on Annie."

"You get anything outta Annie?"

"Yes. She says that her mother told her that she was going

to see a man named Todd. Todd is a freelance driver for Max-imillian Escorts. Marigold used him regularly. I would have followed that down already, but I feel like my most important job is taking care of the girl."

"I got it covered, Olo. You just keep doin' what you're doin'."

I went back to the office to calm down and think.

The experience of my arrest had hit me hard. In most cases you have to be arrested before you can be incarcerated, but from there on it's a straight fall. I knew this from bitter experience. They could beat you off-camera, give your cellmate a script to follow for the courts if he wanted early release, move you from one place to another to keep your legal representation from getting to you. They could call you nigger and slit your throat with the rusty and ragged top of a tomato can. Blind Justice wouldn't see that you're broke and can't pay your bond. She wouldn't notice that the public defender might not lay eyes on your case for months on end. No one talks about the con-on-con beatings, the epidemics of diarrhea, flu, or STDs from daily rape. There's no, nor will there ever be, succor from a faulty heating system or filth. From cloudy water to fungus-encrusted American cheese, prison life offers few alternatives.

I had to repeat that mantra a few dozen times before getting down to the problems at hand.

Google is a silly word. Sounds like something a baby might say about a butterfly in the window or the smell of her feet. But in the twenty-first century it's like the Magic 8 Ball of the epoch before. I typed in the words *marigold hart* and waited for a reply.

On the twenty-seventh screen of mostly house and garden information, I came across an entry that was little more than a notation. Using expertise that most men of my age do not have, I worked my way into a more shadowy version of the baby's exhortation.

There I found a picture of Hart along with the following notation: **LOOKING FOR HER IN THE NYC AREA. WORTH $$$ IF SOMEONE CAN PROVIDE INFORMATION**. The return e-address was most probably a non-specific area of memory on a device in some lax-lawed country across an ocean somewhere. Communication with that address could not be traced. I might not have been as good as my daughter's friends at the Digital Path, but I could stir up some bits and bytes when I had to.

Not that I was happy about the discovery.

My next call was to the offices of the Maximillian Escort Service.

"Services," a young man's bright voice chirped.

"Hi. My name is George Westerly. I had a lunch meeting with one of your representatives the other day and she gave me a ride in her limo and—"

"Hold on, Mr. Westerly," the young man said, "I'll send you to the right line."

The Muzak was classical harp. I liked it.

"Hello?" said a woman with a deep voice.

"Hi. My name is George Westerly. I had a lunch meeting with—"

"Marleigh Mann," she cut in. "How can I help you, Mr. Westerly?"

"Ms. Mann offered to give me a ride downtown after the meeting and I just realized that I must have dropped one of my cell phones in the limo. I was hoping that you could ask them if they found it."

There was a brief pause, then: "The limo service Ms. Mann uses is independent of Maximillian. We don't have any way of making that request."

"Would you happen to know the limo company's name?"

Another moment of corporate reflection, then the rich voice said, "Shorter Car Service."

That was an afternoon of telephone work.

"Daddy?" Aja answered.

"Hey, child, how you doin'?"

"Good. Granddad has great stories, Grandma B is really happy, and Roger has been laughing a lot. I think he's having as good a time as they are."

"Sounds great. I should be there with them."

"Yes, you should," she agreed. "Is that what you called about?"

"Partly. I also want you to make a call to a number I'll be texting you."

"And what do you want me to say?"

We talked back and forth for a while and then I let her go to perform her magic.

Henri Tourneau was the next call on the list.

"Mr. Oliver," he answered.

"Joe," I corrected.

"How can I help you, sir?" he said, and I gave up on making us equals for the moment.

"I need some help on a couple of things I'm doing."

"Let's have it."

"First I need you to find out what hospital a shooting victim named Felix Corn is being kept in, and then I'd like you to get me a pass in to see him."

"Okay. What's this all about?"

"Nothing serious. Just mayhem and murder."

Henri was born in the U.S. but his rich laughter belonged to his ancestral Haiti.

"This is serious, young man," I warned.

"You know that I'm a cop, right?"

I was getting a call from my daughter then.

"I need to go, Henri. I'll call you later."

"Looking forward to it."

I switched calls and said, "Hi, honey."

"I did what you asked, Daddy. He'll be there tonight at nine."

"You see," I schooled. "PI work without the danger."

"If you don't give me a real job, one day I'll go to work for one of your competitors."

"Tonight, at nine?" I asked, skimming over her threat.

"Uh-huh."

"Thanks so much."

"Does this have to do with Miss Hart?"

"It do indeed."

After all that plotting I needed a break.

"Hello?" she said after the ninth ring.

"Hey."

"I was getting out of the shower. You rang a long time."

"Want to go to the UN apartment and eat leftovers?"

She guffawed and then said, "I can meet you there around seven."

22.

NEW LOVE, ESPECIALLY if it has yet to take itself seriously, is like an idyll on a perpetual afternoon by a lake in the middle of nowhere.

Leaf tongued and then bit my left nipple.

"Ow, that hurt."

"Oh? Let me try the other one, then."

My breathing was deep and yet contradictorily hollow, like the exhaustion one might experience after spending an entire lifetime trying to attain a particular moment of grace.

After a little gnaw on my right nipple, she sat up straight on the living room couch.

"Okay," she said. "It's eight thirty-one. What happens at nine?"

"Nothing important."

Leaf's shrug told me she didn't mind being kept in the dark. She didn't consider herself my keeper.

"I was in love with Gatormouth," she said. "His mind was something wonderful whenever he could get ovah bein' so scared."

I didn't know if she was trying to get a rise out of me, but my heart was the soul of kindness right then.

"I can honestly say that I loved that man," I rejoined. "He gave me his copy of *Adventure Comics,* number 247, I mean in almost mint condition."

"So?" she asked, just to wheedle me. "Is it worth a lotta money?"

"Today it could get twenty thousand."

"Fo'a comic book?"

"Yeah, but I'd never sell it. That was the first appearance of the Legion of Super-Heroes. For me, that's a piece of literary history."

"A comic book?"

I smiled hopelessly and she descended for a real kiss.

We were on about the seventh or maybe eighth kiss when my cell phone chimed.

"You need to get that?" Leaf asked, pressing her body down on mine.

"I guess."

After hurriedly putting on my shirt and pants, I retrieved my Walther automatic and headed for the door.

"Not gonna put your shoes on?" Leaf called at me.

"Don't need 'em."

The limo was an upscale black BMW M8 Competition Gran Coupe that was parked with the passenger's side to the door. I hurried out, opened the back door, and slid in.

"Mr. Dubois?" the driver asked with deference.

I pressed the muzzle of my PPK to the side of his neck and said, "Todd?"

"What the fuck, man?"

"Gimme your wallet."

"Hey—hey, man, you got the—got the…"

I thumb-cocked the hammer and he went silent.

"Wallet."

He reached into a back pocket, coming out with a bill-fold made from bleached and scaly snakeskin leather. This he held up to the side that held the gun.

"Other side," I directed.

Holding the wallet so that the night-light from the apartment door shone on it, I could clearly see that my driver was Todd S. Breakman, twenty-six years old, and a resident of Queens.

"Okay, dude, now lemme go," Todd said, trying to somehow take charge.

"Not quite yet."

"What else you want from me?" Breakman whined. "You already got my wallet."

"What I want is Marleigh Mann, aka Marigold Hart," I said. "Alive and unharmed."

"I—I—I—I…"

"Not you, brother. Her. And don't fuck with me. I could kill you right here, drop your body in the East River, and sell this car so that it'a be in Qatar by the end of the week."

I always find that it's good to prove your criminal bona fides up front so that the people you're talking to believe in any threat you pose.

Todd Breakman began to cry. It started out as mere sobbing but soon rose in volume. The cry became a wail, and even though we were sitting in a secure and mostly isolated area, I worried that somebody might hear his increasing bellow.

The second item I had brought out from the red trunk in my storage space was a small electric stunning device supposedly used by British intelligence. In my left hand I held this surprisingly small gadget, which looked most like a gag handshake buzzer. This I pressed firmly against the back of his neck.

Like a stick puppet he danced around for a few seconds or so and then slumped sideways.

It was a short zap and so Todd woke up soon enough. I was hoping that the jury-rigged electroshock therapy would calm him down a bit, and luckily for him, I was right.

"I got her tied up at this electronics warehouse over in Queens," he said before I could ask the question again.

"They pay you yet?" I asked.

"How you know about that?"

"Computer Jesus told me. Now answer my question."

"No, I haven't been paid yet."

"When's that gonna happen?"

"I meet a guy tomorrow and he's gonna pay me when I turn her over."

"How much they payin'?"

"Fifty."

I had to hold back from shooting him in the leg.

"Okay," I said. "Fine. Take me to where you got her."

On the ride I called Leaf.

"Yes?" That one syllable carried the weight of a much larger question.

"I thought it was gonna be easy, honey, but I prob'ly won't be back till morning. I'm sorry."

"How sorry?"

"How about a trip to Paris, first class?"

"Paris, Texas?"

"No, the old one."

"Okay. Talk to you in the morning?"

"Yeah."

"I bet you wish you took your shoes now."

"I wish I'd never left."

"Okay."

I swear I could almost taste the smile on her lips.

The entrance to the warehouse was on an alley off Ninety-Ninth Street in Ozone Park. The building sat about thirty feet back from a locked gate.

"How we get in, Todd?"

"I got the key. You want it?"

"What I want is to put a bullet through your eyeball, that's what I want more than anything."

He shuddered.

"I—I—I could unlock it."

"Maybe in a minute. First why don't you tell me where we are and how the fuck you got Marigold in there?"

"It belongs to these Russian guys. They used to have a business where people assembled electric tools and stuff that come from China. But it got too expensive, and they had to shut down."

"And how come you gotta key?"

"My cousin Percy is like the groundskeeper. He checks it out every week or so but he's on vacation with his wife, so I told him I'd take care of it."

There were two very different Joes in my head. One was

cold and calculating. He wanted to find the woman and get her back with her daughter. The other Joe wanted to slaughter Todd right then and there. Kill the motherfucker.

"All right," I said. "Let's go. But remember, I got this gun, and I am not afraid to kill you."

Todd let loose with a ripping fart, telling me, bodily, that he was most definitely my bitch.

First, he and I got out of the car and unlocked the gate. The big building beyond seemed to be constructed mostly from aluminum and glass. We both returned to the limo, drove through the open gate, then we climbed back out the car and I reattached the padlock.

There were a few doors and double doors that led into the factory, but Todd led me to the nicest-looking one. This primary portal was made from wood and had been painted a forest green.

Todd was fidgeting with the lock when I, once again, pressed the muzzle to his neck.

"Open it or die."

He did as asked.

The room was vast, dark, and silent.

"Turn on some lights," I demanded.

He found a switch and a whole rafter of lights shone down from the ceiling at least forty feet away. The huge space was mostly empty except for discarded pieces of furniture, tools, and electronic components that were covered with a thick coating of dust. In the center of the room sat Hart. She was tied to a chair, gagged, and with eyes so wide I could see them clearly.

"Look, man," Todd said, already bargaining for his life. "I come see about her every day..."

I pushed him in her direction.

"She only been gone one day."

He went on with the explanation as if he hadn't heard me. "...I give her water and a toilet and everything. I ain't done nuthin' to her. I ain't."

I shoved him again, and after a dozen steps or so we'd reached her.

"Cut her loose."

He was crying again, trying to think of a way to survive his expected and well-deserved death sentence.

Todd had gagged Hart and then tied her ankles to the front legs of the chair and her hands to the armrests. It was top-notch work. First, he bound her arms and legs with heavy-duty tape and then he knotted medium hemp over that. It was such a good job that he had to cut both rope and tape with an X-Acto knife that we found in a nearby tool closet.

When her gag was removed Hart cried out, "Oh, God!"

After her arms and legs were free, Hart rushed to hug me, but I straight-armed her.

"After we take care of him," I explained.

Todd actually gulped.

Pulling out a pair of handcuffs that I'd brought along for fun, I threw them to her.

"Put your hands behind your back, Todd," I instructed. "Hart here's gonna cuff you to the backrest of that there chair."

With Hart glued to my side, I managed to find the stash of tape and rope, made Todd sit in the chair he put Hart in, and proceeded to bind and chain him properly.

Only then did I embrace Marigold Hart. She cried and shook and held on for dear life. I didn't have the heart to chastise her.

After a few long minutes she let go.

"What are you gonna do with me?" Todd asked when the tearful reunion was done.

"That's a very good question," I said. I spied another chair in a far corner, strolled over, and then, taking my own sweet time, I dragged it screeching back to our prisoner.

When I finally sat down in front of the kidnapper, he was crying and farting up a storm.

"That's a very good question," I said again. "I'm gonna ask you somethin' in return. And I want you to answer me honestly. The more honest you are, the better it'll be for you. Do you understand?"

"Yeah, yeah."

"I don't want you to tell me what you think I want to hear," I said. "I don't want you tellin' me what you hope I'll do. I want you to say what you would do to me if I had taken one of your loved ones and then did what you did to Marigold. And also, what you planned to do with her."

Todd's face was long and good-looking, like one of those cowboys who catch the girls' fancies. He had a freckle or two and honey-colored eyes. His brown hair was cut short.

He stared at me, moving his lips silently, as if, maybe, speaking to God. Then, finally, I think, he came to understand my question. The answer, he knew, was not in my eyes but in him.

Three or four minutes passed. Todd was staring at his lap while Hart wandered around the huge space. It was like she was savoring the mere act of perambulation.

I was looking at her when Todd finally began to speak.

"I'd kick the shit outta you. Then I'd hogtie you to a rusted-out radiator and beat you a few times. I'd cut you." At this point a rage started building up in the prisoner's tone. "Bleed you and piss on you. I'd cut your dick off and make you suck it. Then I'd cut your wrists and watch you slowly die."

When elocuting the last two words he hiccupped. That little cough was the perfect punctuation to his inner rage.

After this passionate confession, Todd regarded me, little tremors passing through his body.

I wanted to speak but could not. Todd's answer had perfectly preached my own rage, my own dark instinct.

"Hart," I said at last.

"Yes." She walked from a far corner back to the site of her captor's humiliation.

"What size do you think his shoes are?"

"I don't know, eleven or twelve."

"Yeah. Take 'em off and bring 'em here to me, please."

As she was doing this I began to speak.

"That was the right answer, Todd. It's exactly what I would'a done. I'd'a beat you so bad that the only way they could know you was human would be because'a your clothes. You deserve to die for what you did and what you planned to do. Only reason I'm not gonna kill you is that you know you wrong." This was true. "Now, you have to understand that I've already saved your life once tonight. Because if you had brought the men who are supposed to pay you to this building, they would have left your dead body here. Fact. I mean, who needs a witness? And then there's the fifty thousand.

"So, I'm gonna make you a promise. You're tied up good. I'm gonna gag you and leave you here, just like you did to

Marigold. Then I'm gonna go out against these people you made the deal with. If I survive, I will send someone to cut you loose and our business will be done. If I die you better hope Cousin Percy gets back in time."

No more begging or flatulence from the limo driver. He knew that this was the best he could ask for.

I laced on his black leather shoes and then lashed the gag he used on Hart around his own head.

23.

"WHAT WERE YOU thinking?" I asked Hart on our way to Staten Island.

"Todd called me," she said. "He told me that he saw my face printed on a leaflet at limo headquarters. He took it down and then used a web link they had and ended up on the dark web, or something like that."

"Did anybody else use it?"

"Todd was my only driver," she said, shaking her head and sneering. "He was the only one who knew what I looked like."

"So he got in touch with them online?"

"I think so. They made like a phone connection and the first thing they did was to get Todd to prove that he knew me with a photograph."

"And he had one?"

"From the camera in his limo. After that the man he spoke to said that I was his wife and he wanted me back. He said that he'd pay a reward for information leading to me and— and Annie."

"You already knew all that."

"I know. But I figured I better find out what else Todd knew."

"So you went off with him alone. Why you trust him?"

I glanced over and saw the flash of guilt in her eyes. That one mournful look said it all.

She'd chosen Todd as a driver because he was brash and young, good-looking and a little bit bent. Now and then she'd go with him to some motel, or maybe even the back seat of his car, like she did with me in my room at the end of Penitents' Hall.

"I—I thought that he was a friend," she said.

I could have been hard on her. I might have asked if she thought sex meant more to him than money. But what use was there in accusations when it didn't matter?

"Well," I said. "You're lucky I figured out how to get to you."

"How did you find out about Todd?"

"The same way you'll be saved again and again through the rest of your life. Antoinette will always be there."

We got to Melquarth's chapel just shy of two in the morning.

His high-tech garage had equipment that could tell whether the limo was bugged.

"Clean," Mel announced after a few minutes. "Makes sense. It's his own car. Why would he want somebody else having a map of where he goes?"

Olo had taken Hart to some room where she and the child could help Hart relax and freshen up.

Mel went back to bed, and I made a call.

"Hello?" she said.

"All finished."

"I won't ask you what you were doin'," Leaf replied. "No tellin' who might be listenin'."

"Can we try this again tomorrow?"

"What's the matter with right now?"

An hour or so before sunrise, we were both naked and at ease. Her wild mane was nestled in my lap, and I felt again as if I were very far away from my dangerous life.

"So, are you fuckin' her?" Leaf asked, talking about Hart.

I could have said no because we'd only had one night together, and I had no intention of continuing that trend. But a lie would have shattered the illusion of distance and safety.

"Yeah. One time."

"That's all it took?"

"All it took for what?"

"For you to go out barefoot in the middle'a the night riskin' life and limb to save her."

"I'd decided to help her days ago," I said. "When I realized that I was being used to set her up to get killed."

Leaf rose from my lap, twisting around to kiss me, the buttress of her lips covering mine. When she leaned back her face seemed much younger, innocent.

"What was that for?" I asked.

"You don't know?"

I had no answer. She had nothing to add.

Lying back on my lap she said, "I don't know if I could be with a man who out there like you are."

"That's why I don't give the details of what I do to the women I date."

"Then why tell me?"

"I don't know." This was another truth.

"Because," she said, "you know, I don't try and get all in a man's business like that. I mean, I guess if we had kids or somethin' I'd need to know if he was gonna go out one night and never come back, but other than that..."

"So, you think that there is a man out there somewhere that you *could* be with?"

"I'ont know, but if there was, he'd be a lot like you."

"Me without the bare feet."

"Where'd you get them shoes anyway? No stores open."

"The man who took Hart wasn't gonna use 'em for a while, so I borrowed 'em."

"You killed him?"

"I wanted to, but that was a little too much just for a pair of shoes."

Leaf laughed out loud.

"Stole the mothahfuckah's goddamn shoes!" she cried out and then laughed some more.

I was drowsing when she said, "Joe?"

"Yeah?"

"I was tryin' to figger sumpin' out."

"What's that?"

"I was thinkin' that I had never been with a man like you. I've known women that are kinda like you but not really."

"So, what are you figuring?"

"Well, I thought that you were a different kinda man but then I realized that it's me that's different. I usually pick a guy for what I like and that's it. Like with Andrew. But...when I'm lyin' here next to you it feels like it's me that's changed. You know?"

I chuckled and said, "Yeah. It's like Albert Einstein imagining a train being hit by two bolts of lightning."

"Huh?"

"He was the genius. The train and inclement weather just happened to be there."

She splayed her hand on my chest, and all was right with the world.

I woke up about noon, staggered into the kitchen, and made a strong cup of black coffee.

Hunkered over the counter next to the sink, I realized that I needed to jump-start my work and so called Aja.

"Hi, Daddy, how are you?"

"Hey, girl."

"You sound like you just woke up."

"I'm not all the way awake yet."

"What can I do for you?"

"On the night that Ira Gross was murdered he was at the Working Circle workplace in Queens. There was a guard on duty that night. I'd like you to find his numbers."

"All right. I'm on it."

After that I used the cell phone to pick up my e-mails. There was an odd address with a lot of question marks, ampersands, asterisks, and dollar signs. The content was an American Airlines flight landing at 20:46 at Kennedy. I should go to baggage and hold a sign for the Platts.

This posed a conundrum. Ogre Orr had already tried to go around me. He was also expecting his people to meet with Todd today. But Todd could only promise to deliver Marigold. Maybe Orr had asked him to grab the child and he demurred. Maybe he couldn't figure out how to get Hart to bring Antoinette with her. It could have even been that Todd lied and claimed to have the child.

No matter what it was, Orr was lying to me. I didn't hold that against him. I was lying too.

But this was a most delicate moment. The millionaire killer had taken two moves at once on the chessboard. I was at a serious disadvantage and so made yet another call.

It wasn't a long conversation. Just a few words and a forwarded e-mail.

After that I made toast and jam like I was a kid again in Chief Odin's home.

"Mornin'," Leaf greeted. She'd come in from the back room much more light-footed than I.

"Hey."

She kissed me on the right side of my neck and then on the cheek.

"How long you been up?" she asked, taking my bread and biting a hearty chunk out of it.

"Maybe an hour."

"What you been doin'?" She took a swig of the coffee and made a sour face.

"Plotting a coup."

"Against what country?"

"The dynasty of Orr."

"That mean sumpin'?"

She was wearing a blush-colored silk T-shirt that came down to the tops of her thighs. The darkness of her skin forced me to smile.

"Your nose openin'," she observed.

"You have nice skin."

"What you goin' up against?" she insisted.

"Hart's husband wants to kill her, and he wouldn't mind shootin' through me to do it."

She studied me for maybe half a dozen heartbeats, then said, "You have kids?"

"What's that got to do with it?"

"Do you?"

"A daughter."

"What's her name?"

"Aja-Denise. She's nineteen and enrolled at a nonresident university in Detroit."

"Asia like the continent?"

"Only she spells it *A-J-A*."

"That's a nice name."

"She chose it when she was just a kid named Denise."

"She knows what you do?"

"She works for me . . . in the office."

A few beats of heartfelt silence and she asked, "You been lookin' for a girlfriend?"

"Not anymore."

"Just close the door when you leave," Leaf said to me on her way out. "But take what you need, 'cause the alarm will be set."

"You don't have to go," I said. "I got a little time."

She said that she had business in the city and gave me one of her all-encompassing kisses. When she left, I could almost feel the vacuum.

Aja called a few minutes later.

"His name is Finn G. Fergeson," she told me. "I couldn't find what the *G* stands for but he left Working Circle and now is a nighttime guard at some kind of specialized wing of this private hospital in Montclair, New Jersey. Divorced with three kids, he lives on a yacht at the Seventy-Ninth Street Boat Basin."

"A yacht? He's a minimum-wage yacht owner?"

"I knew you'd ask that, so I looked up the docking agreement. He doesn't own the boat, just lives on it."

"Who does own it?"

"A man named Carson Barthelme. He lives in Europe mostly but keeps the boat."

"What's the name of the yacht?"

"*Lancer.* You need anything more?"

"Nothing I can think of, honey."

"Are you going to talk to Finn?"

"Yeah. Why?"

"It's not far from here." This was a suggestion.

The gatekeeper of the marina was an ex-cop named Al Blanton. He wore a uniform for his entire career, and we had been paired on a couple of successful busts. He was retired now and made his *vacation money* either turning people away from or ushering them through the marina gate. He was red-faced, reedy, and rheumy, five-eight and most probably armed.

"So, you wanna talk to Finn," the ex-cop surmised after I asked about the yacht *Lancer.*

"You know him?"

"I know everybody lives here. Finn does the same kinda work as me. He don't have no cop's pension so he's always lookin' for a side hustle. But he's not bent, at least not much. What you want with him, King?"

"He was a witness to a murder in Queens a few years ago and I want to ask him some questions. That's all."

The boat Finn Fergeson lived on was both motorized and wind-driven, over a hundred feet in length and multileveled.

I walked up to the gangplank and called out, "Anybody home?"

After some seconds, a head popped out on the topmost stage, probably where the navigation apparatus resided.

"Who is it?"

"Name's Joe Oliver. Finn?"

"Yeah," he said hesitantly. "What do you want?"

"I'm a private investigator. I work for the estate of Ira Gross, the man that got murdered at Working Circle a few years back."

"I remember. What you need from me?"

"Not much, just to hear from you what you saw, just in case we'd want you to tell the law firm this or that."

Finn stood up to a higher level then. He was wearing white shorts and a Hawaiian-like shirt. His hair was blond with a good deal of gray in it and his skin seemed to be slackening a bit.

"I'll talk to you, but I don't want anything recorded."

"Okay."

"All right, come aboard. Use the stairs on the left."

I climbed up to the space that contained the ship's wheel, but it was empty. Leading down from there was a lounging area where Finn and a lovely young brown woman in a white bikini were relaxing on blue-and-green-strapped-vinyl set of long aluminum chairs. She seemed to me to be from the South Pacific somewhere. Her eyes would not meet mine, but it felt as if she were watching.

"Welcome, Mr. Oliver," Finn said. "This is my friend Chrisanthe Mafi."

When her name was spoken the thirty-something islander

glanced at me and briefly smiled. I nodded and she looked away.

"Have a seat," Finn offered.

The chair was wicker and slathered with a kind of sealant that probably made it completely waterproof.

I sat and said, "This is really nice. You take it out to go fishing?"

"I couldn't sail this thing out the slip."

"No? Seems kinda odd to live on a boat and not be able to navigate with it."

"Guy who owns it, Barthelme, wants me to safeguard the place, but he's got a pilot on call if it needs to be moved."

After pausing to consider this claim I said, "I guess that makes sense. Otherwise, he could come back and find his boat gone."

Finn grinned. He had probably been a beautiful young man. But, when the hide of old age is laid upon that which was once ravishing, it turns out to be kind of sad. Even his smile appeared to be basking in bygone splendor.

"I've had drug traffickers offer me a hundred thousand dollars just to let 'em take *Lancer* out for three weeks," Finn said. "But I knew that that kind of windfall would blow me over."

I smiled at his wisdom.

Chrisanthe nodded at me.

"So, what do you want to know about the shooting?" Finn asked.

"You see the guy's face?"

"That depends on what you're asking."

"What does that mean?"

"It was dark and down two flights of stairs," he said. "He turned his face toward me for maybe half a second."

"But he was Black?"

"About your color."

"Did he have a white beard?"

"Not a white one. I'd'a seen that. I mean, if his beard was dark I might not'a noticed. But white? Uh-uh."

"So, when the DA showed you a picture that he thought might be the man, he didn't have a beard?"

"No."

I had an old snapshot of my father on my phone.

"Is this the man?" I asked Finn.

"I'm pretty sure that that's the man they showed me."

And now I had shown it to him.

"You tell him to stop?" I asked.

"I said, 'Stop or I'll shoot.'"

"Did that mess with him?"

"He shot his own pistol over his head. I fell back into the upper room. A few seconds later I heard a car take off. By the time I made it to the parking lot he was long gone."

"Was anything stolen?"

"All I can tell ya was that the Black man was lugging a suitcase about the size you carry on a plane."

24.

I CALLED HENRI but he told me that there was no official paper on what hospital Felix was in. So then I called Padma, and a few minutes later she called back with an Eighty-Fifth Street address located on the Upper East Side.

The building might have been classified as a triple-wide six-floor brownstone. I took the black stone stairs three at a time, pushed the mahogany double doors open, and approached a long and thin Black man seated on a high stool behind a raised podium.

Looking down on me, the man, who was somewhere between an old thirty-nine and a young seventy, asked, without words, what the fuck was I doing there?

"Felix Corn," I replied to the wordless inquiry.

The Black Cerberus of the Josephine Weingarten Convalescence Clinic was surprised that I knew one of the secret words in his precious entry log.

"What about Mr. Corn?" He slid off his high stool and came around the podium to further investigate.

He was taller than I but weighed less. It seemed to me that

he was so closely identified with that job that losing it would have killed him.

"I'm supposed to visit with him."

"Are you family?" The guardian widened his eyes, using them for punctuation.

"No."

"What is the purpose of this visit?"

"All you need to know is that I am not an insurance agent, an ambulance chaser, or a lawyer of any kind."

"Then why are you here?"

"To speak with the man in question."

My time was short, but I was enjoying this tête-à-tête. I had the feeling that from then on, any disagreement I had would have to be backed up with bruises and blood, broken bones and maybe even death.

"What's your name, brother?" I asked.

His downward stare wanted to say, *I am not your brother,* but his lips uttered, "Enoch Williams the third."

"Well, Mr. Williams, my name is Joe King Oliver, the first. You will find me on your visitors list. Mr. Corn's charity, CCH, called ahead."

The ancient elevator, built for four, ran smooth and straight to the fifth floor.

When I got off, I was confronted by another guardian. This one was all white except for her near-black eyes. Her hair, nurse's uniform, nail polish, and skin shone like alabaster, enslaved America's worst nightmare. Sitting behind a lacquered black desk, for contrast, it seemed, she looked up at me, like Enoch had looked down, with the unspoken question in her eyes.

"Are your shoes white?" I just had to ask.

Snowy eyebrows creased.

"May I help you?" These words had to pry themselves out from between her lips.

"Joe Oliver for Felix Corn."

Nurse White referred to the iPad set upon her desk.

"Name?" she asked, still looking down.

"Joe Oliver for Felix Corn," I reiterated.

"To the left and then the third door on your right."

I knocked on the blue door.

"Come in," a familiar gruff voice called out.

He'd been reading a newspaper, sitting up in a big bed that belonged on the upper floor of a mansion somewhere. There was a vase with at least three dozen roses, in as many hues, decorating a round table set at the bay windows looking down on Eighty-Fifth.

"King." Felix still looked hale but there was something about his eyes, something soft and unfocused.

"You look pretty good for a man left for dead."

He nodded and then chuckled lightly in reply, put down his newspaper, and said, "Sit."

There was an elegant whitewood chair at the flower table. I pulled this over to the big bed and sat.

"The doctor said that the bullet probably had a low velocity and so stopped when it hit a rib. Knocked the wind outta me, though. And I guess, when you get this far up in age, it takes a while to get it back together from a bump in the gut."

"I don't know, Felix," I opined. "Some young people trip on a shoelace and never come back."

"Yeah," he agreed. "Some people just have bad luck."

"Not you," I complimented.

"They say you saved my life," the man with eyebrows like antlers shared.

"It was Padma had the key."

"She's a wonderful young woman," he agreed.

We sat silently for a bit after that kind truth.

Finally, I asked, "Who shot you, Felix?"

"I don't know," he said, the embodiment of a truth teller.

This man had been to prison. Saint Peter could not have caught him in a lie.

"Yes, you do. There's no way in the world that you're gonna let somebody you don't know in your apartment in the middle of the night."

"He said that he'd come up to fix the plumbing. He knew the super's name and everything."

"Well," I judged, "at least that's better than sayin' it was the pizza deliveryman."

"I told the cop that that's what I thought he was when I heard the knock on the door. Idiot."

It took a few minutes for me to figure a way through the elder's lies. I couldn't threaten him, and I really had nothing against him.

"It's just," I said, "it's just that the man that killed your old partner was not Chief."

"What's that got to do with the man who shot me?" Felix demanded.

"You guys had been partners and then you were at odds. Ira wanted to horn in on your business and he probably had backing."

Felix studied my face the way all cons studied anything new that finds its way onto the yard: with hope for a dividend and suspicion that the hammer might drop at any moment.

"But the guy who shot Ira was Black, right?" Felix ventured. "My guy was white."

"Maybe they'd been working for the same concern."

"You think it's like a mob thing?"

"I think the man who shot you is the answer to my questions. If I could put a name and face on him, then Chief might not have to run and hide for the rest of his life."

Again Felix deliberated, playing out the entire game in his head.

"Chief is my friend," he said. "He's stood up for me more than once and never, even after me and Ira testified against him, did he betray us to the law."

"All that and now you're gonna kick him to the curb without even tryin' t'help?"

"I got no other choice." These words contained a tenor of truth.

"No?"

"No."

"Is that what you want me to tell Chief?"

A little paroxysm of pain, not fear, crossed the old crook's face. His expression turned into a sneer, and he said, "You tell your father that I did everything I could, everything. You tell him that I almost died, that I might still die. I would do anything for him, anything I could. But there's nothing to be done."

It felt as if there was an answer to my question in this denial; a moral dilemma that kept Felix from helping Chief. There was a tantalizing whiff of truth in his words. But I couldn't quite decipher the content.

"You know they intend to put him down over this," I said.

The pain in Felix's face almost made me feel sorry for him.

"Can't he run?" the prison-plantation master asked. "He was always talking about the people he had in Africa."

"What good's that gonna do his ninety-four-year-old mother and his children...and his grandchildren?"

Like the Black and white attendants guarding the doorways and halls of the Josephine Weingarten Convalescence Clinic, shaking his head, Felix wordlessly imparted that he'd come to an end, that there was absolutely nothing else he could do. I accepted this impediment. I knew I could not breach his refusal. But still I sat there, hoping for some kind of miracle. At this time, more than any other, I understood that I was a child again fighting for my father, for my blood.

"All rich people ain't white people," my father said to me when I was maybe ten. "And all white people ain't rich. That leaves you with whole big cities lived in by poor people of every color. And the one thing you got to know is that poor people, no matter what color they are, is always hustlin' round for money. Maybe money is a job, maybe it's twenty dollars on red in roulette, maybe it's a Swanson's TV dinner slipped down into their underpants. It all depends on how soon you need the cash. And it's always cash they after. Money in hand. The best way to get money is work. A job for some company or maybe sellin' a product on the street. Whatever it is, poor people always sellin' what their bodies can do: guardin' a door, liftin' heavy loads, or travelin' here and there droppin' things off and pickin' things up. And it's usually not just one job. Sometimes a man or woman need to have two or three different jobs just to make the rent. Don't matter if you sick, don't matter if you tired. It makes no nevermind if you don't like the people you work for or work with. A job ain't about friends. They don't care about you, only what you could do. They like it if you make things easier. But that's hard too. Sometimes workin' fast makes it easy, sometimes it's workin' slow. It's different in every situation and you got to know how to read it every place you alight, and, on top'a all that, you always got to be on guard because every day is always different."

I remembered that parental speech on my drive out to the airport. Once again it came to me how much of my life was dictated by the lessons my father dubbed me with. He wasn't my enemy or even my friend but more like the ground under my feet, the air I breathed, and the water I drank. That was my father.

I parked my tiny Italian car in the airline parking structure. Before getting out I put the parking ticket and the ignition key in the glove box.

Then I made my way to the baggage area. The arrivals board registered carousel 9 for the LAX flight into JFK. I located carousel 9 and then went upstairs to wait an hour and a half before the flight was due in.

I'm always early if I have control. *On time is late and late is dead;* that's another thing my pops used to say. He wasn't really a criminal, but he was willing to bend laws when those laws would leave him and his out in the elements to starve.

There was a bench set up across from where the first-class passengers came to drop off baggage and to pick up tickets. I had the seventy-five-year-old Chester Himes paperback in my pocket but I didn't want to read. I was there to get Ogre Orr off Hart's back, and so my mind needed to be absolutely clear.

In order to achieve this state of mind, I allowed in the fluo-rescent lights and the travelers' noises, the flitting birds that had taken up residence in the airport and the sonorous PA announcements coming through the many speakers embed-ded all around. I imagined that this broad mode of percep-tion was like a worker ant might feel at midnight and at rest in a hive of tens of thousands.

At 20:46 I took the down escalator to baggage, walked to carousel 9, and took out a mini iPad from my shoulder bag. I held up the little device that now read—PLATT.

I stood there watching the workers and families, the indi-viduals waiting for bags, looking for people they were there to meet and those who were looking for customers, or marks.

"Who do you work for?" asked a thirty-something man in lime-colored pants, well-worn leather flip-flops, and a black-and-white-striped shirt.

"Brandman Department store," I said.

"Then why do you have that sign?"

"Why would you care?"

"I work here," the man said.

"And?"

"It's against the law to offer unreserved rides at baggage."

"What if the Platts come and I help them with their bags?"

"You're here to meet the Platts?"

"That's what the sign says."

"You know them?"

"I know they're gettin' off the plane."

"You have some identification?"

"Not for you."

He didn't like me. I didn't like him. But I was in the right.

The only way he could eject me was if he could witness me trying to get business from someone other than the Platts.

The minutes passed by. The undercover security man moved around the area. I held my sign. A couple of people walked up to me asking if I was there for them. I asked, was Platt their name, and they moved off.

Finally, two men in sports jackets approached me.

"For Orr?" the taller, mustachioed man asked me.

"Indeed."

"We have a car waiting in the parking structure."

I put the iPad in my shoulder bag and said, "Well then, let's go."

25.

WE THREE DID not share names, not at first, so I started to think of them as Cain and Abel.

Cain was the taller one with the mustache. He was easily six-five in his sunflower-colored jacket and medium-blue pants. Abel was shorter, five-ten, and wider, with the largest hands I'd ever seen. His sports jacket was dark gray to go with his pale gray trousers. Cain walked next to me on the left side while Abel lagged a step behind on my right. We had to walk up two flights and across the third-floor lot before coming to a black Chevrolet SUV.

"Let me hold your bag," Abel said.

I handed it over.

"Jump in," Cain said.

"Um," I replied.

Meanwhile his partner was rifling through my shoulder bag.

"What's wrong?" Abel asked. The words carried a threat along with the question.

"Why I got to get in a car with you?"

"So we can go someplace where we could do our business in private," Cain said.

I looked from one thug to the other, treading water.

"I can write down what you need, and you can hand me the money," I told them. "I'm not ashamed to be seen doin' business in public."

"Get in the car, Joe," Abel commanded, holding out a hand that looked most like a plank of ridged hardwood.

"You armed?" I asked.

"We just got off a plane," Cain announced. "Where would we get guns from?"

I wanted maybe ninety more seconds and so asked, "Where you want me to sit?"

"Why don't you and Maxie sit in the back," Abel said of me and Cain. "I'll drive."

I considered the offer, then nodded.

I got myself behind the driver's seat and Cain/Maxie clambered in on the other side. His legs were so long that he had to slant his knees toward me. There he sat, watching my hands.

As soon as we passed the ticket kiosk Cain reached into the pouch behind the seat in front of him and came out with a quite compact pistol.

"You armed?" he asked.

"I am not."

"Put your hands up and touch the roof."

After I did what he asked, he ran his hands along my belt-line, up both sides and around to my back, and then he ran his free hand over and between my legs.

"You know you're gonna have to buy my dinner after all that."

The big man smiled at my attempt to keep things amenable.

"He got anything?" Abel called from up front.

"Not that he can reach."

We came to a dark and completely characterless building near Spofford Avenue and Bryant in Hunts Point in the South Bronx. When we approached, a garage door rose and the SUV glided through. That's when my heart started experimenting with new beats.

Our vehicle drove the length of the floor, coming to an elevator door.

"Get out," Cain directed.

The elevator took us up to the sixth or seventh floor; I couldn't be sure which because the buttons didn't have numbers and there was no display to chart our passage.

When the door came open Abel pushed me out, proving to me that those big hands were not just for show.

I was herded down a weakly lit and empty hall lined with closed and darkened doors. At the very end there was a door on the left that Cain pushed open.

I had to concentrate on keeping my breathing under a bellow.

"Climb in," Abel said with a smile.

The air in the room was stale, stagnant. But it was a bright, clean space. Nearly square, it was about twelve by fifteen. The ceiling was low enough that Cain could have probably laid his palms flat against it. The walls were white and the floor brown wood.

There were three chairs set out for us, telling me that everything was prepared for my demolition.

"Sit, "Abel instructed.

I took the chair that sat farthest away from the door. Cain took a chair too.

Abel stayed on his feet.

"So, now, Mr. Oliver," Abel said. "We've brought you here so that you can give us what we want with the least, uh, struggle."

"Where my money at?" I responded.

Abel smiled. Cain leaned back in his chair.

"There is no money," Abel replied.

"Why the fuck not?" It was easy to channel indignance when I was already scared for my life.

"You have to understand, Mr. Oliver, we do this for a living. When Maxie here and I were young men, we liked to cause pain, to hurt people, even to kill when it was called for. But nowadays we simply have jobs to do. Our job right now is getting the address of Mrs. Marigold Orr and her daughter, Antoinette. No money, and, if you're smart, no blood."

"Anybody ever call you a pussy?" I asked Abel.

Cain sat up. His partner's big left hand clenched into a fist.

"The fuck you say?" asked Abel.

"I didn't think so," I said. "You see, I made a deal of good faith with Mr. Orr. I said that I'd turn over his estranged wife for a reasonable fee. I'm not no pussy neither. I give my word and I do what I say. You understand that, don't you?"

"There's no money, Mr. Oliver."

"I heard you. But the question is did you hear yourself?"

"What the fuck?" said Cain.

"The fuck is," I answered, "that we, us three, are on the same side. We do this kind of work and expect honest pay. Tony's using you to duck out on payin' me. What you think he gonna do with your money after you do what he asks?"

Maybe, for half a second, Abel entertained the question. But then that was gone.

"Either you tell us where she is or we beat on you till you do," he said.

"I understand that. But I'm not gonna tell you shit. And for every time you hit me the price is goin' up. Because I ain't bendin' ovah. That's a fact."

"You're not the only way we can get her," Abel said, unable to suppress a smirk.

"Yeah, I know."

"You know what?"

"I know that you think Todd Breakman, the limo driver, got her."

Cain and Abel looked at each other, then honed their serious eyes on me.

"What you know about him?" Abel asked.

"Just the fact I know his name makes me ten times more important than when you brought me in here."

"Maybe so," Abel allowed. "But that's still a hundred times less than you need."

"All I need is Melquarth Frost."

"What you say?" Cain asked in a voice an octave higher than the one he used before.

"I heard about your friend," Abel said with a sneer. "He don't scare me. I'm a bad motherfucker too."

With that the smaller thug hit me in the chest with a vicious left uppercut. The force of that blow knocked me off the chair and back a few feet before I hit the floor.

Things moved fast after that.

A contained explosion blew the door off its hinges in a way similar to me flying from my chair. It seemed as if Mel and Olo came through the doorway at the same time but, of course, this was impossible.

Mel was holding a flat, rectangular firearm that was larger than a pistol but unlike any rifle I'd ever seen. He pointed the weapon at Abel and then at Cain, who grabbed at his left upper arm. Abel reached for something in his jacket, but before he got there, Olo executed a frighteningly powerful roundhouse kick that connected with his diaphragm. He fell against the wall, attempted to stand, failed at that task, then tried to go for whatever was under his jacket, but by this time the drugged dart Mel shot him with was having its effect and his hand had lost its dexterity. He looked at Mel, seemingly realizing that maybe he should have been afraid.

Cain was on his knees next to his chair trying to stand. This hopeless task ended with him in a long-limbed heap on the swept wooden floor.

It was then that I began to feel the pain in my chest. Abel must have practiced that punch every day. I was having a little trouble breathing and my legs absolutely refused to heed my command for them to stand.

Olo got her shoulder in my right armpit and stood up, bringing me along with.

"Hey, Joe," she said.

"Wow, you guys really know how to make an entrance."

"We used this tube thing to watch and listen," she said.

Mel ducked out into the hall. In his absence I tried to keep watch on both my unconscious captors.

"Don't worry," Olo assured me. "They'll be out for hours."

Mel came back dragging a drab green duffel that was at least eight feet long. He dumped out a very large spool of taupe-colored fabric. Olo moved me over to a chair where I could hold myself up using the backrest.

That's when the swaddling began. Mel unspooled five or six feet of the fabric. Then Oliya rolled Abel onto it. After that she traded places with Mel. Olo pulled the fabric bobbin back and forth and Mel continued the body-roll process until the man I'd named after Adam's innocent son was no more than a cocoon.

Then it was Cain's turn.

Something about those featureless sheaths made me understand the emotional disconnect in Melquarth's mind. It wasn't that he couldn't have empathy for others, but that his baseline for human interaction was desperate in the same way as all wild creatures. Survival trumped most softer feelings and nearly all others were either enemies or subjects; sometimes they simply represented food.

Olo and Mel dragged the manlike casings down the hall to the elevator and then out to a different SUV. They put the men into the back.

Mel and I sat side by side in the featureless dark blue van. Olo had driven my car and so followed us to bring my Bianchina along, and also to back us up in case of trouble.

It was a simple series of acts that brought us together that night. I had called Mel and asked him to double-cover me at the airport. That meant that Oliya would stand around the periphery of carousel 9 while I waited for Orr's thugs. Mel waited nearby in his blue van, and I helped by putting a transmitter in my shoe. That way Olo could call Mel when we left the car park and then follow in the car I'd left in the lot.

* * *

I rode shotgun next to Mel while practicing deep breathing.

"What was that place?" I asked when I'd gotten my respiration under control.

"It's what people like these do," Mel explained. "They find a bent night watchman that rents out rooms on those nights when the building they're supposed to be guarding is empty. Works pretty good unless you got me and Ms. Ruez on the job."

"The guard was there?"

"Sure was."

"What you do with him?"

"After he told us where you were we left him tied up."

I went over the scenario in my head. The nighttime guard might lose his job over the damage, but he wouldn't give up Cain and Abel even if he knew who they were.

"Who's the alpha?" Mel asked me.

"The shorter one."

"What's his name?"

"He didn't say."

"How you wanna play it?"

"What you knock them out with?"

"Nitazene."

"That shit is strong. You could kill somebody with that."

"I could kill somebody with my thumb but that don't mean I will."

"How long before they're conscious?"

"Anytime you want."

"Okay, then let's go out to Staten Island."

26.

IT WAS LATE by the time we were all set up. Little Antoinette was asleep in a room in the Penitents' Hall and Olo was in the room next to her with Hart, preparing her for a possible visual encounter.

Mel and I were in one of his basement *workrooms* standing over a gurney upon which Maxie/Cain lay. Mel was giving the kidnapper an injection.

"How long?" I asked.

Just then Maxie opened his eyes. He tried to grab me but found that both his wrists were manacled to the chrome litter.

"What the fuck?"

"Hey, Maxie," I said.

"Where's Rudy?"

"Where you most definitely do not want to be."

Fear registered in the big man's eyes.

"What do you want?" he asked.

"We want you to do what we tell you to do," Mel said.

Judging by the prisoner's expression, it seemed as if my friend's words carried more weight than mine.

"Anything you say," Maxie promised.

*   *   *

Half an hour later we were all, except for Antoinette, standing in a fair-size room. Hart was tied to a chair wearing
makeup that made her look as if she'd received a hellacious
beating. We'd also fed her a quarter-dram of opium, making her more than a little loopy. Theodore Maxwell "Maxie"
Cummings was still wearing his garish suit, holding a cell
phone the size of a breast pocket secretary wallet.

When I said, "Okay, make the call," he looked to Mel, then
hit a tab on the phone, which began to ring.

Olo, Mel, and I went behind a freestanding wall opposite
the area where Maxie and Hart were.

Rudy/Abel had told Maxie that the call to Orr would be
scrambled, and they could say anything without being mon-
itored or tracked.

At the end of the third ring a familiar phone voice said,
"That you, Mr. Carr?"

"No, sir, it's me, Maxie."

"Where's Rudy?" Anthony Orr asked.

Olo, Mel, and I were connected to the call by headphones.
We could see Maxie and Hart on a small monitor.

"He's dead, sir."

"What happened?"

"We grabbed Oliver like you told us to. He knew about the
guy you found, the man Todd. But he said that he'd still give
us your wife if we'd let him go. Rudy tried to get him to tell
us, but he said that he had to take us there. He took us to this
warehouse out in Queens but when we got there, he got to a
gun he was hidin'. He shot Rudy and then I shot him."

"What about the woman?" Orr demanded.

"Rudy's dead," Maxie said, going a bit off script.

"Did you get Marigold?"

"Yeah, yeah. She was tied up."

"Use the video function," the millionaire ordered. "Show her to me."

Maxie disconnected the audio call and then called back for video. When they continued the conversation, we still heard it.

"Hey, Mrs. Orr," Maxie said, pointing the camera lens of the phone at her.

I could see her bleary visage as she raised her head.

"Hart," she slurred. "I'm not no fuckin' Orr. Or what…" She laughed in derision and said something else that was unintelligible.

Maxie turned the phone so that it was inches from his face, then he turned his back to Hart. He knew that Orr couldn't get any hint of us. He knew what Mel would have done in that circumstance.

"What about the child?" Orr said. "What about my daughter?"

"I questioned her," Maxie complained. "You could see that. But she won't say."

They were both quiet a moment.

"Now what, Mr. Orr?"

"Kill her."

"What?"

"Do you understand English? I said, kill her."

"What about your daughter?"

"I know the address where he picked her up," the ogre said. "After I see her dead, I want you to go there and suss it out."

"I'm not killin' this woman," our pawn said bravely, and also according to script this time. "Fuckin' Rudy is dead and—and now you want me to do her? Fuck you."

Maxie disconnected the call.

"Yeah!" Hart blurted out. "Fuck you!"

Olo brought Hart to a bed in the hall set outside Annie's room, there to wait until the narcotic wore off.

Melquarth and I took Maxie to a subterranean room where we had Abel/Rudy locked into an extremely small cell.

"Rudy!" Maxie called out. He had believed that his partner was dead. After all, Mel had a reputation.

Rudy Carr didn't say anything.

"Sit down," Mel told Maxie, pointing to a dungeon chair.

This was probably the most difficult task I faced over that entire time. Mel was a scorched-earth kind of guy. He had nothing against the assassins except for the fact that they threatened people he cared for. He had nothing against them, but killing them made more sense than setting them free.

With deep reservation, I agreed.

Mel had a .45 automatic in his left hand. He was ambidextrous.

"So, what are we gonna do?" I said, starting the convo.

"The job's done, man," Maxie said. "You won. We're goin' back to Cali. Right, Rudy?"

Mr. Carr remained silent sitting there inside his phone booth–sized cell.

"Rudy?"

"Shut up and let the man finish."

"I don't want to have to kill you," I said.

Silence.

"So, can we let you go and call it quits?" I asked.

"We don't have a contract no more, and we don't do nuthin'

for free." Rudy said this with his mouth, but his eyes did all the talking.

I turned to Mel and said, "Well?"

"Let's go outside and talk about it."

Locking the steel-reinforced door behind us, Mel didn't talk but rather pressed a button on a panel next to the door. I knew that the gas released was odorless, but maybe our guests could hear it escaping. On a tiny screen we could see Maxie jump to his feet and throw his full weight against the impregnable portal. There was no sound, but we could see that Rudy was yelling.

Thirty seconds later they were, once again, jangled heaps on the floor.

"I hope this works," said Mel.

The next morning our cracked little family sat around the breakfast table. Antoinette was sitting on her mother's lap, making sure she couldn't get away.

"I'm so sorry," Hart said to the assembly. "I shouldn't have run off like that."

"Not a problem anymore," Olo said, and that conversation was over.

"You make the call?" Mel asked me.

"Yeah. Henri is on it."

"He's not comin' here, right?"

"No."

I called Leaf. She answered but was down in Philadelphia with Luwanda. She was coming back up that night.

"You wanna get together then?" she asked.

"If I'm still breathin'."

I decided to go back out to Kent Street in Newark. Etta-Jane wasn't there. Through the closed door of her guardian's apartment, I heard no sound. Maybe Mama Beah had taken the clan out to beat up a park somewhere.

"Who is it?"

"King."

The door swung open and Andrew "Gatormouth" Williams stood grinning with a vestige of suspicion undergirding the mirth.

"How you doin', boy?"

"Can I come in?"

"Sure."

My father's oldest friend moved back, and I walked past.

"You hear from Leaf?" he asked, following me into the avant-garde living/dining room.

"I was gonna ask the same thing of you," I said, hopefully avoiding an answer.

"What you mean?"

"I wanted to talk to Luwanda, but I don't know her number."

"Oh." The pain he felt was palpable. "No, no. I haven't heard from neither one."

"Okay. Maybe you could help me."

"You want some water?"

"Sure."

Sitting in my father's friend's room, on a chair without a table, I felt guilty, like Judas on the road to ignominy.

"Got no ice but the tap is cold if you let it run long enough," Andrew called as he reentered the blue-shade room.

I took my blue plastic tumbler and said, "Thanks."

"Sure. Now, what can I do for ya?"

"So, you know Felix, right?"

"Yes, I do."

"You think he might try and frame Chief?"

Andrew's frown made him look as if he were about to cry. He moved his head from one side to the other and back again.

"Man, King. That's a hard question. I mean, you know, anybody could be a snitch if you push him hard enough. I been there. And there's folks out there who hate Chief just because he got so much dignity. But I don't see Mr. Corn doin' nuthin' like that. He got enough money and it's better to have Chief as a friend than a enemy."

Andrew looked at me like a man might watch a snake rising on the coil of its own body.

My next stop was the palatial home of King Silver on the Upper West Side, there to find my father once again engaging his mother's boyfriend in a game of chess.

"Where's Brenda?" I asked either man.

"She was tired and went to lie down for a nap," Chief Odin said.

"Sick?"

"Nah. We went to the Brooklyn Botanic Garden and walked around a lot."

"How is she?"

"The tumor pressin' on sumpin', so it hurts some. But she seems happy to see me."

"I need to talk to you," I said.

"Okay. Wanna go to the summer tent out back?"

What Roger referred to as his backyard could have been measured in hectares rather than acres, it was half the size of Morningside Park. Most of the trees were cherry with a pine or two mixed in. The lawns were vast. The largest of these had a fancy octangular pavilion with a turret roof that housed a rose garden. The inner space of the gazebo could have easily seated a dozen diners. And there were benches along seven of the eight sides.

Chief led me to one of these benches and we sat.

There was a near-full moon in the eastern night sky and maybe a dozen jets floating in the atmosphere above the city, their lights blinking at regular intervals. Side by side we were more like family right then than we had been in many a year.

"You come out here a lot?" I asked Chief.

"To smoke," he concurred.

"That shit'll kill ya."

"Ain't the worse way I could'a gone. I might not nevah seen my mother again in this life; not nevah known how beautiful my son become."

I appreciated his joy and gratitude, but there were still problems to solve.

"A Black man killed Gross," I said. "Shot him and then shot at the security guard."

"Wasn't me."

"Do you know who it was?"

"Not for a fact."

"What the fuck does that mean?"

"At one time I thought it'd be Carney did it. But when I thought it through, it didn't make any sense."

"The giant? Why him?"

"The day they put him out in population, the brothers, Vatos, and Aryan Nationals all was lookin' at him like he was Christmas dinner. And, man, when I tell you that he wasn't scared, that's exactly what I mean. Four dudes flanked him, four! He stood there just as calm as Big John in the Jimmy Dean song. He wasn't scared but he knew what was comin' down. That's when me and my little ragtag crew got involved."

"He told me about that. But what's that got to do with Gross?"

"Carney donated to Felix's charity. Havin' been in, he knew what was right."

"You think he might have paid for a hit on Ira?"

"That's just it, son," my father said. "Carney didn't know nobody to pay for sumpin' like that."

"Somebody did."

"Not me. And not him neither."

"Well, well, well, if it ain't my beautiful boys."

The darkness she came out of took on the quality of myth.

"Mama," Chief said, jumping to his feet. "Come on, darlin', sit with us."

He guided her by one shoulder to the space between us on the bench.

She wore a dark blue shawl over a dull orange dress. Sitting there with us she looked from side to side, her smile growing with each sway.

"I never thought I could be this happy again," Brenda Naples claimed. "My boys."

"How you feelin', Mama?" Chief asked.

"Like I died and got resurrected. Like a Black man found innocent in the white man's court."

"You hungry?" I asked.

Shaking her head, she said, "Full."

"It's not too cold for ya?" Chief asked.

"A cold day in hell."

"So, this is where everybody goes to hide from me?" yet another voice asked.

Aja-Denise wore a mini-gown of silver and red. She moved like a woman of high fashion, or from great wealth. I brought her to my side of the bench so that she could sit down next to Brenda.

"We would never hide from you, child," Chief professed. "This little gatherin' just happened."

Aja took my hands in hers and grinned.

"Who killed Ira Gross?" I said out loud, not wanting to become maudlin when our reunion could still turn dark.

"Forget about that, King," Grandma B said. "The man is dead and at the end of the week your father will be in Accra."

"Roger?" I asked her.

She nodded.

"It's for the best, son," Chief added. "There's a wife waitin' for me over there. And I'm told that I've had a talking drum made just for me."

Though unconvinced, I could see that there was no use in further discussion.

After an hour or so Cousin Rags found us, and the stories began to flow.

From the deep past that Brenda had access to, to a dark future that Aja and her generation prepared for, memories of blood and hopeful laughter filled the night.

27.

A LITTLE AFTER 10:00 p.m. Cousin Rags drove me out to Queens to look in on Kidnapper Todd, only to find that the limo driver had somehow smashed his metal chair on the back wall and made his escape, handcuffs and all.

The desperation and tenacity of this getaway made me smile.

"Can't say I blame him," Rags said, echoing my own thoughts.

"No. I hope he has the sense to keep his head down after this, though."

My cousin grunted and nodded.

"But you know," he said. "Once you get to speed goin' downhill, it's a motherfucker and a half to stop."

We searched around for a while, not looking for anything in particular. Maybe an hour later Rags was driving me up to my apartment/office spaces in Brooklyn Heights.

"You want me to come in?" Rags offered.

"Naw. I can take care'a myself on home ground."

*   *   *

Despite my bravado, I went around the back of the building through the underground garage. Climbing the back stairs, I peeked out to see a form waiting beside my door, hunched down in a corner.

"Leaf," I said, approaching her.

She rose to her feet so easily it was as if gravity was some afterthought of some long-ago existence. She was smiling, wearing a royal blue shift that made my heart thrill.

She kissed me and I kissed her back. She put a cold hand down the front of my pants and grabbed on.

"I could work you here and now," she cautioned, "right out here in this hall for anyone to see."

Searching my eyes for an answer to this claim, she broke out into a grin.

I put my hands on her shoulders, and she took a deep breath.

"Let's go inside," she said.

Our passion settled into a wait pattern when we faced each other across the red table at the huge window of my apartment.

"I don't want anything from you, Joe King Oliver," she said, seemingly out of nowhere.

"I don't understand."

"I don't want your money or to meet your friends. I don't need you to save me or teach me or believe in what I can do."

"Do what, exactly?"

"Anything." It was a big word in her mouth, like a promise, an oath.

"What if I needed something?" I asked.

I could see that this reply surprised her.

"What could you need that you ain't already got?" she asked.

"I might not be a cop anymore, but I'm still a detective."

"What's that got to do with me?"

"You're a part of what's been happening, and you got eyes all around your head."

When Leaf's expression got serious it revealed what she'd look like when she grew older. If anything, the woman she'd become would be even more beautiful and engaging.

"Why did you break it off with Gatormouth?" I continued.

"That's what you're detectin'?"

"He doesn't drive, does he?"

"No. I mean, he can drive but he lost his license over DUIs, and he never got it back. What's that got to do with anything?"

I could hear that protective sheath of anger coming up in her voice.

"Nothing," I dissembled.

Leaf gave me a wan smile that was like a thank-you.

"You know, everything is all right," she said.

I considered these words. They came at me like an enigma that was older than humanity, deeper than the question — Why?

"What?" she asked.

"They say that an octopus got nine brains."

"Nine?"

"One in its head and one for each arm. Some people say they got even more."

"So?" she questioned, hunching her shoulders as if to add, *Why don't you come over here and kiss me?*

"When I read about octopuses' brains I wondered if those nine minds always agreed with each other. You know, like if arm number two tells the main brain everything is all right but arms four and five say the opposite."

"So that's what it's like bein' you," she said.

"That's exactly what it's like."

"I'm arm number two?"

"My favorite one." I reached across the table to caress her forearm.

"Okay. So, what do you need from me?"

"Do you know Carney?"

She took a long pause before saying, "Met him."

"What did you think of him?"

"He's tall."

"Anything else?"

"I don't know. When you talked to him it was like he felt that he was a failure. Like he just stopped one day, looked around, and realized that he'd gone the wrong way for the most'a his life."

"You ever see him with Chief?"

"Once, out at that warehouse'a his."

"They get along?"

"As far as I could tell. But why?"

"Wanna go to bed?" I asked.

"Finally, sumpin' make sense."

Creature comfort. That's the best way I can explain how I felt around that woman. There might have been the stirrings of love, but being with her wasn't about love, it was being in the right place at the right time when you felt ready to fight, fuck, or flee. It didn't matter what you did because, whatever it was, it would be the right thing.

"You sleep?" she asked.

It was late and I wasn't aware of being awake, but Leaf's question seemed for some reason to be right on cue.

"No."

"I heard somethin'."

Hearing these words, I realized that same sound had roused me.

I leapt from the bed, grabbed my pistol from the night table, and moved quickly toward the rope ladder that led down to my office.

And there we were, me butt naked with a pistol in one hand, my cell phone in the other. I was closely followed by Leaf, who only wore the sheet from our bed over her shoulders.

The sound we'd heard was the feeble tinkle of three bells designed not to sound like an alarm, not to be heard beyond the steel-hearted door.

"Can they hear us?" Leaf whispered in my ear.

"No," I said, just as softly. "It's metal on the inside but the sheath is soundproof. I put it in after a client's daughter broke in one time."

At eye level, on the far left side of the door, was a little peephole. When I moved to take a peek, Leaf put a hand on my shoulder.

"Won't they see your shadow?"

"No. The outside peephole is in the center. It's got mirrors that connect 'em."

*   *   *

There was enough light in the hall that I could make out the two men investigating the lock on my barricade. Rudy Carr, whom I'd dubbed Abel, was there for revenge and also, I believed, due to an outsize and misplaced feeling of professional pride. It was no surprise to see Abel. For that matter it was no revelation that Cain/Maxie wasn't there. Cain didn't seem to want to do anything but get away from Orr's machinations.

The real shock was that Anthony Orr was standing next to the big-handed killer.

"Can you flip it?" Orr asked Rudy, referring to the door lock Big Hand was fumbling with.

No, he couldn't. The only thing he managed to do was to set off the feeble alarm that played throughout my office and upstairs apartment.

Because the alarm was set off, a microphone was engaged. It broadcast their conversation over a small speaker next to the peephole.

"No," Rudy unknowingly agreed with me. "I can't even figure out how it works."

"We should try the crowbar," Orr asserted.

"What if someone's in there and they hear it?" Rudy reasoned. "All he'd have to do is shoot us through the door."

"I thought you said that if we could get in there, we could catch him by surprise in the morning?"

"*If,*" Rudy said.

"Well, what now?"

At that moment my cell phone throbbed. I'd turned the ringer off when approaching the door. I didn't think that the ring could be heard through the soundproofing, but there was no reason to take the risk.

"Hello? Henri?" I uttered softly.

"Where are you?" the detective first grade asked.

"Standing at the inside of the door to my office."

"Your guy Rudy and some other man are probably on the other side."

"You got that right."

"You want us to grab 'em?"

"No. They can't get in and you wouldn't have enough charges to hold them overnight."

"Okay."

By the time I got off the phone, I'd missed whatever the crooks had discussed. When I looked back out the peephole, they were half the way down the hall.

"What did they say?" I asked Leaf.

"One of 'em wondered if they should wait in the hall and the other one said it was too risky. Who was that on the phone?"

"A guy I got following the guys at our door."

"They're a little late."

"That's why I always have a backup plan or two."

"Did those men have anything to do with Carney?"

If I said yes, she might have opened up to me. But with unconscious tenacity I had decided, as much as possible, not to lie to Leaf Alyssandra Morton.

"No," I said. "This is about Marigold Hart and her ex."

"The man wants to kill her?"

"Oh yeah."

"He thinks that she's here?"

265

Shaking my head I said, "Yes or no, he needs to deal with me too. I know what he's planning, and even if I can't prove anything, he'd like to play it safe and see me dead."

"You wanna go back to bed?" she asked after a short pause.

Right time. Right place.

The phone the next morning didn't wake Leaf. She slept right through five rings and by then, I answered.

"Glad?"

"In the telephonic flesh."

"It's six thirty. You once told me that you never even finished vomiting before nine."

"It was the same gun that killed Gross and shot Corn," he said. "Same damn gun. Weird motherfucker too. The guys in ballistics say that it's ammunition for an old German Mauser; king of the guns back before it was replaced by the .357 Magnum."

"Was it the same one that Chief shot 'em with in the first place?"

"There's no ballistics record on those shootings, and the evidence is gone."

"And Chief was no fool. You never found the gun he shot them with in the bodega. He'd never hold on to evidence like that."

"Can't take that to court," Glad opined.

"But you hear what I'm sayin'."

I went down to Aja's workspace on the second floor. I made instant coffee and sat behind the receptionist desk. There I drank the born-again bitter brew and wondered about endings.

Usually, I would have gone across the street to Manzo's

bakery to work out my problems, but Rudy was a stone killer and Ogre Orr was crazy.

After Mel gassed Cain and Abel in their cell, he had two guys he knew take them to an SRO in East New York. They'd be out for hours more, giving Henri and his pickup task force time to put them under surveillance. Mel would have preferred killing them but was convinced to let it play out my way.

I decided that the killers after me and Hart should be dealt with first, and so I dug out a phone number that Aja had sent me and pressed the appropriate digits.

The phone rang eight or nine times before he answered, "Who is this?"

"It's me, Todd, Marleigh/Marigold's friend."

"How'd you get this number?"

"It's my practice to keep tabs on my enemies."

Todd took this threat seriously. I could tell that by his heavy, breath-laden silence.

"We're through with each other," he said at last. "You got the girl and I'm in a place you'll never find."

"But then what am I gonna do with this ten thousand dollars got your name on it?"

"For what?"

"I want to get to the guys you were supposed to turn Marigold over to."

"Why?"

"Do you care?"

After another breathy pause he said, "Twenty thousand. Twenty thousand and I want my car back too."

"I could maybe push it up to twelve, but no more than that. Car's no problem. No problem at all."

"What makes you think I know how to get to them?"

"You talked to the husband. He expected you to meet his people when they got to town."

"So?"

"Talk to him again. Tell him I'll be willing to hand over his wife for a hundred thousand dollars and assurances that he'll leave me be."

"And you're only going to pay me twelve?"

"A bird in the hand, my friend."

"I need to have this bird in my fist before I do anything for you."

I had him.

"We got to meet each other halfway to do this," I said.

"What's that supposed to mean?"

"We meet somewhere. I give you half the money. You bring me to Cain and Abel, and I give you the other half."

"Bring you to who?"

"Detective Tourneau," my second call answered.

"Hello, Detective."

"Mr. Oliver. Sorry, but we lost Rudy and his friend. They had a Zipcar, jumped out at a subway entrance in Times Square and hustled away before we could get to them."

"That's okay. It wasn't a sanctioned operation anyway. But I think I'll have a place where they'll meet me in a day or so."

"You're not gonna go there, are you?"

"Yeah. I think I'll have to. But your people'll be there to cover my ass."

I was thinking about my next call when Leaf came down from the apartment clad in a rose-colored sheet that she'd pinned to make a kind of formal robe. One leg was visible and the other covered. The bodice hung low and loose, but she was still what my grandmother would call decent.

"Hey," I greeted.

"You workin'?"

"Tryin' to live long enough to get to know you better."

She took my banter seriously enough to kiss my lips.

"We could go to Paris now," she suggested.

"Love to, but no. I got to make sure that all my ducks are in a row."

"Leadin' where?"

"To a place don't make me wake up in a cold sweat in the middle of the night."

She gazed at me with indecipherable intensity.

"My head," she said, "is tellin' me to run. But my breast wants to stay right here."

"Your car down in the parking lot?"

"Yeah."

"Wanna give me a ride out to Carney's?"

"If that's what you want."

28.

HUNKERED DOWN IN the back seat of Leaf's Buick Century, I was avoiding detection and studying my phone. The news had nothing to do with me or with people I knew. This much was good.

The call came through when we were maybe six blocks or so away from my place.

"Todd," I said.

"There's a statue called Cleopatra's Needle; do you know it?"

"I do."

"Meet me there at six thirty, bring my money, and I'll take you to the men you want to see."

"Half up front and the other half when I see 'em."

"Six thirty," Todd the chauffeur said, and then he disconnected the call.

I reached out to Detective Henri Tourneau, giving him the same information the chauffeur had given me.

"You need to be careful, Joe." It was the first time I could remember Henri using my proper name.

"Don't worry. I got plans for later tonight."

*   *   *

Once again Carney opened the door to his warehouse home before I could knock.

"Joe," the colossus greeted. Then, looking down at my de facto driver, he asked, "Leaf, isn't it?"

"Hi," she said. "You sure ain't got no shorter."

This brought forth a great guffaw from the sad ex-con.

"Come on in," he said. "Come on."

Back in the kitchenette that had no walls or ceiling we three sat. Leaf, as usual, kept her own counsel. I chattered on, confident because of the Walther PPK in the right-hand side pocket of my blue sports jacket. Carney, still dressed like an oversize Boy Scout, leaned back in his chair studying my words and, beyond that, my manner.

"...so, you see," I was saying, "it's really important that I find out who killed Gross."

"I don't understand why," Carney argued. "He was a piece'a shit deserved to be killed. Anybody did him earned himself a get-out-of-jail-free card as far as I'm concerned."

"True," I agreed honestly. "But now that Chief's back in his mother's life, you can see that it makes her so happy, she glows."

Carney nodded, swayed by the power of unobtainable familial love.

"If I can't at least find somebody else to blame, then Chief's gonna have to escape to Africa, leavin' Grandma B to face her cancer with a broken heart."

These words had the biggest impact on Leaf.

"That's how we need to love our elders," she added, almost to herself. "You got niggahs out here goin' through they mama's purse when she's layin' up on her deathbed. You got young mothers leavin' their babies off at their grandmother's house 'cause they wanna spend a weekend in Vegas with some crackhead."

Carney's eyes shifted to Leaf.

"You want me to confess to doin' it?" he asked me while still looking at her.

"Did you?" I asked.

"No. No. I would'a done it if I could'a been sure that it would have solved Felix's problem. But Gross wasn't workin' alone. I was pretty sure'a that."

"Then why would you confess?"

"Because I owe your father," he declared. "And if I could pay him back by bein' there for his mother...shit, that's what the Jews call a mitzvah."

Leaf's eyes had filled with defiant tears.

"I'd take you up on that," I said. "But they got an eyewitness who swears that the killer was a Black man."

"Maybe he's lyin'," Carney suggested.

"Maybe. But I got to prove that before you could do anything."

"Yeah," Carney agreed reluctantly. "And they serious about hangin' Chief, ain't no mistake about that."

"So, you don't know nuthin' 'bout it?" I asked.

"No."

"Did anybody talk to you about doin' somethin' to solve Felix's problem?"

Carney shook his head.

"Did Felix ask you for anything? Anything at all?"

There was a flicker, a half a flicker of hesitation in his deep-set eyes.

"No, King, no. I don't know nuthin' about what happened that night or what Felix might'a been tryin' to do."

He did know something, but the gun in my pocket wasn't strong enough to get at that truth, I was sure of that.

"We should go," Leaf said.

"I'm sorry I brought you," I told Leaf as we headed for Manhattan.

"But you didn't bring me," she said. "I was the one brought you."

"Yeah, but I could see how much that hurt."

"It's just that I hadn't thought about your grandmother. I kept thinkin' that you were trying to save your father, to prove that he was the kinda man you believed he was. But when you were talkin' in there, I realized that it was all about her."

"Like with your mother?"

Leaf rubbed her thumbs on the steering wheel. She looked out at traffic and sniffed.

"I got a older brother," she said. "When Mama was already dyin', he robbed her. Took her savin's, her jewelry, and the only thing she had left from our father, a beat-up old stamp collection. He took it while I was asleep. When I heard her screamin', I jumped out the bed. She was standin' in her living room over a open drawer where she kept Daddy's stamp collection. She cried until she fell asleep, and then she slept till she died."

"What's your brother's name?"

"I never speak it."

It was about 4:45 when we reached the heavily wooded outskirts of the ancient Egyptian obelisk called Cleopatra's

273

Needle, in the heart of Central Park. Now and then someone walked past, but that particular park monument was fairly isolated. I couldn't see anyone who might have represented the NYPD, but that was probably for the best.

"So, you're gonna meet the white woman's husband here?" Leaf asked.

"No. Her chauffeur, who also kidnapped her there for a while, is meeting me here and then he's supposed to take me to her husband."

"The husband that wants you dead?"

"Most likely he does."

"Is that smart?"

I could tell that I was nervous because her sarcastic question almost made me break out in laughter. I took in a deep breath and then let it out very slowly.

"If I play it right," I surmised, "they'll be armed, and the cops can bust 'em. One of the guys workin' for Orr doesn't feel committed and so he's likely to turn on his boss. And the driver is a straight-up coward...he's bound to snitch."

"But the husband wants you dead."

"He wants his wife more dead."

"So, you sayin' you don't think he'll kill you till he can get to the wife?"

"That's about it."

"If we ever get together, are you gonna bet the rent on thirteen black?"

"When we get together you can be in charge of the money."

"I'm goin' down there with you."

"No, you're not."

"How come?"

"Because if you were there I'd be distracted, worried about you bein' safe."

She mulled that explanation over for nearly half a minute before nodding.

"I don't want you gettin' hurt, now," she said. "I got plans for tonight too."

"Go back to the car and wait there. I'll come meet you as soon as this is all over."

Showing her elder face, Leaf winced and then nodded. Then she walked away.

The best-laid plans...

Standing at the outer edge of the display area of Cleopatra's Needle, I was thinking that Hart was right about me and my friends. We were abnormal, atypical, unusual, and strange. How else could I explain myself, thinking that this was the best path, the best plan to be following?

I was more like my father than not. This thought brought a smile to my lips. I backed up next to a great willow, secreting my presence behind its low-slung branches and leaves. There I counted my breaths and waited.

At 6:26 it was dark enough to be called night. I headed down to the ancient Egyptian stone. One minute after that Todd strolled up. He was wearing his chauffeur's suit without the cap. I could see that he wanted to jump me but there was too much at stake for petty payback.

"Where's my money?" he demanded.

I had the envelope in my pocket. This I handed over and waited for him to count it — twice.

"Okay," I said. "Where to now?"

"Follow me."

Eleven steps beyond the obelisk and we were at the edge of the woods: not deep forest but a dense stand of cherry trees. Todd slowed a bit as I entered the stand. The sound of West-Side traffic did nothing to make me feel safe.

"Hey, you," a man said with outsize emphasis.

Seeing Ogre Orr approach sent a thrill through my shoulders.

I was already too deep in the trees to run, but I didn't want to run. There was a gun in my pocket. At least three times a week I practiced grabbing the pistol, lifting it while still in the cloth pouch, and pulling the trigger. I was good at that maneuver, and it took all my self-control not to execute it along with Anthony Orr; the police should have been around there somewhere, and me shooting a man for calling out to me would not have gone down well in a court of law.

"Stop right there," Orr said.

He strode right up to me, a very-long-barreled pistol down at his left side. For some reason it surprised me that this human container of stoppered rage was left-handed. I usually thought of left-handed people as more creative and sensitive. This distraction was short-lived, because coming up behind Orr was tall Maxie, the mustachioed man I'd thought of as Cain when we first met.

I looked up beyond the gunsel, expecting to see big-handed Rudy—but he wasn't there.

I did see a furtive group of shadows among the trees behind. These were probably Henri's men. This would have made me happy if Rudy wasn't on my mind.

"Where is she?" Ogre Orr asked Todd.

"I—I don't know, sir," the hapless chauffeur said. "He told me that he was gonna bring her."

With amazing speed and accuracy Anthony Orr swung up his gun and fired twice into Todd's handsome but stupid face. The shots made the sound of sharp puffs through the quite efficient silencer employed.

Without volition my head turned toward the crumpling corpse of Todd S. Breakman. Before he'd settled, I turned my eyes back to his killer, wondering what was driving him. Why would he go to such great lengths to get his daughter and wreak vengeance upon his fugitive wife, when he could have just called the police and charged her with kidnapping?

Why hadn't I asked this question before then?

Orr moved the barrel of his pistol to my nose.

"Okay, now you're gonna—" he managed to utter.

At that instant I let my legs go limp, falling to the lawn as seven pops sounded. I was on the ground, face-to-face with Todd's demolished visage. Anthony Orr lay next to us, gasping his last breaths. A few feet away Maxie/Cain was on his knees with his hands over his head.

Scrambling to my feet, I rushed at Maxie, grabbed him by the lapels of his windbreaker, and lifted his face to mine.

"Where's Rudy?" I demanded.

"I don't know," he said. "For true."

"You bettah tell me sumpin', bitch."

Maxie didn't know who had shot Orr from the trees. The last time he saw me I was in the company of Melquarth Frost. And if that was still the case, his life was in great danger.

"When—when—when Orr saw that the woman wasn't there, he made a real short call. That might'a been to—to Rudy. I don't know."

I hit him. I didn't intend to. I didn't even want to. But I hit him hard enough that I think I might've broken his jaw.

"Joe," Detective Henri Tourneau called. He was rushing out of the cherry trees followed by three officers in battle gear.

"No time, Detective. I'll call you in an hour."

There wasn't another cop on the NYPD, other than Gladstone Palmer, who would have let me run off like that.

I ran out beyond the obelisk, out to Central Park West, and then down half a block to Leaf's fancy car. I jumped into the passenger's side and said, "We gotta go!"

It took only fifty-five minutes to make it to the deconsecrated church on the outskirts of Pleasant Plains, Staten Island.

That was fourteen minutes too late.

I called Melquarth twenty-seven times on that ride. His automatic answering service provided no message, just a solitary beep.

An armored van had knocked in the front gates of the courtyard. I thought the dogs were all dead but later realized that Rudy had used some kind of gas that had rendered the Rottweilers unconscious. The door to the nave had been hammered down by a mechanical battering device that Rudy had discarded upon entry.

Gun in hand, I ran inside and found that Hart had made it into a seat and was leaning over, holding her head. Daisy was growling at Rudy's corpse and Mel was laid out between pews.

The way I saw it, Rudy and Mel traded shots. Rudy got the

upper hand, hitting Mel in the chest. Then he advanced on Marigold. She got in front of her daughter, but Rudy laid her low with a big hand slap.

That's when he made a mistake that he couldn't have planned for; when he reached out for Antoinette, Daisy leapt from shadow. The guard dog dug her teeth into Abel's throat and all the strength of his great hands was not enough to dislodge her.

Most of the details of this misadventure I learned after the fact.

"Where you been?" That was Mel, sitting up from the place I thought he'd died.

"I thought you were dead," I said.

"Uh-uh, no, Teflon don't beat Kevlar, not no double layer. All he did was to knock the wind outta me."

"Mel!" little Annie shouted, running to hug him. Daisy joined her bloody tongue into that celebration. After that the four of us went to comfort Annie's groggy mom.

Leaf came in with a nickel-plated snub-nosed .32 in hand. It was no surprise that she hadn't told me about the gun, she was the kind of woman who kept her own counsel.

Oliya came through the door maybe ten minutes later.

"I told you, you need to keep the outer stone doors closed," Olo chastised her *not-boyfriend,* Melquarth Frost.

"You were right," he said in a rare show of humility. "Any cops come?"

"No. The crash was probably muffled, and nobody could see from the road."

"Then we have some work to do."

"How'd you know to come here?" I asked Olo.

"There's an alarm that communicates with my smart-watch. It went off but I got stuck in a traffic jam."

"I wanna get Annie's mother to an emergency room," I said to one and all. "Rudy hits hard."

"I'll text you an address," Mel said, a slight wheeze in his voice. "It's a woman I know in St. George. She's a doctor that doesn't report to cops."

"Can you walk?" I asked Hart.

"I think so."

"Don't go, Mommy!" Antoinette pleaded.

"I'll be right back, baby," the bruised mother said. "Mel and Olo will take care of you till then."

"I'll wait here," Leaf told me while handing me the keys to her car. "Maybe Annie and me can play hopscotch in the yard."

29.

ST. GEORGE IS the administrative hub of New York City's fifth borough, the dock of the famous Staten Island Ferry and still the most densely populated area of SI. On our way there I decided to set things straight with my *client*.

There was a darkening bruise on the left side of her face, and she seemed to be in pain, but still I asked, "So, why you wanna lie to me?"

"What?" she responded weakly.

"Naw, naw, naw. Answer my question."

"Lie to you about what?"

"It dawned on me when your husband shot Todd in the face and was about to do the same to me. I asked myself, how crazy would a rich motherfucker have to be to travel across an entire continent and leave a trail of bodies more than a year after being abandoned by his wife? I mean, if he wanted his daughter back, all he had to do was call the cops. If he wanted you dead, he could'a done whatever he did with the first wife."

"He was crazy," she explained.

"He was scared," I corrected.

"Scared of me?" she said incredulously.

"Look, woman, you have to admit, you're a dangerous piece of business. You almost got yourself, your daughter, me, and my friend killed. You did that because you got sumpin' that your now ex-husband would kill over; sumpin' he wanted so bad he needed to get it from you before he got rid'a you. He needed to be the only one who knew what it was you had."

I was angry with Hart but still I appreciated the amount of pressure she was able to hold up under. She raised her hurt eyes to engage me, saw that I understood her deceptions and faults, and, at the same time, capitulated to my accusations.

"I never meant for everything to go so wrong," she said, seemingly resorting to truth. "But when you told me that Tony knew I was in New York and that it was only because you were willing to do the right thing that me and Annie survived, then I knew I had to do more."

"Why not tell me about what the problem really was?"

"I didn't know you, Joe. I mean, you said your name was George and you were a banker. My daughter's life was on the line, and I had to play it the way I saw it."

"Okay. All right. You were in a bind, I admit that. But why call me back and pull me in if all you really had to do was run?"

"When we were first together," she said, "even before we were married, Tony got a note in our mailbox. There was no stamp on it, and it only used his first name. I thought he was having an affair or something and I wanted to know what it was. He wasn't home and I—and I steamed the envelope open. It was a letter from a man with the initials L.R.M. He said he had proof that Tony hired him to take care of his first wife."

"Natalia Henly," I said, just to show that I paid attention.

"Yes. I took a picture of the note with my cell phone, then I reattached the seal and put it back in the mailbox. I left to go shopping in Beverly Hills, that's what I told Tone, but really, I just went to the library there and tried to figure out whether or not I should turn him in.

"I wanted to tell the police, but I was pregnant, and after thinking about it I realized that that letter didn't prove anything."

"And he was rich," I suggested. "Life was going to be lovely if he didn't kill you along the way."

Hart looked down at her lap, moving her bruised head from side to side.

"Four weeks later I saw that he had a Cleveland newspaper on the table in the tearoom," she continued.

"And you read it?"

"I was too afraid. I just got the date of publication and picked it up from one of the international newsstands downtown...It—it had an article on page seven that told about the killing of a man named Lawrence Molorton. He'd been shot, gangland style, the article said. It also said that he'd been arrested for assault and attempted murder at different times in his life."

By then I'd pulled up to the curb on Montgomery Avenue near Fort Place. There was a nameless alley there that Mel had given me directions to.

"So," I asked, "what was the plan? You wanted me or Mel or Olo to kill your husband?"

"I was just trying to get away."

"You say that, but the story doesn't make sense. Something's missing."

"What do you mean? I told you everything."

"How did Orr find out about the picture of the blackmail note?"

Hart became very silent and still, stock-still like a deer in the deep wood that just heard the hiss of wolf fur rubbing against bark.

"Is the doctor here?" was her reply.

"Talk and then doctor."

She wanted to argue but my tone left no room for dispute.

"Four months after I left Tony, I sent to him asking for money. We were broke and Annie had an infection."

"How'd you send this request?"

"I set up a temporary e-mail address in Columbia, South Carolina."

"What was his answer?"

"He said that if I came home, I could have all the money I wanted."

"I bet that went over big."

Giving a wan smile she said, "I sent another e-mail with no words, attaching a copy of the note that L.R.M. had sent."

"And what did he say?"

"Two words, 'How much?' "

"And what did you have to say to that?"

"Two hundred fifty thousand. Cash. We set up a meeting at the Santa Monica Pier. I paid a girl with a telephoto camera to film the place where he was going to meet me. The only ones to show up were two guys. One of them was the one that slapped me. Neither one of them was carrying the briefcase that Tony and I agreed on."

"So, after that you ran and took up the old job. And when I told you about him you kissed me a couple of times and let me play hero."

"Yes. But—but—but I tried to tell you how dangerous he was too."

"But what you didn't tell me was the truth. He was after you because you had his ass in a sling."

"I didn't know what to do. Are you . . . going to turn me in?"

"For what?"

"For not telling the police about the note Molorton sent."

"You don't know for sure that Molorton sent that note or that he killed Natalia for that matter."

"But—but Tone killed Todd and tried to kill you."

"That's his crimes, not yours. All you did was to make men wanna protect you. If that was against the law, we'd have to have a lot bigger prisons."

"I did what I had to do."

"Let's go see that doctor."

Halfway down the alley on the left side was a weathered wooden gate that had no latch or handle. When I knocked, a very angry hound dog began to bay. The dog was the doorbell. That was the first smile I'd had in some hours.

Hart was leaning against me. Maybe it was because of the concussion. Maybe she was still angling for my sympathy.

"Who his it?" a probably older woman with some kind of Eastern European accent called out.

"Red," I said. That was Mel's code name for me.

When the latchless door swayed inward a very large dark-on-light-brown bloodhound blundered through, still baying and using his sad nose on me and Hart.

"Enough of that!" a sixty-something woman shouted, coming out into the alley after the dog.

She was short and stocky, with straw-like gray-brown hair and swarthy skin. Her ankle-length dress was formed from teetering patches of bright colors against a dark background.

I could see that she had one gold tooth and a ring of some sort on every other finger. If I had to place a people on her I would have said Romany, but I was no expert on the multitude of communities that inhabited that faraway continent.

"Enough of that!" she shouted again, and the hundred-pound dog ran to her left side and sat, looking up apologetically.

"Breena Codona?" I asked.

"Mr. Red?"

"This is Hart," I said. "She got hit in the head and Mel said you might be able to look at her."

"Come on in, come."

The yard that led to Breena's door was a dried-up summer garden waiting for the spring. Her back door (or maybe it was the front door) was constructed from eight square panes of glass held in place by cracked blue slats of wood.

We entered a spacious kitchen. The dining table had been cleared off and then set up with various medical paraphernalia. There was a magnifying monocle, a hand-pump blood pressure device, various hypodermics, and a beaker filled with water and set upon a hot plate.

"Sit," Breena said to Hart.

Hart lowered herself into a whitewashed wooden chair that was of a design that was a close cousin of the kitchen table. She smiled at Breena, who nodded as if in reply. The old woman picked up the monocle and examined each eye. Then she had Hart follow the tip of her finger from side to side, up and down, and finally in a curlicue-like circle.

After these exercises she prepared Hart a cup of tea.

"Drink," Breena said, "drink. It will calm you."

After Hart had imbibed maybe half the Pyrex cup of rosy-brown liquid, Breena took her arm, wrapped it in the rubber sheathing, and pumped it up. Releasing the pressure, she gauged the heartbeat at the wrist.

"Good," the secret doctor said. "You have had a shock to your brain but not so bad, I think. I have a room that is very quiet and can be kept dark. You should sleep there for maybe twelve hours and then take it easy for a few days. I think you will be fine after that."

"But I'm not tired," Hart said pleasantly.

"You will be," Breena promised. "The darkness of the room and the tea will call forth dreams. They may be disturbing but don't worry." She reached down to scratch her hound behind his big ears. "Manfri will be with you and no man or ghost would dare hurt you when he is nearby."

I went into the bedroom with Breena and Hart. The elder helped Hart off with her clothes and dressed her in a thick cotton robe that was white with prints of little blue flowers all over.

Marigold Hart obediently got under the fluffy blanket and allowed Breena to fuss over the bedding for a while.

When the doctor was finished Hart asked, "Can I speak to Mr. Red alone?"

Breena gave us an inquisitive look and then said, "She needs rest, not pleasure."

"Not even a smile," I promised, crossing my heart.

Not completely convinced, Breena made her exit.

"I don't know how long I can just lie in this bed," Hart whispered as I pulled up a stool. "I'm not tired." Then she yawned. "I'm not tired at all." She yawned again.

Manfri the bloodhound put his chin on my lap, making sure, I thought, that I wouldn't try any monkey business.

"I'm sorry," Hart said.

"You don't have to be. I would have done what I did no matter what I knew about you and him. I would have done it for your daughter alone."

"You're very kind," she said on the third yawn. "I don't deserve it. I was so dishonest with you."

Manfri simpered. I imagined that he was warning me not to trust his patient.

I said, "I would take the kind of dishonesty you dish out eight days a week."

"Not anymore, I think."

Before I could come up with some kind of response, she was asleep.

I took a sip of Hart's tea and then went to sit in a stuffed chair set in a far corner of the small room.

I fell into a light sleep, the kind where dreams come at you more like thoughts. I could see Hart and her UCLA film student friend, who in the dream was named Tracy and wore a dark red one-piece swimsuit. Hart was telling Tracy that what she needed to see was a briefcase about half the size of a travel bag.

I came awake so suddenly that Manfri leapt to his feet and stared at me.

"That was some strong tea," I said to Breena in the kitchen.

"Herbs designed to help with healing," she said. "My people have been using them since before Jesus."

It was just the right touch of blasphemy; just what I needed for the next phase of my investigations.

30.

IT WAS EVENING by the time I'd made it back to Mel-quarth's church. Olo and Mel were constructing a jury-rigged fix to the gate that Rudy had knocked in. Annie was watching them work, closely guarded by Daisy and Leaf.

When I got out of the car, Annie ran up to me, followed by her human and canine protectors.

"Mommy with you?" Annie asked.

"She's at the doctor's house, taking a nap," I said. "I'm sure Oliya will take you there. But if she's sleeping you can't wake her up."

"Yaaaa!" the child cheered.

"But you can't shake her or call out her name if she's asleep. The doctor said that she has a bruise in her head and that it has to heal if she's gonna be all right."

Antoinette frowned but nodded.

"You have to promise," I pressed.

"Okay. I promise."

Oliya grinned at me over the child's head.

"You got somethin' t'eat?" I asked Mel.

He nodded and put down his wire cutters.

"I guess I'll go with Oliya to check on Annie's mom," Leaf said as I was about to follow Mel. "Will you be here when I get back?"

"If not, I'll call."

In the kitchen Mel pulled out a tray of maybe half a dozen raw chicken thighs from an outsize refrigerator. He dredged the cutlets in a mixture of white flour, salt, pepper, cayenne, and granulated garlic. He placed a big cast-iron skillet on the gas stove and filled it halfway with a mixture of Crisco shortening, bacon fat, and olive oil. As the oil heated, I probed him for any unexpressed complaints.

"I'm really sorry about bringing trouble to your house, Mel."

"It's okay, bro."

"He broke down your fence," I countered. "He shot you."

"Shot my vest," he stipulated. "All I got was a few small contusions. Maybe a cracked rib or two."

"You could'a been dead."

"And I thank you for that," the consummate killer obliged.

"Thank me?"

"Look, Joe, I spent nearly my entire life buildin' a rep. When I was in middle school, I'd pick fights with high schoolers. By the time I got to prison, wasn't one out of nearly a hundred that'd fuck with me."

"And?"

"It's one thing when somebody else believes you're some kinda superhero, but that goes wrong when you begin to believe that shit yourself."

"So, let me get this straight. You're sayin' that because I

created a situation where somebody almost murdered you, you're happy because it revealed your own vulnerabilities."

"That's part of it, but not all."

"What else?"

"Your girl Hart is not perfect, but she's all right. Her daughter was good enough that my killer dog took her in. You brought them both here, we had a good time, and nuthin' went wrong—not really, I mean, nothing permanent."

I didn't say anything, but I'm sure the confusion showed on my face.

"Part'a why Oliya likes me," he offered in explanation, "is because she respects your opinion. Put all that together and you come up with a real friend who can test you. You know how many people have put me to the test and survived?"

It's a rare thing in life when you get a list of compliments like that . . . from the devil himself.

When the oil was hot Mel spooned the thighs, one by one, into the bubbling cauldron.

While the chicken fried my host brought out a premade salad and tossed it with a real oil, wine vinegar, and garlic French dressing.

After he served the meal, we talked a little more.

"I'm, um," he said. "I'm, um, changing. At least I'm trying. I guess it's because of Oliya. I mean, she says that she can't be my woman until I come over to her side of the tracks. Do you understand what that means?"

"If you don't, then the whole process is hopeless."

"Yeah. I get it. But what could I do with Rudy that's on her side?"

"What did you do with him?"

"Let's just say he's well on his way to being in liquid form, soon to be discovered by krill along the Atlantic shore."

"It's an old world," was the only reply I could come up with.

"That's a fact."

After our meal, Mel went back out to check on his work. I got on my cell phone.

"Hello?" she said on the fourth ring.

"Padma?"

"Mr. Oliver?"

"My friends call me Joe."

"They call me Vicki."

"Okay, Vicki. Do you have a little time to talk to me?"

"When?"

"Tonight."

"Now? On the phone?"

"It's gotta be face-to-face."

"Oh. You mean like a date?"

"No. You're a lovely woman and I'd love to get to know you, but right now I'm still on the job."

"Okay. There's a little Chinese restaurant down the block from my house called Happy Moon," she said. "It's on Eighteenth. We could meet there."

"I won't be very hungry, but I'd be happy to buy your dinner. Wanna say an hour and forty-five minutes from now?"

"I'll make the reservation and bring my appetite."

Melquarth had access to the cloud and beyond. I plucked out five photographs and downloaded them to my ever-more-important iPad.

Mel was finishing the entry gate when I came out into the yard.

"The job over yet?" my friend asked.

"Half of it."

"Half? What else you got to do?"

"Prove that my dad didn't murder Ira Gross."

"Damn, Red. You know I never worked that hard for less than half a million since my twenties."

"Capitalist," I spat.

Happy Moon was a small joint. It had three rows of tables, three tables per row. It wasn't a fancy place. As a matter of fact, you might have called it a dive if it weren't so clean.

The first two tables of each row sat four. The end tables were set for two. At the back of the row to the far left sat Padma Vyas. As I approached, she stood up from a lacquered black chair, wearing a little black dress with a sewn-in semi-transparent red midriff, maybe nine inches in width.

She was stunning.

"Hi," I said and then kissed her cheek.

"Hi."

Her smile was as thin and potent as a paper wasp's hive. Not deadly or threatening, she had transmuted from a highly sophisticated form of beauty that spanned over two thousand years to the sting of the world we lived in right then.

Sitting down she said, "I hope you like this place. The owners are from Sichuan and the food is authentic for those who know what to ask for."

"Is it spicy?" It was my habit to ask questions I already knew the answers to.

"As much as you want," she promised, her eyes engaging mine.

"Well," I said, still taking in her beauty, "you can order for me because I just ate three pieces of chicken. I'll taste everything and bring whatever's left over home."

The waitress who served us was about Vicki's age. She wore a midnight-blue button-up silk blouse and black pants, the cuffs of which stopped a few inches before reaching her sockless ankles. Her shoes were white and reminiscent of ballet toe shoes.

The ladies spoke in a dialect that I couldn't identify.

They laughed and haggled about the order.

When the hostess went away, I stated, "You speak Chinese."

"A Han dialect. Mei Wei puts up with it and I've gotten a little better...and a little fatter."

"Fat like a young woman's kiss." I couldn't help it.

Vicki smiled but then a shadow fell over her cheer.

"I saw Mr. Corn today," she said.

"I saw him a day or so ago. He looked pretty good."

"He does. But when I saw him, it reminded me of all the blood."

I reached to put a hand on hers. I'm pretty sure I did this to comfort her. I'm completely sure that she was comforted.

"Felix has had a checkered past," I said. "You live like that and, sooner or later, you got to pay the check."

"Is your life like that?"

"Yeah."

The look in her eyes was a little saddened, I believe; it said that she liked me but abhorred bloody wounds.

"What did you want to talk to me about?" she asked.

"A few things."

Before I could begin, Mei Wei brought us two fairly large bowls of hot-and-sour soup.

When she was gone, I said, "The first question is simple. What's with Dorothy Ridges other than she's a stuck-up bitch?"

Vicki stifled a laugh and then turned serious.

She said, "Mr. Corn promoted me and had me fire her."

"Why?"

"I didn't give her the reason, but Mr. Corn said that he had found out that she was making reports to the police about any Black friends or acquaintances he had. I think it had something to do with your father. Do you know what that is?"

I told her the pertinent parts of my father's story as far as Ira and Felix were concerned.

I ended by saying, "But why would a socialite like her be worried about Felix's Black visitors?"

"I can't be sure, but I've heard around the office that her son had been arrested for dealing heroin, but he never went to trial."

She gave a hapless little shrug and I nodded, agreeing with the unspoken explanation.

"Do you know the men that Dot was reporting on?" I asked after all that.

"Most of them. Dot had me make reports to her whenever she was out on one of her long lunches. I really wouldn't have done it if I knew she was a spy for the cops. I hope you don't have to tell Mr. Corn about that."

That's when I took the iPad from my shoulder satchel. I called up the gallery of photographs I downloaded at Mel's and handed the device to the child of many cultures.

"Do you recognize any of these people?"

Studying the photographs, Vicki pointed out the only two

that concerned me: Ruby Lee and Andrew "Gatormouth" Williams.

"Anybody I didn't include?" I asked.

"There was this one white guy," she said, "that the cops wanted to know about. I think his name was Carey, something like that. He was very tall and had shaggy hair."

"Huh. What about him?"

"Dot wanted to know what him and Mr. Corn talked about."

"Did she have his office bugged?"

"Not exactly. There's a toilet under Mr. Corn's office where, if you stand on a chair near the vent, you can hear what they're saying. Not that she'd be caught dead climbing up on a toilet chair."

"And she had you listen to the tall shaggy guy?"

"Yeah. But I didn't tell her anything. I mean, I like Mr. Corn. He always asks about my grandmother and—and when Dot wanted to fire me, he said no."

"Do you remember what Carney and Felix talked about?"

In the time Vicki/Padma considered answering my question, a young man in a white jacket came up with Mei Wei. He carted away our soup bowls as she placed a big bowl of garlic and chili noodles between us.

When they were gone Vicki said, "I guess it'd be all right to tell you. I mean you are Chief Oliver's son."

"I am that."

"Mr. Corn told Mr. Carney that Ira Gross wanted one hundred and fifty thousand dollars to back off from getting involved in his prison labor market."

"What did Carney say?"

"He asked what the assurance would be, and Felix said that that was the problem."

Nothing is easy. Everyone on my list was a friend of my father's. I couldn't just go against them without at least his okay.

"Anything else?"

"How did you get that scar?"

"I used to be a cop. Then they put me on Rikers Island. They don't like cops around there."

She reached across the table and ran her slender, dark-honey-colored finger down the jagged seam.

"I think it's beautiful," she said.

I fell in love three times that week; four if you included the Daily Grind.

"Anything special about the man or woman in these photographs?"

"The guy came around a lot. Mr. Corn liked him. He'd say, 'How they hangin', Gates?' and the guy would answer, 'Lower every day,' and they'd both laugh."

"You'd bring the guy back to the office like you did me?"

"Always."

"Anything ever happen then?"

"Like what?"

"An argument or maybe Felix would give Gates something?"

"Most of the time Mr. Corn would give the man an envelope. Sometimes he gave the lady one too. The lady wasn't as friendly as the man. One time she told Mr. Corn that he could do more than he was doing."

"Do more about what?"

"I don't know."

That was when Mei Wei brought us the Sichuan pork. I didn't need to, but I ate it all.

31.

LEAF WAS STILL at Dr. Codona's, so I made my way there.

The good doctor was asleep and so even the hound kept, more or less, quiet. Leaf guided me back to the kitchen table where she'd been laying out tarot cards in haphazard order.

"You read these?" I asked after our third kiss.

"Not really. I just like shufflin' 'em up and then layin' 'em out next to each other and makin' up my own stories."

"Really?"

"Yeah. When I was a little girl and my mother and father were together, my dad used to tell me everything was a story: fairy tales, Bibles, medical reports, even mathematical equations."

"What did your father do?"

"Pickup construction work. He could speak a little Spanish, so they hired him to translate for the bosses."

I let that sink in a minute and then I asked, "Where's Annie?"

Leaf pressed her right point finger against her lips, took me by the hand, and led me into the room where Hart slept.

In the tarnished light that listlessly made its way in through the window shade I could see, in the stuffed chair across from the bed, Oliya asleep with the slumbering child draped across her lap. It was an idyllic scene, worthy of an old master's oil painting. Leaf and I were backing out when: "Joe?"

Hart's eyes were glittering, ever so slightly. I moved softly to her bedside, sat on the stool, and took her by the hand.

"He's really dead?" were her first words.

"He is."

"And the — and the cops killed him?"

"Yeah. We told Annie that he had a fall down a rocky beach outside of Santa Barbara. You can decide when to tell her that he died."

Somehow hearing my words as an accusation, she asked, "What else could I have done?"

"I don't know. Going to the police with a picture of the blackmail note probably wouldn't have worked. You could'a tried to kill him yourself but there'd a been a good chance you'd get caught and Annie would have lost both parents. But we don't have to talk about this right now. The doctor says that your brain needs rest."

When I moved to stand, she grabbed my hand again and said, "I already knew you would help me when I made love to you, Joe. It wasn't some kind of bribe."

"I know," I lied.

"You did things for me and Annie that my own parents wouldn't have done."

"It's all okay now, Hart. Maxie will testify against Orr and Rudy, and seein' that they're either dead or missing, his will be the only testimony. There won't be any charges against you."

I didn't add that she stood to inherit her husband's millions. I didn't need to. And it wouldn't have bothered me if that was her plan all along.

Anthony Orr was a bastard.

"What?" Leaf asked of my deep silence.

We were laid up in my bed in the wee hours. No sex that night.

I was staring at the bilious ceiling, wondering how to take the next steps.

"I don't want to lose you," I said.

"Why would that happen?" she asked, laying her splayed hand across my chest. "Whatever either one of us done on our own or with anybody else don't count. I mean, we not married or nuthin'."

"No," I agreed.

"So, what's the problem?"

"Nothing, I guess."

The next day I found myself on the road to Newark, New Jersey, once more.

Instead of the regular country soundtrack coming out of Mama Beah's first-floor apartment there was a clear, solitary child's voice singing "Will the Circle Be Unbroken." It was so lovely. Etta-Jane hadn't mastered her voice yet, but her passion for the words resonated in my chest.

I knocked on their door.

Mama Beah answered. When she saw me, she smiled.

"Hello there, Mr. Oliver."

"Wow."

Etta-Jane ran headlong into my leg and hugged me.

"Hi, Mr. Joe," she said. "Did you hear me singin'?"

"It's beautiful."

"They said if I could get the notes right then I can be in the Easter concert."

"After that they'll have you singin' for the president and the pope."

"Yeah," she said, knowing that these must have been very important music critics.

"Thank you," Mama Beah said, laying a hand on my forearm. "It's a blessing for her."

I knocked on Gatormouth's door and waited a good three minutes.

When he finally opened up, we could both tell that something was different.

"King."

"Gates."

"What you want, man?"

"Can I come in?"

He looked down at both of my hands and then asked, "For what?"

"Talk."

"Talk about what?"

"Talk about things you don't want nobody behind one'a these doors to hear."

With the back of a hand, he wiped away the moisture forming on his lips. Then he smiled.

"'Course you could come in, King. Come on."

He let me go by and closed the door behind. I wondered, as we walked toward the living room, would he shoot me in the back?

We sat across from and diagonally opposite each other at the nonexistent dining table.

For a while there we reclined in silence.

"You helped Mama Beah get her li'l granddaughter into singin'," Andrew said. "I been livin' in this apartment for eight years and I ain't done that much for a soul."

"She babysittin' for her parents?"

"Naw. Beah's daughter was a single mom who died from too much livin'."

"Are all the kids in her place her blood?"

"Uh-uh. She babysits for all the single mothers and fathers in the neighborhood. Two dollars a hour for each child, plus food and breakage."

I grinned at the word *breakage*. This allowed Gates a brief smile.

"Eight years, huh?" I asked.

"Just about."

"I never asked you before, but what you do for a livin'?"

Staring me in the eye he said, "I used to work in a garage but there was a accident and now I got disability."

"How long ago you hurt yourself?"

"Um...A few years I guess."

"Just about the time Ira Gross got killed," I surmised.

"Huh? Oh yeah. I guess that's right."

"You and Felix pretty tight, right?"

"I wouldn't say that. I went to see him for Chief mostly. You know, when Luwanda or Leaf would ask."

"That's not what I heard."

"You heard what?"

"They say you were pretty much a regular over at his Bowery place."

"What you gettin' at, man?"

"I just wanted to know why the fuck you kept the gun," I replied.

Gatormouth's eyes became very large—very. You could almost see the heated breath coming out from between his lips.

"What gun?"

"The Mauser."

"Like a cat?"

"It's all because Felix became one of those born-again kinda Christians, right?"

"What you jabberin' about, King?"

"I bet he go to service Sundays *and* Wednesdays."

"I wouldn't know."

"True," I agreed. "There's a lot you don't know. But when Felix called you and said he needed you to take somethin' out to Queens for him, when he said he'd give you enough money to maybe take Leaf somewhere nice—"

"You been fuckin' her?" he asked, partly to throw off my questions, but mostly because he wanted to know.

"Why you try and kill Felix, Andrew?"

"He said that?"

"No, he did not. But when you know all what I do, then it's the only thing makes sense."

"What you think you know?"

"First," I said, holding up an instructive finger. "When I was ten years old and my mother had gone to Nashville to see her mother who was dyin', my father pulled out this old pistol that his father brought back from World War II. He told me that it was a Mauser and that it used 7.63 ammunition."

"So?" He might as well have said, *Please stop.*

"Ira Gross was killed with a bullet from that gun. Felix Corn was shot with one."

Andrew had to wipe the moisture from his lips again.

"Didn't Felix see who shot him?" Gatormouth begged.

"He told the cops that it was a white man."

"That ain't me."

"Yeah, but there's enough of prison left in Felix that he ain't no snitch. He wouldn't tell 'em about you. But he asked you to come over 'cause he knew what you did. He knew it and he wanted you to make it right."

"You crazy."

"Three years ago, he had given you a case or somethin' with a hundred and fifty thousand dollars in it," I said, pressing on. "I figure he got that money from Carney. He wouldn't'a had it himself because his kind of Christianity wouldn't let him steal like that. He let you take the money because Chief trusted you. And maybe you really could be trusted, but after you handed the money to Ira, I bet he told you that he was gonna take Felix's business anyway.

"That's when something inside'a you broke. You let down Chief, Felix, Leaf, and my grandfather too. It wasn't your fault, but you took it all on yourself, pulled out my father's antique automatic—"

"What's all this shit about me and some old war gun?" He almost sounded as if he were angry.

"My father shot Felix and Ira back in the day. He prob'ly took the Mauser with him because he had a few old guns that he took along on what he called serious business. If he didn't use the gun, then he brought it back home. If he did—now, you got to understand, my father told me this when I was a child—if he did use a throwaway gun, then he always got rid of it."

"What the fuck any'a that got to do with me?" asked Gates, a flimsy paper ribbon stretched out to stop a speeding train.

"I figure Ruby Lee called you 'cause Chief was shot, and he gave you the Mauser to throw it off some bridge or sumpin'. But you liked the feel of that piece. You liked it that Chief had used it to draw blood. You kept that motherfucker until Felix sent you out to Ira. You was feelin' all gangster and shit. And when he told you that you was a bitch, you shot him in the head, in the eye, and killed him. You were lucky 'cause the bullets had lost some'a their umph and if you shot him anywhere else the shit would'a probably stopped short like it did on Felix's rib.

"You had Leaf bring you out there but then you made it home on your own."

"So, you *are* fuckin' her," Andrew said like the man he'd always wanted to be.

"No," I said with a resolve just as strong. "She didn't tell me about bringin' you out there. I asked her if you drove, and she said you knew how but they took your license away for DUIs."

"What if she did drive me somewhere? That don't prove nuthin'."

"No," I agreed. "I can't prove a damn thing. But I know Ira told Felix he'd take one hundred fifty thousand dollars to stay outta his business. I know that Felix was prouder than a peacock that he gave all the profit he made off'a convict labor to help them and their families. I know that when you killed Ira you still had his money.

"What you do? You tell Felix that you paid Ira off and then after that somebody must'a stole it? He might'a believed a lie like that. But even if he didn't it wouldn't'a mattered 'cause with Ira dead he had more time to try an' save his business."

"I ain't done nuthin'."

"You killed Ira Gross and let the cops think it was Chief."

"You tell Chief that?"

I shrugged. "Wouldn't make any difference. Chief wouldn't turn you over. He wouldn't come after you for killin' a dog like Gross. My problem is that you gonna make my family leave the country because you too much of a punk to pay for what you done.

"When you went to Felix and he asked you to do the right thing, you shot him too. You probably worried about him tellin' Chief. You probably thought if no one knew what you did wrong, then that would be like bein' innocent. Too bad you never learned from my grandfather what it really is to be a man."

Gates tried to swallow but his throat was too tight. He took in a staccato breath and considered doing something; I don't know what. But that didn't matter. Here, a man I loved had destroyed my life when I didn't even know I had a life left to destroy.

It was as if I was the prisoner in a detective's interrogation room, but the truth didn't matter. As a matter of fact, the truth would have hurt me more because Chief would not turn on his friend and if Leaf found out I'd turned on Gates she'd give up on whatever we might have had.

Nothing was going to save Grandma B's life. Nothing.

I looked down at my hands as Andrew had done. They were still empty, and I was more helpless than Mama Beah's whole clan.

The only difference was that there was no one to take me in and pay for the breakage.

When I looked up, I saw that Gates was holding a gun, a German-made automatic that I hadn't seen in more than thirty years, pointed right at my eye.

32.

IT WAS A cockeyed confrontation. There I was, all puffed up and angry, hands empty and helpless. And there was Gates, scared shitless, with a gun older than he was rattling in his hand because he was shaking so hard.

"You gotta believe me, King," he begged. "I didn't mean to shoot Felix. I didn't mean it. When he looked at me all hard and said that we needed to help Chief, I just lost it, like you said."

"None'a that means shit to me, Gates. You sittin' up here feelin' sorry for yourself, spendin' money you stoled from a man only tryin' to help others. You puttin' my father out the goddamned country and leavin' my dyin' grandmother with a broken heart. And on top'a all that, here you are pointin' a mothahfuckin' gun at me when my grandfather should'a shot you dead up in Maine twenty-five years ago."

There was rage in me, stupid rage. I believed my own bull-shit about the ammo in that Mauser, that it was too weak for anything but soft flesh. I believed that I could reach for the gun in my sports jacket while falling to my left and firing at the same time—all without receiving a fatal wound.

"So, tell me the truth, man," Andrew "Gatormouth" Williams requested. "Are you fuckin' Leaf?"

That was the most skewed part of the little drama we were playing. I was more than willing to risk my life just to see that old man die. I was just about to make my move. But even though I wanted more than anything to see him dead, I didn't want to break his heart over a woman deserving of any man or woman's love. Suddenly my rage became a kind of tamped-down indignance.

"That's where your problem is," I said in a surprisingly calm tone.

"What you mean? You sayin' I don't deserve her?"

"What I mean is that it ain't about fuckin'. You could get a woman to fuck you every night with the money you took. But you don't want that. What you want is a woman to love you, to look up into your eyes and smile because just the seein' feels good.

"No. I am not fuckin' your girlfriend. And maybe, if you stop thinkin' about her like that, then she'd be here helpin' you figure this shit out."

That was the proverbial straw that broke the real camel's back.

Gates lowered his pistol and I held myself back from shooting him. Then I stood from the empty table space and walked away.

"What's wrong, baby?"

"Nuthin', B," I said to my grandmother.

Rags, Brenda, Roger, Chief, and I were sitting at the Silbrig Haus dining table eating boeuf bourguignon and French bread. Aja had gone home since Anthony Orr and his crew had been negated.

"Nuthin' my ass," my genteel ancestor noted.

"That's right, Grandma, your ass ain't got nuthin' to do with it."

It was a deep pleasure to hear Brenda laugh, not giggle, chuckle, or snigger, but a real belly laugh like when you're a child and so happy that you can't contain it. She laughed so hard that Roger got up and stood next to her, placing a hand on her shoulder.

"That's okay, honey child," she said, patting his concerned knuckles. "King just knows how to make me happy; not that he knows how to do it for hisself."

Going back to his chair, Roger said, "You do look a little grim, Joe."

"It's been the only time in my life that I've been with this much family. And I know I'll be losing it soon."

"Maybe not," my step-grandfather said. "The new doctors say that she might dodge the bullet. If that's the case, we can all go to Ghana anytime we want."

It was one of those times when I couldn't tell what my face was saying.

"We all die sometime," Chief said to the face he saw.

"I know. But it's like with Mama."

"What you mean, son?"

"They took her away to the asylum and she just died. By the time I could look for what happened to her, the place was gone and the records lost under the ruins."

I slept in the room my grandmother had designed, based on the shotgun shack she and my grandfather lived in outside of Jackson, Mississippi. The thin mattress didn't bother me, and the soft lighting subsided automatically at 10:00 p.m.

As I lay abed, wide awake and wondering if the pain I felt would ever subside, it was no surprise at all when Brenda's orange phone rang.

"Hello?"

"Hey, Joe," said Forthright Jorgensen.

"What time is it?"

"Three forty-nine."

"And there's some reason for us to be talking this time of morning?"

"Henri Tourneau."

There was a hard-and-fast rule at Silbrig Haus that no one was ever to allow police entrée without a warrant and at least two of Roger's lawyers present.

So, across the street from the Great Wall of the mansion was a good-size home used for meetings that might be had off-site. They called this house the Cottage. That's where I found Detective First Grade Henri Tourneau.

He was standing at the window of a large sitting room looking at the dark street.

"Hey, Henri," I said, entering the chamber.

He turned to greet me. His dark skin and definitely African features always made me smile. He was America even if the country didn't know it . . . yet.

"Hey, Joe," he said. "They call this a cottage?"

"You should see the house."

"Damn."

"You got the graveyard shift?"

"No."

"Then why ain't you at home with your people?"

"Andrew Williams."

"What about him?"

There was a sense of empathy about Henri that made him a superior cop. He was aware of the line where the trouble either ended or began and so was able to make negotiations there, at the place few others even knew existed. He took out a small iPad, touched three or four patches of light, and then held out the ensuing video.

It was a nighttime view of a Manhattan street, from about two and a half stories up. There were police cars parked horizontally at the curb and very few pedestrians were out. After a few seconds a skinny Black man in a yellowy gaberdine suit walked up to the curb carrying, by their handles, a duffel bag in his right hand and a soft-sided briefcase in his left.

It was Gates. I could see, by how loose the suit was on his frame, how much smaller he'd gotten over the years. He looked up at the camera, then got down on his knees. He separated the long clasp of the case and brought out my father's old Mauser. Quickly he turned the muzzle of the gun to point at his right eye. Then, I suppose, he wrapped a thumb around the trigger and pulled. For long seconds he stayed semi-erect upon his knees, then he fell forward, his forehead banging down on concrete.

When the video was about to repeat, I handed the iPad back to Henri.

Taking the device he said, "Bullet went right through his head and hit a pedestrian in the arm across the street. If he lives, he'll be charged with assault."

"He's still alive?"

"He is."

"And what brought you here to me?"

"He left a note, the gun, and sixty-seven thousand dollars in the duffel bag. You are who the note is addressed to. I called your emergency line; Aja called back and told me what to do."

Then Henri fumbled around the virtual keys of the iPad until getting where he wanted to be. After all that he handed the gadget back to me.

> This is the last will, testament, and confessions of Andrew Coster Williams, AKA Gatormouth, AKA Gates. I am writing this testimony for Joe King Oliver who asked me a question and now I am giving my answer. Three years ago I was given a large sum of money to deliver to a man named Ira Gross. When I went to give him that money, we had a disagreement and I shot him in the same eye that I will shoot myself in tonight. He died and I ran. Somehow my friend Chief Oliver was blamed for the crime and I was a coward and didn't confess. This is my confession.
>
> The gun I kill myself with is the gun I used on Ira. The money in the duffel bag is mine and I bequeath it to Leaf Alyssandra Morton. Tell her that I'm sorry that I could never get on the right track and that I don't hold anything against her for being with Joe.
>
> Andrew Coster Williams

"You can't tell anybody you read this," Henri said.

"Okay. Are you going to question Leaf?"

"You know how to get in touch with her?"

"No."

"Well then," the excellent NYPD detective said, "I'll tell her when I find her. Did you know anything about what he did or was going to do?"

"It's like Gates said: I asked him if he knew anything about the charges against my father, and he said he'd have to think about it.

"The bullet went through his skull, huh?"

"Yeah. That mean anything to you?"

"No. Nothing at all."

33.

THE NEXT DAY I went to the hospital room where Roger Ferris had Andrew installed. Leaf was sitting in a chair next to his bed. Looking at the back of her wild mane, I remember thinking that she'd been living a life of loss since she was a child.

"Hi," I said to her.

She glanced at me and then looked out the hospital window.

I pulled up another chair to join the vigil.

Gates had tubes running up his nostrils and down his throat. Over these was an oxygen mask. There were three IVs, one in either arm and another inserted into an artery in his upper right thigh. There were pinging electronic measuring tools connected to two fingers of his left hand, and there was another machine somewhere humming.

I hadn't slept much and so when I closed my eyes the electronic sounds lulled me.

"Is this why you said you didn't want to lose me?" she asked in the darkness.

"I think so."

"You don't know?"

Opening my eyes I said, "I didn't know when I said it. It was just...Andrew meant a lot to me when I was a boy. He was like a kid himself and so I identified with him. I loved him and he loved you and you seemed to love us both. And then there was my grandmother who needed her son, my father, who I hated for years.

"I mean, how can a mess like that turn out right?"

That question brought a smile to Leaf's lips.

"I drove him there that night," she said. "We pulled up in the back parking lot and he told me to go, that he might be a while. But I stayed. And when he came runnin' out still dragging that suitcase, I knew he was in trouble."

"So, you knew who killed Ira."

"You see?" she replied. "It's me who should'a been worried about losin' you."

"I guess. But what else could you do? You and Gates were together. If you turned him in, his life would have been shattered."

"Shattered," she repeated.

"At least Chief Odin had a way out and there's not much either of us could do about my grandmother's cancer."

"That all sounds very reasonable, Mr. Oliver."

"I still don't want to lose you."

She pushed back her wild hair and stared at me as if I was from some conquering tribe attempting by force to undermine her beliefs in her people's gods.

"Chief called me this morning," she said. "He told me that the doctors said Andrew's brain is all tore up and there's no coming back for him. He told me that he knew how close me and Andrew was and so they were gonna leave it up to me when to pull the plug."

"So, what's your call?"

"I cain't," she said. It was the first time I'd seen her with such vulnerability. "Will you do it for me?"

"Why don't we work it out together?"

"How?"

"I don't know. But Andrew deserve to have somebody put some thought into his last breath. I mean, he did his best — killed hisself in order to save Chief and he left you because he couldn't find it in his heart to be the man you needed him to be."

"How long would it take to figure it out?"

"I don't know. One day, one month, as long as it takes."

She turned her gaze toward the window again and said, "After that I'm'a go to Alaska for a bit."

"You got people there?"

"No."

"Then why Alaska?"

"It's far away from here."

"You know, the cops will never let you have that money."

"I got my own money," she said with sudden conviction. "And I can work too."

Six weeks later we buried Andrew Coster Williams. We put him in a plain pine coffin because that's what my grandmother wanted. She was the only close family member not there because she'd had her operation and was in the hospital, hopefully healing. Rags was there along with Leaf, Ruby Lee, Roger, Luwanda, Aja, Felix, Mama Beah, and her grandchild.

Etta-Jane had spent her time perfecting her performance

of "Will the Circle Be Unbroken." It was lovely and plaintive and made me cry.

After the service Leaf insisted on going to the airport alone. She said that she needed to start her journey right then. The rest of us went to Silbrig Haus to toast Gatormouth.

Raising a glass, Roger Ferris, the richest man in the world, said, "Usually, when a man passes people get together and lie about the life he lived. They say what a good man he was and how much he loved and was loved. They say these things for each other but it's never the truth. The truth is that we're all flawed and lost, failures and unfulfilled, lovers undeserving of love. But...through all that some of us manage to make some little mark on the world; a squiggle scratched on a stone lost in a desert or under some nameless building.

"Andrew Williams was such a man. He gave the only precious thing that any creature, anywhere, truly possesses, his life, for the love of a friend. It took him an entire lifetime to fuck up and only one moment to make it all right."

As my grandmother would have said, *It wasn't nuthin' new, but it was true,* and so we drank and felt that that was the best that could be done.

"Son," my father said to me on the porch of Roger's mansion.
"Yeah, Dad?"
"You got plans?"
"Not really."
"So, you wanna take a ride?"

It took almost two hours to get there. We didn't talk very much on the way. Gatormouth's death and departure felt like the disappointing end of a story that might have turned out better.

When we finally got to Carmel, New York, it was night-time. Chief directed me until we arrived at a true cottage that sat atop a lawn that was also a small hill.

"You go on up," my father said to me.

"What is this place?"

"You'll find out."

"What about you?"

"There's a bar in the next town ovah. I go there sometimes."

"And what about me?"

"You go on up. I'll take the car and you can call me when you want to leave."

There were lights on in the house and the sounds of a TV and maybe a radio too. I stood there at the front door, hesitating, thinking about Chief. He'd always been like that, bringing me a brown paper bag and saying to look inside.

The doorbell was three notes—high, low, high.

After a minute the porch light came on. Then the door opened.

A white woman in her late thirties answered. She was plain, pear-shaped, and mild of expression.

"Yes?" she asked with no hint of fear or suspicion.

"Hi," I said.

"Are you here for Missy?"

"Yes," I answered because it didn't seem like *no* would get me anywhere.

"Come on in."

There were two small children, maybe seven and nine, sitting on a short couch in front of an old-fashioned TV. There was some kind of cartoon show playing but the little white children's eyes were glued to me.

"Minnie, Floyd, this is Mr. . . ."

"Oliver," I said.

"What do you say?" the lady asked the kids.

"Hello, Mr. Over," Minnie, the older child, said.

Floyd continued to stare.

"Come with me, Mr. Oliver," the thus-far nameless woman invited.

We entered a longish hallway that had an open door at the far end. From the partially open doorway yellow electric light poured out. Walking toward this light I felt the prickling of fear along my scalp.

When we got there, my guide called out, "Missy?"

"Yes, Maud?"

"Someone to see you."

With that, Maud stood away from the entrance and nodded for me to go through.

It was a very small room that had a bare wood floor, furnished with two stuffed chairs and a small table that could serve many purposes. In one of the chairs sat a small Black woman with a radiant face and eyes that showed no fear.

"Mom?"

Her smile was receptive. *At last,* that grin imparted.

"Joey."

It was a struggle for her to stand from the soft seating, but she managed it. Her hug was strong the way I remembered it from so long ago.

*   *   *

"...I fell in love with the janitor at the asylum," my mother was saying. "His name was Claude, and he was Maud's father. Her mother had died from pneumonia and poor Claude didn't know what to do with a child."

"How come Dad knew you were here?"

"Chief ain't such a bad man. He knew that the life he lived was too hard for me. He knew it."

I didn't ask, that night, why she hadn't gotten in touch with me, who else knew that she was alive, or what had happened to cure her. I didn't need to know any of that.

About the Author

WALTER MOSLEY is one of America's most celebrated writers. He was given the National Book Award's 2020 Medal for Distinguished Contribution to American Letters, named a Grand Master of the Mystery Writers of America, and honored with the Anisfield-Wolf Award, a Grammy, a PEN USA Lifetime Achievement Award, the Robert Kirsch Award, numerous Edgars, and several NAACP Image Awards. His work is translated into twenty-five languages. He has published fiction and nonfiction in *The New Yorker, Playboy,* and *The Nation.* As an executive producer, he adapted his novel *The Last Days of Ptolemy Grey* for AppleTV+, and he serves as a writer and executive producer for FX's *Snowfall.*